Praise for Dorien Grey's Elliott Smith Mysteries

His Name is John

"In the hands of Dorien Grey, the master story-teller of the Dick Hardesty tales, this story sails smoothly along from beginning to end. He adds in more than enough mystery, suspense, and even romance to satisfy any reader."

– Joseph DeMarco
Mysterical-E

"A welcome addition to the mystery genre for it's humor, creative plot and well-written scenes and descriptions. This one isn't just for fans of Grey, it's a terrific entry point for new readers to discover a true talent."

– Jay Hartman
Untreed Reads

Aaron's Wait

"Grey provides a well crafted, fast paced, action-driven account filled with deceit, greed and treachery all created through unforgettable writing skill."

– Molly Martin
Compulsive Reader.com

"...definitely worth reading more than once."

– *Rainbow Reviews*

ALSO BY DORIEN GREY

The Dick Hardesty Series

The Bar Watcher
The Dream Ender
The Angel Singers
The Secret Keeper

The Elliott Smith and John Series

His Name Is John
Aaron's Wait

DORIEN GREY

CAESAR'S FALL

An Elliott Smith and John Mystery

ZUMAYA BOUNDLESS
AUSTIN TX
2010

This book is a work of fiction. Names, characters, places and incidents are products of the author's imagination or are used fictitiously. Any resemblance to actual persons or events is purely coincidental.

CAESAR'S FALL

ISBN 978-1-936144-08-2

Look for us online at
http://www.zumayapublications.com/boundless.php

Library of Congress Cataloging-in-Publication Data

Grey, Dorien.
Caesar's fall : an Elliott Smith and John mystery / Dorien Grey.
p. cm.
ISBN 978-1-936144-08-2 (trade pbk. : alk. paper) -- ISBN 978-1-936144-09-9 (electronic)
I. Title.
PS3557.R48165C33 2010
813'.54--dc22

2010035693

To Norman, who was part of my life longer than my parents were, and who died February 18, 2010. I miss him.

ACKNOWLEDGMENTS

To the usual suspects, whose support and unflagging willingness to share their knowledge add hopeful verisimilitude to all my books. And with special thanks to friend and stamp expert Anthony (Tony) Mason.

“The Supernatural is the Natural, just not yet understood.”

-- Elbert Hubbard

Chapter 1

"And how's Steve?"

Elliott rolled his eyes toward the ceiling, glad his sister couldn't see through the phone. Suppressing a smile, he replied, "He's fine, Sis. He's exactly as he was yesterday when you asked."

"Well, he could have been hit by a bus, and you'd never volunteer the information."

"Hardly."

"Well, I really like Steve."

Elliott resisted an ironic *Like I don't?* and said instead, "I know you do, Sis. And he likes you, but I really wish you wouldn't be in quite such a hurry to get me married off."

"Elliott, you're thirty-nine years old. I'm just worried you might lose Steve if you don't let him know how you feel."

The smile became a grin. "He knows how I feel, and I know how he feels, and God's in His heaven and all's right with the world. Really. Neither of us has a train to catch, or a biological clock, so there's no great rush." Deciding it was time for a subject change, he said, "And speaking of Steve, he's the reason I'm calling. He's thinking of getting Brad a new tackle box for his birthday and wanted to make sure he hadn't gotten one recently."

Brad, his sister Cessy's police detective husband, was turning forty-five, and Cessy had planned a surprise party at one of his favorite restaurants.

"He doesn't need to get him anything. Just a card would be fine."

"Yeah, well, he wants to do a little more than a card. The last time he and Brad were talking about fishing, Brad showed him some flies from an old battered tackle box, and Steve thought he could use a new one."

"I'm sure he'd love it–he's had that same one since before BJ was born–but Steve really doesn't have to–"

"I know. So, seven-thirty at Monestero's?"

"Yes, and I really hope Brad won't be upset with me for doing this."

"You know he won't."

She was referring to the expense of renting a banquet room and paying for a catered buffet. She was always very conscious of Brad's pride, and of his unspoken discomfort over his wife's having, through her wealthy parents, far more money than he would ever earn. She'd discussed the idea of the party with Elliott, who encouraged her to go ahead with it.

"What's the good in having money if you don't ever spend it?" he'd told her. "It's not like you're buying a closet full of mink coats. And Brad deserves something special for his birthday."

She'd reluctantly agreed and had arranged for the party, limiting the guest list to close friends and a few of Brad's fellow detectives.

"So, we'll see you Saturday night, then," Elliott said.

"Yes, but I'm sure we'll be talking before then."

Knowing his sister, he hadn't a doubt in the world.

❦

As he did nearly every time he talked to Cessy about Steve, Elliott felt a wave of guilt. He and Steve had been seeing each other for a year, and he still couldn't bring himself to share the largest secret of his life with him.

How could he possibly explain that he had a friend named John who just happened to be dead, and with whom he conversed frequently in his sleep? Elliott had at last reached the stage himself where he fully accepted the situation without fearing he was insane. He knew the time must come when he had to tell Steve about John, and Steve already suspected something odd was going on.

Sighing, he realized he'd not picked up his mail on his way upstairs from the underground garage. He was expecting a bid for some tile work on his nearly completed current renovation project, so decided to go down to see if it had arrived. Checking the oven timer to verify he had enough time before his TV dinner would be done, he headed for the elevator.

After the usual interminable wait, the elevator door whooshed open, and he stepped in to join the car's only other occupant, a newcomer to the building. He and Steve had ridden the elevator up with the man on their way back after a night out the previous Saturday. He'd been with a very nice-looking young guy both Steve and Elliott instinctively knew was not a relative. Elliott had suspected he might be the man who had just bought the condo left vacant by the death of one of the older residents.

Living in a large condo complex was a little like living in a small town, in that everyone tended to know everyone else, at least by name.

After the obligatory exchange of greetings, Elliott said, "Are you by any chance the one who bought Forty-J?"

The man grinned. "Yes, I moved in about two weeks ago."

"Welcome to the building. I'm Elliott Smith, Thirty-five-J."

The man extended his hand.

"Bruno," he said, not indicating whether that was his first or last name. "I guess we're vertical neighbors."

Taking quick stock, Elliott estimated him to be between forty-five and fifty, graying short hair, about five-foot-eight, stocky. He looked somehow familiar, though Elliott couldn't immediately make a connection.

"How do you like it so far?" he asked.

"I love it! I've never lived in a building this big...or so tall. As a matter of fact, I've never lived above the third floor before. I really don't like heights, but when I saw the view..."

Elliot smiled. "I know what you mean. It was one of the main factors for me, too. I think it's one of the best in the city. "

"I agree," Bruno–again, Elliott wondered if that was a first or last name–said enthusiastically. "I don't think I'll ever get used to it. I hope I don't."

The elevator reached the lobby.

"After you," Bruno said with a sweeping gesture of one hand.

Bruno followed him through the inner lobby, where they both said hello to Marco, the doorman, then into the outer lobby, where Elliott turned left toward the mail alcove. Bruno did the same, echoing Elliott's reaching into his pocket for his keys.

"Forgot to get my mail earlier," Elliott said, as they went to their respective boxes.

"Me, too, though I haven't really been here long enough to get any, thank God."

Elliott thought that a rather strange thing to say, but let it pass as he extracted his mail and went quickly through it looking for the bid. Finding it–or at least an envelope from the company making it–he put it on top and turned back toward the elevators. He was a little surprised to see Bruno still pulling mail out of what seemed to be a full box.

Seeing Elliott's look, Bruno grinned.

"Looks like they found me."

Elliott had no idea what he was talking about but didn't want to appear nosy, so said nothing.

Bruno caught up to him in the outer lobby and waited while Marco pressed the buzzer to open the door. An elevator was waiting, and this time Elliott gestured for Bruno to get on first.

"Was that your...partner...I saw with you Saturday?" Bruno asked.

"We're getting there," Elliott said with a smile. "Not living together, though." He deliberately avoided adding "yet" and wondered why. "And you? That was a really nice-looking guy you were with."

"He was, wasn't he?" Bruno said it in a way that reminded Elliott of a proud little boy who'd just received an A on his spelling test. When he didn't volunteer any other information as to the young man's identity, Elliott let it go.

When the elevator reached his floor, Elliott got out, turning to say, "It was nice to meet you...Bruno. I'm sure we'll be seeing each other again."

"I hope so," Bruno replied, smiling broadly as the door closed.

❧

He'd just finished dinner and was looking over the tiling bid when the phone rang.

"Elliott Smith." He'd never cared much for "Hello."

"Hi, Ell, how was your day?"

Even if he hadn't immediately recognized the voice, Steve was the only person Elliott allowed to call him "Ell." He didn't consider his insistence on being called by his proper name an affectation; he simply preferred it, and made his preference known politely but firmly.

"Coming right along. I should be ready to start looking for another project before too long."

"So, did you get a chance to ask Cessy about the tackle box?"

"Yeah. She says you don't have to get him anything, but that he'd be happy to have it."

"Good. I'll stop by and pick it up on my lunch hour tomorrow. Nothing else new?"

"I met the guy we ran into on the elevator last Saturday. The one with the hot 'friend.' I was right, he is the one who bought Forty-J. Seems like a nice guy, but there's something a little...different?...about him."

"That's cryptic. Different how?"

"Hard to say. Sort of like he's a kid in a candy store, somehow. He's all excited about living here, like it's out of his element."

"Well, it's sure out of my element. You rich kids live in a different world from us working folk."

"Yeah, yeah, you're breaking my heart. So, dinner Friday? Maybe a movie?"

"How about I cook and you bring some DVDs?"

"That'll work. I'll give you a buzz tomorrow."

⁂

Elliott's current project was a relatively small one, and a definite departure from his usual pattern. It was the first time since he'd gotten into the business of renovation that he was, in effect, doing a project for someone else. He had always before done everything for himself–finding and buying a property, renovating it exactly the way he wanted it with the help of his crew, then selling it.

But when two of his friends, Jesse Lambert and Adam Burton, bought an early twentieth-century frame two-flat and asked if he would be willing to renovate it for them, he'd hesitated only briefly before agreeing.

The building had originally been a private home but had been converted to a two-flat probably sometime after WWII, Elliott estimated. Jesse and Adam had bought it with the intention of restoring it to a single-family home. They'd originally planned to do the work themselves but quickly realized that, having no real experience in home renovation, they might be in far over their heads and called on Elliott. He and his crew had taken a look at it, recognized its potential then reviewed and largely approved of the sketches Jesse and Adam had made of what they wanted.

That, too, was a departure, since Elliott normally worked from his own ideas. But after pointing out a few impracticalities in their plans and receiving their assurance they wouldn't second-guess him, he gave them an estimate, which they readily accepted. He then drew up a new set of plans with the agreed-upon changes, which they approved.

While he couldn't foresee doing this kind of thing on a regular basis, he'd convinced himself he was not only doing a favor for friends but would be saving both the expense of buying a property and the time, trouble and expense of selling it when he was finished.

The job was now about two-thirds complete, and Elliott was ready to start looking for his next project.

Friday night, coming home from a particularly labor-intensive day and badly in need of a shower, he opted to avoid going through the lobby by walking the stairs from the garage to the second floor to catch the elevator. He was in a hurry to get home, get cleaned up and head out again for Steve's. When the elevator doors opened, he was surprised to see Bruno and a tall, almost skeletal, redheaded man he'd never seen before. The man looked at him with mild curiosity and gave him just the hint of a beatific smile.

Bruno indicated the man beside him. "Elliott, I'd like you to meet my sensei, Dr. Clifford Blanton. Sensei, this is my downstairs neighbor, Elliott Smith."

"Nice to meet you," Elliott said, extending his hand and wondering what kind of a doctorate would be required to be a sensei. He tried not to let his curiosity show.

"My pleasure," Blanton responded, shaking hands.

"We're just going up for our session," Bruno said, and Elliott felt his eyebrow rising. Noticing, Bruno grinned broadly. "Meditation," he explained.

"Ah," Elliott replied, unable to think of anything better to say. "Sounds interesting."

"Oh, it is. I can't tell you how much it's changed my life. I'm sure I'd be a basket case without it." There was only a slight pause before he added, "I'm glad I ran into you. I'm having a party tomorrow night and wondered if you and your friend would like to come."

"That's really nice of you to ask, but we're going to a surprise birthday party for my brother-in-law. A rain check, maybe?"

Bruno smiled. "Sure. I'll probably be having another next Saturday, too. We'll see."

"That'd be great. Thanks for asking."

The elevator reached thirty-five, and Elliott got out after exchanging goodbyes. He didn't know quite what to make of the encounter and brief conversation. Sensei? He understood it to mean "teacher," and associated the term with kung-fu films. He'd never thought of it in terms of meditation. Still, he acknowledged, there was a lot he didn't know.

And while it was nice of Bruno to invite him and Steve to a party, the fact he'd said he was likely having another the following week struck Elliott as perhaps a bit excessive. Two parties in two weeks?

Well, he *had* said "probably," not "definitely," but Bruno hadn't struck him as the party-boy type, so it did seem a bit unusual.

⁂

Elliott spent the night at Steve's, and if he hadn't been tired before he got there, he was totally exhausted–although very pleasantly so–by the time they finally got to sleep.

Since Steve wanted to spend Saturday afternoon working on a painting, Elliott returned home shortly after breakfast, with the agreement Steve would pick him up and drive to Brad's party. Elliott spent the afternoon doing cost analysis paperwork on his current project and was happy to determine he was running slightly under his projected estimates.

As he passed through the lobby to wait for Steve, he noticed three men–one about sixty and two cover-model types in their twenties–standing at the desk as Marco picked up the house phone and said, "Mr. Thorne, Mr. Alvarez and Mr. Greenway to see you, Mr. Caesar." He then put the receiver back in its cradle and said, "Forty-J, gentlemen."

One of the should-be models gave Elliott a definite and none-too-subtle once-over as they passed.

So, Bruno's last name was Caesar, Elliott mused. Interesting name. And he suddenly smiled to realize why he'd thought the man looked familiar–Bruno was a dead ringer for a bust of the Roman emperor Tiberius in his father's study in Lake Forest.

⁂

The birthday party was a big success, and Brad professed total surprise, though Elliott knew not much got by him. He was a homicide detective, after all, and chances were he'd either known about it or suspected long before they arrived. But even if he did know, he also knew Cessy had to have gone to a lot of trouble, and he played along perfectly, if for no other reason than to please her.

There were several of Brad and Cessy's friends, most of whom Elliott knew, and several of Brad's friends from the force, all with their wives. The only one of the police contingent he knew was Brad's partner, Ken Brown.

Brad did his best to deflect attention away from himself by offering a toast and congratulations to one of his fellow detectives–his first partner–who was retiring from the force to move to New York.

Elliott and Steve were the only male couple there. This did not escape the attention of one of the officers, who appeared uncomfortable when Brad introduced them. Noticing the man had his arm firmly around his wife's waist, Elliott was strongly tempted to slide his around Steve's, but resisted for Brad's sake.

The food more than lived up to Monestero's reputation, and Elliott ate far more than he'd intended.

"Hey, slow down," Steve teased as Elliott got up from the table to head back to the buffet for another slice of ham. "The warden isn't coming to get you at midnight." Grinning, he added, "But grab me another roll while you're there."

Brad seemed truly pleased by the tackle box, and the tickets Elliott had gotten him for the next Blackhawks game. He was a huge hockey fan, and Elliott had been tempted to get him season tickets but, like Cessy, didn't want to flaunt the Smith family wealth.

They left the party around ten and returned to Elliott's to spend the night. As they entered the lobby, two men had just been cleared by the doorman and directed to 40-J. Somewhat to his surprise, Elliott recognized Button and Paul, regulars at the Anvil, a nearby gay bar. He'd met them there some time before but couldn't recall when he'd last seen them.

Spotting him, Button said "Elliott!" in a tone usually reserved for greeting long-lost friends."What a surprise! Going to the party?"

"No," Elliott said, "I live here." Button, he noted, was as always his impeccably groomed self, dressed in a very expensive suit and tie.

They converged on the way to the elevators, and Elliott introduced Steve.

"Well," Button said, "we wondered why we hadn't seen you in a while." Giving Steve an exaggerated head-to-toe scan, he added, "Now I see why. Why go out for hamburger when you have steak at home?"

Steve grinned as the elevator door opened, and they all got on.

"So, how do you know Bruno?" Elliott asked.

"Everyone knows Bruno," Paul volunteered, the roundness of his face accented by the roundness of his wide-open eyes, which always gave the impression he had just been surprised. "He's like a shooting star, suddenly appearing out of nowhere to streak across the firmament of the Chicago gay scene."

Elliott and Steve exchanged a quick glance, and Button said, "Once a publicist, always a publicist. And he's hardly a shooting star. I've known Bruno for centuries."

"Maybe so," Paul said firmly, "but that's before he won the lottery."

"He won the lottery?" Steve asked, obviously impressed.

"And not just any lottery," Paul said. "The MegaBucks, no less! Fifty-nine million!"

"Wow!" Steve said.

The elevator stopped at 35, and the door opened.

"Why don't you come up with us?" Button asked. "I'm sure you'd be welcome."

Elliott, standing in the door to prevent its closing, said, "Bruno did invite us, but we had a birthday party and had to decline."

"It's not too late," Paul suggested.

Since Steve had already stepped out of the elevator, Elliott looked quickly to him for confirmation, then said, "Not tonight, I don't think. Maybe next time."

They all exchanged smiles and waves as the door closed, and Button said, "Don't be a stranger!"

"Button?" Steve asked as they walked to Elliott's unit.

Elliott grinned, taking his keys out of his pocket.

"I have no idea where he got the name, but I like it. It fits him."

Steve just shook his head.

Feeling Steve might be curious as to how he knew them, as he unlocked and opened the door he continued, "They're regulars at the Anvil up on Granville. I met them there a while back. Nice guys. Button manages a men's clothing store on Michigan Avenue. I hadn't known that Paul was a publicist."

"And you didn't know this Caesar guy had won the lottery?"

"I didn't have a clue. But that might explain why he seemed a little out of his element when I first talked to him on the elevator."

Going into the living room, Elliott turned on a small light and the stereo system. The overture to *The Man of La Mancha* subtly filled the room.

"Want a drink?" he asked.

"In a minute."

They sat on the sofa, facing the sliding glass doors to the balcony and looking out over the galaxy of lights of the city spread out in front of them. It was a sight, as Elliott had told Bruno, he never tired of.

Steve reached over and took Elliott's hand.

"I don't know whether to envy Caesar or to pity him. From what I've heard, winning the lottery isn't all it's cracked up to be."

"It's nice to have money," Elliott agreed, "as long as you know how to handle it. But to have...what did Paul say it was?...fifty-nine million?...dumped in your lap out of the blue, that can't be easy. I just hope he's smart enough to deal with it. Somehow, I suspect that an endless string of parties isn't exactly a practical way to do it. Maybe having a guru might help him."

"A guru?"

"Guru, sensei...a long story. I'll tell you about it if you're interested. But how about that drink first?"

❧

Steve left for home at around two o'clock Sunday afternoon, wanting to get back to his painting, and Elliott decided to do a load of laundry. His cleaning lady, Ida, normally did it, but when Steve stayed over, the sheets and towels sometimes got a little extra workout, and he did them separately, leaving the rest for her.

He'd just started the washer and was heading for the elevator when a man came in with a laundry basket piled so high Elliott couldn't see who was carrying it. When the basket was set down on a folding table, he saw it was Bruno Caesar, looking more than a little tired.

"Elliott! Hello!"

"How was the party?" Elliott asked with a grin, indicating the towering pile of laundry.

"Wonderful!" Bruno started tossing laundry into a machine. When it was full, he moved on to the next. "I'm so sorry you couldn't make it. I love parties, meeting new people, making new friends. I've always been something of a recluse, and now...well, I'm learning how to really live."

Not knowing how to respond, Elliott said nothing.

"You just have to come next Saturday," Bruno continued, filling a third machine then retrieving a large bottle of laundry detergent from the bottom of the basket.

Elliott wasn't quite sure why the invitation caught him by surprise, but it did.

"Uh, that would be nice," he said. "I'll have to check with Steve, but it sounds like fun."

Bruno smiled reflexively. "Yes, they are fun. They aren't wild or extravagant–no naked go-go boys or couples dragging one another off to the bedroom for sex. That's not me. They're just...well, nice." As he took out his laundry card and went from machine to machine turning them on, he said, "Are you busy right now?"

"Not until the washer's done."

"Can I invite you and Steve up for a cup of coffee? I just made a pot before coming down here, and I could use a cup right about now."

"Steve left for his place a while ago, but, sure, I could go for a quick cup."

He knew his acceptance had more to do with his curiosity to see what Bruno had done with his unit–which he knew had a floor plan identical to his own–than his desire for coffee.

"So, tell me about your work," Bruno said as they got on the elevator. Elliott detected the scent of Old Spice, his own favorite aftershave, though his mother was horrified he would choose something so common, as she called it.

"There's not much to tell," Elliott said. "I renovate small older apartment buildings with a lot of character and sense of history and bring them back to their original glory. Chicago's losing its architectural heritage at a really alarming rate, and I'm just trying to preserve some of it."

"That sounds like a most worthy endeavor," Bruno said. "You'd love the building I left to move here. I'd been there twelve years and really loved it–I don't think I realized how much until I moved. Of course, I love it here, but I still don't really think of this as home yet...not like my last place."

"Then why did you move, if you don't mind my asking?" Elliott asked, although he was pretty sure winning the lottery had a lot to do with it.

"The owner's been talking of selling," Bruno explained, "and I didn't want to risk being evicted if it he did. Besides, I guess I thought it was time for a change."

They reached the 40th floor and went down the hall to Bruno's unit. In the years Elliott had lived in the building, he'd only been to one other unit that was a duplicate of his own, and it had been an almost surreal experience to see what was, in effect, his own home with someone else's furniture and decor.

Bruno also used the door to the kitchen rather than the front door. Both kitchens were identical except for the small appliances and a number of empty liquor and champagne bottles, glasses and bowls lining the counters. The dishwasher door was partly open to reveal what appeared to be freshly washed dishes. One sink was filled with soapy water, and a dish rack on the counter held a large number of washed glasses.

"Sorry for the mess," Bruno said, "but my...overnight guest...didn't leave until after noon, and I haven't gotten everything back together yet. Why don't you go into the living room and have a seat while I pour the coffee?"

Setting his laundry basket against the kitchen door, Elliott strolled into the living room, trying to take in as much of it as he could without being obvious. Going to the balcony doors, he was intrigued by the way the view was subtly different from his own. Approximately fifty feet in additional height did make a difference, if only a minor one.

"Cream and sugar?" Bruno called from the kitchen.

"Yes, please."

Turning back toward the kitchen gave him a chance to take in the whole living/dining area, and again he experienced an oddly surreal sensation. The carpet was a different color than his, and the hallway to the bedrooms was carpeted rather than the hardwood flooring in his unit. The furniture was a strange mix of obviously brand new–and expensive–and older pieces apparently brought from Bruno's former apartment. The paintings tended toward the modern, and he wondered what Steve would think of them. A large baker's rack beside the sliding glass doors to the balcony held a number of African violets and spider plants and some species Elliott couldn't identify.

"Here we go," Bruno said, coming across the room with two mugs.

"Do you use your balcony much?" Elliott asked. "It's still a bit cool out there, but I use mine constantly when the weather allows."

Bruno smiled. "I'm afraid I never use it. I love the view–from inside looking out–but to actually go out and stand at the railing? It sounds strange, I know. I've got three balconies, and I've never set foot on any of them. I tried stepping out onto this one once, but couldn't do it."

They moved to matching leather wingback chairs with the distinctive smell of new leather, which creaked as they sat.

Elliott found it interesting that Bruno had never mentioned the lottery, and while he was curious, he didn't want be the one to bring it up. They talked, instead, of general things. Bruno had left his job as an actuary at a large insurance company in the Loop three months previously, and while he didn't give a reason, Elliott assumed it had coincided with his winning the lottery. He did make frequent references to how much his life had changed "recently," and Elliott clearly sensed confusion and vague disquiet.

When Bruno asked about his family, Elliott gave the basics without mentioning their wealth. Only his reference to having grown up in Lake Forest gave an indication of money.

Bruno, he learned, had been born and raised in nearby Rockford and had gone to Northern Illinois University, then returned home to care for his ailing parents. He had an older brother with whom he was apparently not close, though he seemed very fond of his sister-in-law, and had moved to Chicago after his parents died within a year of one another. Elliott got the impression he hadn't had much of a chance to have a life of his own, which might be why he'd mentioned being somewhat reclusive, and that he apparently didn't have many–if any–real friends.

"So, tell me how you came to have a sensei," Elliott asked. "I gather you're into Eastern philosophy?"

Bruno smiled. "Not really. I mean, not until recently. I met Sensei quite by accident–at a stamp show, of all places. I had just cashed in my lottery ticket the week before, and I was still pretty wound up, trying to come to grips with it all. We got to talking, and he gave me his card. He believes stamp collecting is an excellent form of meditation and calming for the mind. I called him, and we try to get together two or three times a week for our sessions. I really can't describe how grateful I am to him for helping me cope with all this. I don't know what I'd do without him."

"Exactly what kind of doctor is he, if I can ask?"

"He has his Ph.D. in metaphysics."

Elliott had no idea there was such a thing, but let it pass with a simple "Ah."

"You really should consider attending one of his seminars. They're very popular. You can find a schedule on his website."

Before either of them could say anything else on the subject, the grandmother clock on the curio-filled etagere struck the quarter-hour, and Bruno said, "Ah, time does fly when you're having fun. We'd better go check on the laundry. Yours must be done by now." As they passed the etagere, he paused and picked up a framed photo. "By the way, here's a picture of my old building."

He handed Elliott the picture—Bruno standing in front of a seen-better-times-but-still-striking old Victorian. The first floor had obviously originally been a storefront, but what caught Elliott's attention was that what little could be seen of the second floor showed it had an ornate turreted corner, typical of many buildings of the period. There was some sort of bas-relief writing at the bottom of the turret, which he couldn't make out because of the curve and angle of the photograph, though he could see the number 96.

"Where is this place?" he asked.

"On Armitage, not too far from the Brown Line."

"How many units?" He handed the picture back to Bruno, who replaced it on the etagere.

"It's basically a two-flat, not counting the ground floor," he said as they moved through the kitchen, where Elliott picked up his laundry basket. "It was originally the neighborhood grocery. It was converted to an apartment, and the owner lives there now. Why? Do you think you might be interested in it? I can give you his number, if you'd like."

They'd reached the elevator and pressed the button when Elliott said, "Well, I don't know. I hate to just call people and ask if they're planning to sell. That can send the wrong message and make them think

I'm anxious to buy–which, in turn, tempts them to raise the price if they *were* thinking of selling."

The elevator arrived, and they got on, pressing the button for the laundry room on the fourth floor.

"Would you like me to call him and see if he's still thinking of it? I won't tell him I talked to you."

Elliott shrugged.

"Tell you what...why don't I take a drive by and get a look at the place first? Then we can take it from there."

"Sure," Bruno replied as the elevator came to a stop on thirty to admit a red-haired woman with a whippet. They all exchanged greetings and rode the rest of the way to four in silence.

The week passed quickly with the usual number of minor crises at work, phone calls to suppliers and subcontractors, evening calls to and from Cessy and Steve and various friends. Because both Jesse and Adam worked during the day, his personal contact with them was limited to occasional after-work meetings to consult on details about plumbing and electrical fixtures, siding, doors, windows and appliances. Luckily, they deferred to him with most of his recommendations. He didn't have to worry about either carpeting or painting, which Jesse and Adam said they'd decide on and take care of themselves just before they moved in.

He'd mentioned Bruno's former building to Steve and suggested they might drive past it Saturday on the way to an art store Steve wanted to check out. He heard nothing further from Bruno, but when Steve asked Thursday night if the party was still on for Saturday, he said he had no reason to think otherwise.

"Even if it's canceled," he said, "I'm sure we can find something to keep us entertained."

"Yeah," Steve said. "Maybe something involving latex, a sling and whipped cream." They both laughed.

"Well, thank God you and I are normal."

The minute he said it, Elliott felt a quick rush of guilt and wondered for the hundredth time why he'd not told Steve about John.

It certainly wasn't as though he didn't think Steve wouldn't understand–Steve had often expressed his belief in the paranormal. It was just that coming right out and telling someone–anyone–that he had frequent visits and dream-chats with someone who had died more than a year before was something Elliott simply couldn't bring himself to do just yet. He'd convinced himself it was similar to what he'd told Cessy whenever she tried to push him into taking his relationship with Steve to the next level–there was no rush. He'd have to tell him about John sometime...just not now.

While they'd fallen into a comfortable routine of spending most Friday and Saturday nights together, each seemed to be careful not to want to give the other the feeling of being pressured, or of getting into too much of a pattern. So, when Steve said he wanted to spend Friday evening finishing his current painting, Elliott took it in stride, and the conversation ended with the agreement he would pick Steve up Saturday afternoon around four so they'd have ample time to go to the art store, drive by the building on Armitage, and have dinner at Elliott's before going to Bruno's party.

❧

–You're not ashamed of me, are you, Elliott?

Elliott's body jerked, almost waking him up. Despite the countless times he'd had these sleep visits from the spirit he'd first encountered sitting beside him in the hospital following a traumatic head injury, every now and then he was caught by surprise.

–John! You scared me.

–Isn't that what ghosts do? Scare people?

Elliott knew John was teasing. He never referred to himself as a ghost, and Elliott certainly didn't think of him as one.

–Yeah, well, don't quit your day job. Where have you been? I haven't heard from you in...how long?

–I'm not sure. I've told you, my time is different from your time. But it can't have been that long, can it?

–Well over a month.

–You're kidding! Time sure does fly when you're having fun...and being dead helps, I suppose.

–So, where have *you been?*

–I kind of hesitate to say.

–Why?

–I don't want you to think I'm bragging, or for you to ever think that where I am is better than where you are. Let's just say that when you

don't have to worry about breathing or feeling any pain or discomfort, you can do a lot.

–Like?

–Well, I went back to Africa, to the lake where the ferry I was on capsized, and I walked around underwater among the crocodiles and the hippos just to see what it would be like. I didn't stay long. The hippos were kind of interesting, but incredibly messy, and I found the crocodiles every bit as nasty now as when I...before. Not everything's fun, even for me.

–You're serious?

–Would I lie?

–So, are you going to be around for awhile?

–I'm not sure. There are a couple of things I'd like to do around town, so maybe. Now, you really should get back to sleep. You have to work tomorrow.

–Yeah, you're right.

–Oh, and don't worry about Steve. He's not stupid.

❧

Elliott always considered himself lucky in being able to throw himself so completely into his work he seldom noticed the time, with the result that every day passed quickly. It seemed as though he had hardly gotten to work Friday morning when it was time to go home.

As he approached the door to the inner lobby after picking up his mail, he couldn't help but notice a nice-looking kid around twenty standing at the window beside the entry door, asking Marco to tell Mr. Caesar Perry was there. Buzzing Elliott in with one hand, Marco picked up the phone with the other. As Elliott stood waiting for the elevator, the young man–Perry–joined him. They exchanged nods, and Elliott, curious but not wanting to appear too much so, fixed his eyes on the digital display indicating the ascent of the cars. He could feel the kid's eyes on him.

Turning to him, he smiled and said, "So, you're a friend of Bruno's," making it a statement rather than a question.

The kid gave him a small smile. "You could say that."

On closer observation, Elliott decided Perry was probably older than he'd first thought, and his good looks had that indefinable hardness Elliott associated with hustlers. The young man with Bruno the first night Elliott had seen him had borne the same look. It wasn't the hardness of a street hustler but rather a certain self-confident awareness and defensiveness. Elliott pegged him as being a mid-level escort and wondered how Bruno had come across him–on the internet, or through a newspaper classified.

While Elliott had no idea what Bruno's predilections had been before winning the lottery, it was clear he was indulging them freely now. He wondered again about the effect of sudden wealth on those who had never had it before, and hoped Bruno would not follow the path of so many others in his same situation. He'd heard that seventy-five percent of all lottery winners went through every penny of the money they won within five years.

Still, aside from his parties and his indulgence in hustlers, Bruno didn't seem to be throwing his money away.

The elevator's stopping at four to let on a woman with a wheeled cart of laundry precluded any further conversation, and they rode to 33, where the woman got off, in silence. As Elliott got off on 35, he and Perry exchanged nods, and Perry said, "See ya." Elliott rather doubted it.

❧

Sleeping in was a luxury Elliott rarely allowed himself, so he was surprised to awaken to see his bedside clock indicating it was 7:20. He threw on his robe and went into the kitchen to make coffee, then wandered into the living room for his ritual checking of the city, which swept out before him to the towers of the Loop and beyond to the horizon somewhere off to the left.

He could see the scoop of the lake where Illinois became Indiana. The sun was shining brightly, and to the east over the grey-green, whitecap-flecked lake, there wasn't a cloud in the sky. However, to the west, a line of dark and quickly moving cumulus clouds advanced on the city like a phalanx of Hannibal's elephants.

By the time he'd had a glass of V-8, poured his coffee, cut and toasted a bagel and slathered it with cream cheese, the light level in the living room had been reduced by half. A few minutes after that, a gray veil of rain and low clouds obscured his view of the loop.

He went into the den to catch the news while he ate, but he'd missed the headlines so turned the TV back off. On a whim, he went to the bookcase and pulled out a dog-eared copy of his favorite book–*Chesspiece*, by Morgan Butler, whose work he'd discovered while still in high school. He'd read all of Butler's books and two biographies of the closeted writer, who had killed himself in 1953 at the age of thirty-one.

Though Elliott didn't think of himself as a romantic, Butler's life story—his inability to break the bonds of a domineering father and an unforgiving society had doomed his relationship with the man he loved—had for some reason resonated deeply, though he could never understand why.

He was still reading at noon when Cessy called to invite him—"and Steve"—to Brad, Jr.'s, regional high school swim meet the following Saturday afternoon.

"I'll have to check with Steve to see if he can make it, but you can tell BJ I'll be there in either case."

"I hope you both can make it," she said. "It's really important to BJ for the men of the family to be there, and with Brad's job being what it is, there's never a guarantee he won't be called out on some case or other. He hates to miss any of BJ's activities, but he doesn't have a choice."

"I understand." Her implication she considered Steve one of the "men of the family" was not lost on him.

"So, is Steve there now?"

"No, I'm picking him up around four. We're going to a party later here in the building."

"It's too bad you have to go out in this weather."

"Hey, it's Chicago. By the time I'm ready to leave, the sun will probably be out again. Either that, or we'll have four feet of snow."

Cessy filled him in on everything that had happened with the family since last they'd talked—an awful lot of activity, Elliott decided, in the space of two days. They hung up with his repeating his promise to check with Steve about the swim meet and let her know.

Chapter 2

The rain had all but ended when Elliott left the building on his way to Steve's. He'd called just before he left, and Steve was waiting in the entrance to his building when Elliott pulled up.

They drove first to the art supply store on North Avenue, where Steve spent twenty minutes shopping. Elliott used the time to admire the very helpful clerk, who seemed to take a particular interest in assisting Steve to find exactly what he wanted.

They then swung over to Armitage to check out Bruno's old building. Elliot didn't have the exact address but knew he wouldn't have any trouble spotting it based on the photograph. He'd always admired the classic old turreted and domed buildings located along Armitage within a few blocks of the el station. He particularly loved the one immediately to the east of the tracks but had felt it was too close to them to be practical. However, he was pleased when someone else purchased it and restored it very much as he would have.

They'd gone about a block past the el when he spotted Bruno's building ahead on the right–three stories, with the turreted corner siding an alley paralleling the structure. The turret was painted a uniform rust-brown, and the ground floor false front was inexplicably painted purple.

"Purple?" Steve said, echoing Elliott's thought.

But as they neared the building, Elliott could see the rust-brown of the turret covered ornate fretwork typical of Queen Anne "Painted Ladies" of the period, and he could immediately envision the ground floor as some sort of commercial space once the facade was restored to how it must have looked when it was built.

On closer inspection, the turret's top, base and window framing also revealed an abundance of detail work all but hidden by the uniform rust-brown coating. His mind's eye easily envisioned it stripped of the drab paint and the detail work redone in the bright, contrasting and complementary colors it probably had when it was first built.

The ground floor's false front gave little indication of what it had originally looked like, though again the lintels above and around the entrance hinted of details covered over. The bas-relief writing he'd noted in the photograph read "Brisson Block 1896."

Pulling just far enough into the alley to get the rear of the car out of the street while enabling a closer look at the front and side, Elliott turned to Steve for his reaction.

"I like it," Steve said. "The false front is a disaster, but put back the way it must have been originally, and with some creative repainting, it has real potential. But you're the guy who does all the work. What do you think?"

Elliott pursed his lips, thinking, then said, "Same as you."

It had begun to rain again, which dissuaded them from parking and doing a more close-up inspection. Instead, Elliott drove slowly down the alley, trying to take in as much of the building as he could. He was pleased to see typical Chicago-style bay windows on the second and third floors over the alley. He looked for cracks and missing bricks and didn't see any, though it would definitely have to be tuck-pointed. A one-story extension he assumed to be a garage had been added to the back.

As they turned down the intersecting alley, he saw he was correct. Three individual single-car doors, one of them in bad shape, faced the back alley, with an inset not visible from the side for a narrow metal fire escape.

"Can we go around again?" Steve asked.

"Sure," Elliott said, turning left toward Armitage at the next street, then left again to pass by from the other direction.

"Did you notice the park?" Steve asked, giving a head-tilt to the right.

"Yeah. Oz Park. I forgot it was that close. A park is a definite plus. And no one will be building there to block the view."

The rain was much heavier as Elliott turned again into the side alley, once more stopping with the rear of the car just off the street. He had to lean forward to see the top of the building, checking again for cracks or missing decorations. It was hard to tell with all the paint, but he was able to discern even more covered-over detail than before. Again, he had a mental picture of what it could look like when restored.

He continued down the alley and headed back toward home.

"So, you think you might be interested?" Steve asked.

Elliott shrugged. "Hard to say. I've never done a building with commercial space. That's not to say I wouldn't, it's just that they're sort of a different animal."

"I understand," Steve said. "But I liked it–if you squint and ignore the first floor, which is ugly as sin. I can imagine what it looked like originally."

"Me, too," Elliott agreed. "Bruno said it had once been the local grocery, so I could probably make a good guess. The problem with converting it back to commercial space is what might go in there. Mom-and-pop grocery stores went out with the dinosaurs. The same with butcher shops and drugstores, hardware stores, paint stores, appliance stores. They've all been sucked into the black hole of Walmart and K-Mart and Cosco and Target and the other chains. A coffee shop, maybe, or a bar, or a cafe, but..."

"It would make a great place for an art gallery," Steve said casually, looking out the window at the rain.

"Thinking of giving up your day job?" Elliott asked with a grin.

Steve turned to him, returning the grin.

"I wish! Still, no harm in fantasizing. Maybe someday."

After a quick stop at the supermarket for a couple of steaks, they returned to Elliott's. The rain, which had dropped off to an intermittent drizzle while they were in the store, picked up again as they returned to the car, and Elliott was glad he had indoor parking at his condo.

"So, what time is the party?" Steve asked as he helped unpack the groceries, leaving the steaks on the counter.

"He said any time after seven-thirty, so I guess whenever we get there will be fine," Elliott replied. "No rush."

"I wonder if the rain will keep people away?"

"From free booze? Are you serious?"

"Any idea how many are coming?"

"Not a clue, but I'd suspect quite a few."

Elliott fixed drinks then followed Steve into the living room, where he turned on the radio. The overture to *Tannhauser*–one of his and Steve's favorites–was playing, and they sat side-by-side on the couch, sipping their drinks and watching in silence as a rain-blurred dusk closed over the city.

When the piece ended, Elliott asked, "Were you serious about having a gallery?"

Steve gave him a small smile. "I've thought about it, sure, for sometime in the future. I don't have enough of my own work to fill a whole gallery, of course, and I've really been doing well with Devereux's."

Elliott remembered Steve's show at the tony Devereux Gallery in the River North art district not long after they'd first met, and how happy he had been for him. The gallery regularly displayed and had sold several of Steve's paintings.

⁂

They had another drink then went back into the kitchen to fix dinner. Steve set the dining room table–the small breakfast bar between the kitchen and living room was too small to be practical for two people and a full meal–and made a salad while Elliott got the steaks ready and fixed instant mashed potatoes.

They took their time over dinner, the conversation as always touching on a wide range of subjects from Steve's HIV-positive brother Manny, whom Steve was trying to convince to come to Chicago for a visit, to Cessy's invitation to Brad, Jr.'s, swim meet, to Steve's current paintings-in-progress–he was working on two at once.

"I've been meaning to ask you," Steve said as he poured them each another glass of wine, "if it would be okay if I did some sketches from your balcony."

Elliott's face reflected his surprise.

"You have to ask?" he said. "Of course you can. Any time you want."

"Well, I didn't want to impose, and I feel a little awkward saying it, but when I'm sketching, I sort of go off into my own world. I wouldn't want you to think I was ignoring you."

Elliott knew Steve was diplomatically saying he didn't want any distractions when he was working.

"No problem," he said. "I'll stay completely out of your way. You can have the whole place to yourself for as long as you want it, and any time you want it. Tomorrow, if you'd like."

Smiling, Steve said, "Thanks, but I don't have my sketch pad with me. I'll bring one when I come over next time."

Elliott was tempted to say he was welcome to keep a sketch pad and anything else he might need at the condo but didn't. They never left things at the other's place. The fact they wore the same size clothes helped—if a change of clothes was necessary, they would just borrow something.

Cessy couldn't understand why he and Steve never discussed where their relationship was going. While he increasingly, if secretly, agreed with her, neither he nor Steve had suggested such a discussion was immediately necessary, and he assumed that when it became necessary, they would have it. There was no doubt in his mind as to how he felt, and he instinctively sensed Steve felt the same. It was as though they had mutually agreed to take their time enjoying the journey rather than rushing to the destination.

After dinner, Steve cleared the table while Elliott rinsed the dishes and put them in the washer. At around nine, they headed up to Bruno's unit, sharing the elevator with a fifty-something man and two nice-looking younger guys Elliott suspected were not partners. They exchanged cursory greetings then rode the rest of the way in silence.

When the elevator stopped at forty, the three men got off first and turned left to 40-J, which told Elliott they—or at least the older man—had been there before. The kitchen door was open and the front door slightly ajar, and the fifty-something went right in without knocking, trailed by the younger two.

He and Steve hesitated only a moment, then followed them in. Elliott was pleased that the music wasn't set to a window-shaking volume.

As they entered the living room, the fifty-something and his companions turned immediately toward the kitchen, where a bartender was mixing and serving drinks. There were at least a dozen guys in the living room, standing around in pairs and small groups. Elliott saw Bruno in front of the partially open sliding glass door to the balcony, talking with a very handsome young man. Spotting them, Bruno laid a hand on the young man's arm, apparently excusing himself, and came over.

"Hi, guys! Glad you could come," he said with enthusiasm. "Grab yourselves a drink and help yourself to something to eat." He indicated both the bar and a long credenza against the wall nearest the kitchen, on which a stack of plates, napkins and several trays of cheese, vegetables, dips, cold cuts, iced shrimp and small sandwiches were laid out.

"You really went all out," Elliott said, acknowledging the people, the bar and the food.

Bruno again beamed like a small boy who'd just been complimented in class.

"Thank you. I do what I can." Glancing at the young man to whom he'd been talking, who was in the same spot he had left him, watching him and smiling, Bruno turned back and said, "Go–have a drink. We'll talk later."

When he left, Steve smiled and said, "I see you and Bruno share a love of Old Spice."

Elliott merely grinned.

As they turned toward the bar, the fifty-something, drink in hand, moved toward Bruno with his two companions in tow. Elliott heard the man say, "Bruno, I'd like you to meet Cal and Turk..." before the rest were lost in the general murmur of conversation.

Elliott recognized the bartender immediately from one of the bars, though he couldn't immediately recall which one. They exchanged greetings, and Steve ordered a bourbon-Seven.

"Make it two," Elliott said.

Behind the bartender was a serving cart stacked with glasses and liquor bottles, and by the refrigerator, a man Elliott assumed was the caterer was taking deviled eggs from a large Tupperware container and arranging them on a platter. The entire counter near him was lined with containers of various sizes and shapes.

On the top of the serving cart Elliott noticed various saucers of garnishes–lime slices, maraschino cherries, cocktail onions and cannonball olives.

"Can I get a couple of those olives?" he asked.

The bartender didn't bat an eye. Steve looked at him quizzically.

"Olives in a bourbon-Seven? That's a first," he said.

"What do you mean," Elliott replied casually. "I do it all the time."

Steve gave him a raised eyebrow.

"Uh-huh." Turning to the bartender, he said, "Me, too. But give 'em to him."

Skewering several of the huge olives onto two toothpicks, the bartender placed them on a napkin rather than putting them in the drink and handed it to Elliott, who smiled his thanks.

"Can't fool a good bartender," he said as they moved to check out the buffet. Indicating his skewered olives, he grinned at Steve. "Want one?"

⁂

While Steve knew none of the guests, and had met Bruno only once, Elliott had the advantage of knowing three or four people who also lived in the building. He envied Steve's natural ability to appear perfectly at ease surrounded by strangers. Elliott had worked at it over the years, but he doubted he'd ever be as good at it as Steve.

Bruno, he noted, was surrounded by four or five very attractive and attentive younger guys, including the two who had ridden up on the elevator with him and Steve. All of the young men seemed to hang on his every word and laughed a lot, and it didn't escape Elliott that the fifty-something who had accompanied them seemed to keep a close eye on them. Though he estimated at least thirty people were at the party at one time or another, Bruno had very little time to spend with anyone other than his circle of admirers.

Button and Paul showed up shortly after ten, walking in with the tall redhead Bruno had introduced to Elliott as Dr. Clifford Blanton. Both Blanton and Button were dressed to the nines in expensive-looking casual suits. Spotting Elliott, Button came right over, Paul on his heels. Blanton headed for Bruno, leading Elliott to think their mutual arrival was coincidental.

"You made it!" Button exclaimed happily as the four exchanged handshakes. Looking around, he said, "Well, he's done it again. I don't know where all these people come from. I've never seen three-quarters of them before, and for me, that's saying something. I thought I knew everybody in Chicago. I suspect Bruno imports them. I must talk to him about that. And people will come out of the woodwork for free booze." He smiled brightly and added, "Of course, you'll notice I'm here, too."

"Where's our host?" Paul asked.

Steve made a head-up gesture toward where Bruno was talking with the fifty-something and one of the man's young companions. The rest of the clique that had surrounded him now stood clumped together several feet away.

"Ah, yes," Button said. "Rudy and...what's his name?...Turk. Turk dances at the Lucky Horseshoe and Crossroads. He really should never wear clothes. They hide his best assets."

"And who is Rudy?" Steve asked.

Button smiled. "Rudy Patterson. He's the Heidi Fleiss of Boys Town. A...matchmaker...if you will. I've told Bruno to watch out for him, now that he has money. Rudy operates a limousine service and has a large stable of attractive and enterprising young men he hires as drivers. He also introduces them to gentlemen of means, who show their appreciation in the form of a donation to Rudy's favorite charity–Rudy. I didn't know Turk was part of his stable. I must be slipping."

"Do you know the guy who came in when you did?" Elliott asked.

"The redhead? Yes. He's one of Bruno's new acquisitions, and I'm not quite sure what to make of him. Perhaps I'm just being overly protective. Bruno isn't gullible, but he's an antelope at the watering hole for the sort of predators who can smell money from a mile away. Bruno told me about him, but I've not met him before. I'll wager he bought that suit in Taiwan. I can always spot them."

Elliott didn't know if that was meant as a compliment or a slam, so let it pass without comment.

Paul, as usual, didn't say much, but Elliott could sense he was very taken with Steve, as were a couple of the other guests. He was at first oblivious to the covert attention he himself was being paid by one of the members of Bruno's clique, but Steve noticed and called his attention to it with a grin.

Elliott shrugged. "When ya got it, flaunt it."

"So, how's the construction business?" Button asked.

"Keeps me busy." Though he'd never told Button or Paul he owned his own business, the fact he lived in this building probably gave them a clue he wasn't just "in construction" as a laborer.

"And what do you do, Steve?" Paul asked.

"I'm a painter."

"Do you work with Elliott?"

Steve grinned. "Well, we do work well together, but, no. I'm a commercial artist for an ad agency."

"...and far too modest," Elliott added. "He's a damned good painter, and he's got some of his work on display in a River North gallery."

"Really?" Button appeared genuinely interested. "Which gallery?"

"Devereux," Steve said.

"One of my favorites!" Laying a hand lightly on Steve's arm, he said, "I'm impressed. Beauty *and* talent! I'll have to look for your work next time I'm there." He paused, then added, "Your last name is Gutierrez, right? I'm so bad with last names."

Steve grinned. "Well, for only having heard it once, I'm flattered you remembered it at all."

They left the party around midnight. Elliott had hoped to at least mention to Bruno that they'd gone by his old building and to say he might be interested in talking with the owner if the man was, in fact, thinking of selling. However, they only had a chance to exchange an occasional few quick words in passing, so he had shifted his concentration to the party and talking with Button, Paul and several other guests.

❧

Over the next few days, Elliott began to question just how much of his enthusiasm for the Armitage building was due to his liking it for itself–which he did–and how much he was being influenced by how much he knew Steve liked it, and by how much Steve wanted his own art gallery. He was a bit concerned Steve might think he was using the building as a spiderweb to trap him. That was the last thing in the world he wanted.

But he also saw his concern as yet another indication of the need for a serious talk with Steve about where they were headed.

That the Armitage building just happened to come along when it did was, he finally concluded, strictly a coincidence. His current project was at the point where he was starting to look around for the next one anyway. He had tried to contact Larry Fingerhood, his real estate broker, the week before to tell him to start looking for properties, only to learn Larry was on vacation and would be gone for another week.

❧

Monday evening, while checking his mail after work, he ran into Bruno in the lobby, holding a large stack of envelopes.

"Thanks for the party," he said. "We had a great time."

"I'm sorry I didn't have more time to spend with you. I do apologize."

"Not necessary. You were busy. I would have called to thank you, but I don't have your number."

"Do you have a pen?"

Reaching into his pocket, Elliott extracted a pencil stub.

"Will this do?"

Smiling, Bruno took it.

"Sure." He wrote a number on the back of one of the envelopes and handed it and the pencil to Elliott.

"Don't you need this?" Elliott asked, indicating the envelope.

"It's just someone wanting money. Screw 'em."

They got on the elevator and began the ride to their respective floors.

"Steve and I drove by your old building," Elliott said. "It's got a lot of potential."

"Doesn't it? The purple is ghastly, but it was painted that color before the present owner bought it."

"Well, I wouldn't mind seeing the inside."

"I'd be happy to call Marvin–the owner–and see if he's still thinking of selling. And if he is, perhaps I could give him your number."

Elliott realized that, just as he hadn't had Bruno's number, Bruno didn't have his.

"Got another envelope you can spare?"

Bruno's smile was more rueful than happy.

"Pick one. They're all junk."

Elliott took the top one, retrieved the pencil from his pocket and wrote down his phone number.

"Aren't you curious?" Bruno asked.

"About what?"

He indicated the stack of mail.

"About all this crap."

Elliott shrugged. "I didn't figure it's any of my business."

"Right. Sorry. It's just that it would be nice to get a real letter sometime from someone who didn't just want money."

The look on Bruno's face struck something in Elliott, and on the spur of the moment, as the elevator stopped on thirty-five, he said, "Would you like to stop in for a drink? I've seen your place, but you haven't seen mine yet."

Bruno looked just a bit surprised, but then said, "Sure. That would really be nice. I've never been in anyone else's condo here before." Again Elliott got the distinct impression of loneliness.

Entering through the kitchen, they continued into the living room. Bruno looked around slowly, taking everything in.

"Very nice," he said. "It's really strange how two identical floor plans can look so different. All this..." He made a small gesture with the envelopes he was holding. "...looks like it...belongs. Not like my place."

"There's nothing wrong with your place," Elliott said. "You've got a lot of really nice things."

Bruno shrugged but said nothing.

Elliott moved into the kitchen. "What would you like to drink?"

"Whatever you're having's fine." Bruno stopped by the balcony doors and looked out over the city.

"Bourbon-Seven?"

"Fine. You know," he continued without turning around, "sometimes I really think I'm out of my element here."

"How do you mean?" Elliott reached into the freezer for ice cubes. He could observe Bruno's expression by watching his reflection in the glass of the sliding doors.

Bruno's gesture took in the apartment and the panoramic view beyond.

"All this. It's not me. I never would have dreamed in a million years I'd be able to afford all this. Hell, I had a devil of a time just making my rent at the old place. And now...it's all kind of overwhelming."

Returning to the living room, Elliott handed him his drink, gesturing him to the sofa. He took a facing chair.

"I can imagine," he said. "But you seem to be handling it all right."

Bruno shrugged. "Glad it looks that way. I really am trying. One of the first things I did after–I assume you do know I won the lottery."

Elliott nodded.

"The first thing I did was to get a financial manager to handle the money so I didn't blow it. The first thing *he* did was ask me if I had a will, and when I told him I'd never felt the need, since I'd never really had anything of value, he insisted I make one immediately. It was him who told me about this building, by the way. He lives here, on thirty. Maybe you know him? Walter Means?"

Elliott knew him. Means was the multi-term president of the condo's board. He was officious and condescending and, to Elliott's mind, thoroughly dislikable. Means's wife, with whom he and Bruno had ridden the elevator a week or two earlier, was one of the building's more flamboyant characters, noted for her flaming red hair, her whippet Alexi, and her penchant for wearing mink whenever the temperature dipped below sixty.

Means had approached him when he first moved into the building about representing him as a financial manager, and he had been invited to a small cocktail party at the Means's condo. The invitation had been handwritten on embossed vellum by Mrs. Means, who prided herself on her calligraphy.

Luckily, Bruno didn't wait for a reply.

"Anyway, I'm really not an extravagant guy. My only indulgence, prior to...all this...was my stamp collection. But even with a financial manager and my being on the equivalent of an allowance, it's still one hell of a lot of money to deal with. And let's face it, when you've never had much, to suddenly have more than you ever dreamed of is kind of fun. I can give parties and make new friends–I've always been something of a loner, not so much through desire as circumstance. I'm so glad I have Sensei to keep me balanced."

Elliott resisted the temptation to ask exactly how that worked and instead said, "Well, judging from the people at your party Saturday, you seem to be doing quite well as far as making friends goes."

Again a slight shrug, accompanied by a wry smile.

"Having handsome young men falling all over me isn't all that bad, I guess. But I certainly don't kid myself as to why. They wouldn't have given me the time of day six months ago."

"Don't sell yourself short," Elliott cautioned.

"I'm not. I'm just being realistic. And it's kind of nice being the center of attention for a change."

"What about the friends you had before?"

"To be honest, I've never had many. I've always been pretty much a loner, and I've always been intimidated by practically everybody. I think that's why I started collecting stamps when I was a kid. Stamps weren't judgmental or didn't make me feel I was constantly being measured against others. I'm only now learning how to be comfortable around people, thanks to Sensei, and I hope you won't think I'm being arrogant when I say that knowing I can buy and sell most of the people I've always been intimidated by is oddly empowering."

"I was into stamps when I was younger, too," Elliott said. "We traveled a lot, and I took to collecting stamps from every country we visited. I really enjoyed it, but got out of it around the time I started college. I gave them to my sister Cessy for her kids, and I suppose she still has them. So, are you still collecting?"

Bruno gave him a strange little smile.

"Yes. Next time you come up, I'll show you my pride and joy, if you'd like to see it."

Though he wasn't quite sure what Bruno was referring to, he nodded. "I'd like that."

"How about you?" Bruno asked. "Do you have any hobbies now?"

Elliott was rather surprised, not by the question but by the realization that the answer was no.

"I guess my work's my hobby, come to think of it," he said. "I really love what I do."

"Well, I hope you'll decide to take on my old building. As much as I like my condo, it's not the same. The old place had...I don't know...a... charm, a warmth, a feeling these newer places simply can't match."

"Do you know anything about its history?" Elliott asked. "I see it was built in eighteen-ninety-six, probably by someone named Brisson."

Bruno nodded. "Right. The people who owned the building when I moved in were named Taggert, but the wife was the granddaughter of the man who built it. I understand the architect was another relative, who later went on to design several Chicago landmarks. It stayed in the family until about five years ago, when the Taggerts' only son convinced them to sell and move to Phoenix, to be near him.

"Mrs. Taggert was the one who told me the ground floor was originally a grocery store, and was converted to an apartment when the store closed right after World War Two. It still has its original pressed-tin ceiling, and I think she told me they just paneled over the pressed-tin walls. But the upstairs apartments haven't changed all that much since the place was built. They showed me a black-and-white photo of the exterior taken around nineteen-hundred. It was really beautiful.

"It was the son who decided the outside should be painted before they sold it. Unfortunately, the guy must be color blind and have no taste, plus he had a friend who ran a paint store and gave him a real deal on the purple and rust-brown. I know the Taggerts weren't at all happy, but the son thought he was doing them a favor by saving them a lot of money.

"The guy who bought it, Marvin Lamb, is the one who has it now. He works for some brokerage firm, and I think he was hit pretty hard when the bottom fell out of the stock market. As I told you, one of the reasons I left was because I thought he'd probably try to sell it. But maybe he's holding off listing it in hopes the housing market will pick up."

"Good luck with that one," Elliott said. "But I wouldn't mind taking a closer look at it, so if you want to check to see if he *is* considering selling, you might just mention that you know someone who might–emphasis on *might*–be looking, and see what his reaction is."

The conversation then wandered off in other directions until Bruno finished his drink.

"Would you like another?" Elliott asked.

Bruno shook his head.

"Thanks, no. My nephew Cage is coming into town this evening. I haven't seen him in years." He smiled. "I've been hearing a lot lately from the few relatives I have left. I'm sure it has nothing whatever to do with my winning the lottery, of course.

"Anyway, Cage has been emailing me just about every day, hinting that he'd love to come visit for a few days to 'catch up on old times.' Actually, there weren't any 'old times' to speak of. We have almost nothing in common, and we've spent very little time together. But both my brother and sister-in-law are in pretty bad health, and I can understand his wanting to get away for a bit, so finally I gave in. He's arriving at around seven."

"How long is he staying?"

"He didn't specify, but I hope no longer than a couple of days."

"He doesn't have a job he has to get back to?" Elliott asked.

"Cage–his real name's Edmund, but he unofficially changed it when he took up acting–has been living in New York for the past six or seven years, and I'm pretty sure just scraping by. He was in some off-Broadway revival that just closed, and he's back in Rockford. I don't know for how long."

"Well, it's nice of you to have him visit at all. And maybe it won't be all that bad."

Bruno gave him an unconvinced smile. "Maybe."

Both men got up and went into the kitchen, where Bruno set his glass down on the counter beside the sink. Turning to Elliott, he said, "Thanks for the drink. I really enjoyed talking with you."

"Same here."

* * *

Cessy called Tuesday night to re-verify what he'd told her on Sunday–that Steve would be coming with him to Brad, Jr.'s, swim meet on Saturday. He again declined her offer to ride with her and the family to the meet, which was being held at New Trier High School in suburban Winnetka.

"Thanks, sis," he said, "and no offense, but four adults and three kids in one car, even an SUV, can get a little crowded."

"Well, actually, there'd be four kids–the parents of one of BJ's teammates won't be able to come, so we're going to pick him up. But there's still plenty of room."

"That's okay. We'll meet you there. Three o'clock, right?"

"Right. We'll be going early so the boys have time to get ready, but we'll save you a seat."

They talked a few more minutes then said their goodbyes. Elliott had just returned the phone to its cradle when it rang again.

"Elliott Smith."

"Elliott, it's Bruno. I just talked with Marvin, and he is definitely interested in selling. He just lost another tenant, so the building's empty except for him, and I get the impression he's in a lot worse financial shape than I'd thought. When I asked him if he was still thinking of selling, he immediately asked me if I wanted to buy it. I told him no, but that I knew someone who might be looking. He said to please give you his number, and he'd be happy to talk to you, and would be glad to show you the place any time you might want to see it."

"Thanks, Bruno. I appreciate it. Let me get a pencil and get the number." As he rummaged for a pencil and paper, he said, "So, did your nephew show up?"

"About half an hour after I got back to the apartment from your place."

"Everything going okay?"

"About as expected. We're just getting ready to go out to dinner. He wants to try the restaurant at the top of the Hancock. I've never been there, but I understand the view is spectacular. Then he wants to go bar-hopping."

"He's gay?"

"Oh, yes. It's a long story I'll have to tell you sometime."

"I'd like to hear it. But I should let you go to dinner now. Thanks again for getting the phone number for me. I'll give Lamb a call."

He deliberately waited until Thursday to call, so as not to give the wrong impression about either his eagerness to see the building or his possible interest in buying. He waited until he'd had dinner and talked with Steve, who was enthusiastic at the prospect.

"I've got a really good feeling about that place," Steve said. "I hope you like it."

When he called, the phone was answered on the second ring.

"Marvin Lamb?"

"Yes?"

"My name's Elliott Smith. My neighbor, Bruno Caesar, mentioned you were considering selling your building on Armitage."

There was a slight pause, which Elliott sensed was calculated.

"Well, yes, as a matter of fact, I have been thinking of it. I was talking with Bruno a couple of nights ago, and he said he knew someone who was into restoring old buildings. This one's a gem, if I do say so myself, and it's in great shape for its age."

Elliott resisted saying he'd already driven by, again to avoid giving the impression of eagerness.

"Well, I might be looking for another property and wouldn't mind taking a look at it."

"Of course. I work during the day, but any evening–or maybe this weekend?"

"Saturday morning might be good." It occurred to him that maybe Steve would like to go along. Then the fact he'd considered that rather startled him.

"That'll be fine. What time?"

"Eleven?"

"I'll be here. You have the address?"

"Yeah, I got it from Bruno, and I think I know the place. That whole stretch along Armitage is one of my favorite parts of the city, architecturally."

"Then you'll love this place. Built in eighteen-ninety-six."

"I'll look forward to seeing it," Elliott replied. "Saturday at eleven, then."

They exchanged goodbyes and hung up. Elliott thought of calling Steve but then reconsidered, since they'd already talked shortly before. He still hadn't figured out exactly why he'd even thought of asking Steve to come along. He had never taken anyone other than Larry Fingerhood, his real estate broker, with him when he viewed a property for the first time.

He eventually decided he'd had the idea in the back of his head, as soon as he saw the building, that Steve, as an artist, might have some advice on color schemes if he were to decide to buy it. Victorian-era buildings often combined many hues, and while Elliott felt he had a good sense of color, this was the first time he'd had the chance of working with a true Painted Lady. An artist's eye might be helpful.

He deliberately avoided considering the other possible reasons he wanted Steve to go with him.

❧

He mentioned it to Steve when they talked Thursday night, and Steve was pleased Elliott wanted his help in choosing colors should he decide to buy the place.

"I appreciate that, Ell. I'd never have mentioned it myself, but the first time we drove by it, I had some really great ideas."

They agreed to go to dinner Friday night–Elliott suggested the Cornelia just off Halsted, to which Steve had never been. Steve suggested they could then spend the night at his place and go see the building after breakfast. They could stop at Elliott's condo on their way to Winnetka so Elliott could change clothes, and go on from there.

❧

–And you're kidding whom, exactly?

–I don't know what you're talking about.

–Uh-huh. Steve. Remember him?

–Yes, I remember Steve, and if you're going to pull a Cessy on me, you can just forget it.

—Sorry. It's just that you're a little on the stubborn side at times.

—Yeah, and I like you, too. But just let me take this at my own speed, okay? I'll think about it when I think about it.

—You're thinking about it now.

—Give me a break, will you?

—Okay. I really like the building.

—You've seen it?

—Of course. As I say, I really like it. But you can make up your own mind.

—Thanks.

—Any time. I'll let you get back to sleep, now.

Sorting through his mail Friday as he crossed the lobby to the elevator, he didn't see Bruno until he was almost on top of him. Bruno wasn't alone, which was hardly surprising.

The handsome young man beside him was in his early thirties, just under six feet tall with a swimmer's build, black wavy hair and eyes so dark they, too, were almost black. He reminded Elliott of a gondolier in Venice with whom he'd had a furtive fling on one of his trips to Italy with his parents as a teenager. His complexion, Elliott noticed, was flawless, and he couldn't help but wonder if it was the result of nature or of professional-level makeup.

"Elliott!" Bruno said, smiling. "Good to see you."

Elliott felt the nephew's eyes giving him a very slow head-to-knees scan.

As if realizing for the first time that someone was standing beside him, Bruno said, "This is my nephew Cage. Cage, this is my downstairs neighbor, Elliott Smith."

The young man smiled warmly and extended his hand.

"It's nice to meet you, Elliott," he said. "Uncle Bruno has been telling me about you."

The handshake was warm and firm, the kind Elliott called the hail-fellow-well-met handshake—one meant to impress. And, given Cage's overall packaging, Elliott was quite impressed.

As they got on the elevator and pressed the buttons for their respective floors, Bruno said, "So, what are you up to tonight?"

"Steve and I are going out for dinner, then maybe a drink after."

He noticed that every time he glanced at Cage, Cage was looking at him and smiling.

"Cage and I are going out for dinner, too." Bruno paused, then said, "I know this is spur-of-the-moment, and I hope I'm not imposing or being too bold, but would you and Steve consider joining us? My treat. We're thinking of going to that semi-gay restaurant behind Little Joe's bar. I can't remember the name, but it's just east of Halsted."

Elliott smiled. "The Cornelia," he said, "and that's where Steve and I were planning on going."

"Small world!" Bruno grinned broadly. "Poor Cage has been practically shackled to my hip since he arrived. I'm sure he'd welcome spending time with some new faces."

Elliott was somewhat taken aback by the unexpected invitation and the coincidence of the choice of restaurant, though he sincerely doubted, from the looks of Cage, that he was the kind of guy who would allow himself to be shackled to anyone's hip.

"That's really nice of you, Bruno."

Since they were all going to the same restaurant, declining the invitation would be awkward. Besides, he was curious to know a bit more about Bruno's handsome nephew and what he might have in mind regarding Bruno. For some reason, he felt a vague sense of protectiveness toward Bruno, and didn't want to see him being taken advantage of. Whether or not that was Cage's intention he didn't know, but figured spending some time with him might provide a clue.

He noted Cage gaze was still on him.

"Let me give Steve a call," he said. "We'll be staying at his place tonight, so it'll probably be best if we take two cars."

Bruno smiled. "No problem. We weren't planning to leave before seven, but whatever time is good for you..."

As the door opened on thirty-five, Elliott said, "I'll get back to you as soon as I call Steve. And thanks."

❧

Putting his cooler and the mail on the counter near the sink, he reached for his land-line phone–strictly from force of habit–to called Steve.

"Are you up for a change of plans?" he asked.

"What kind of change?" Steve sounded mildly puzzled.

Elliott explained Bruno's offer and the reasons why he hadn't simply declined with thanks.

There was only a slight pause before Steve said, "Sure. No problem. It never hurts to get in a multi-millionaire's good graces. What's his nephew like?"

"We didn't have a chance to talk much, but he seems okay. Really nice-looking guy, early thirties, I'd guess. Bruno told me they've never spent much time together, and I'm just curious to see if there might be any ulterior motives in his suddenly reestablishing contact."

"I can think of fifty-nine million, right offhand."

"Yeah, that's what I'm a little concerned about, even though it's none of my business. But I like Bruno and think I can guess what he's going through with all this. I wouldn't want to see him being taken advantage of."

"Nice of you to feel that way. Should be an interesting dinner. What time?"

"How about seven? I'll pick you up, and we'll meet them at the restaurant."

"Okay, I'll be waiting out front."

Elliott hit the disconnect button and called Bruno.

After dinner, they went with Bruno and Cage to Side Track, one of the largest and most popular bars in Boys Town, for a drink. It would not have been the choice of either Steve or Elliott, neither of whom was fond of crowds; but Cage had heard of it and wanted to go, and Bruno had insisted they join them.

As usual on a weekend evening, Boys Town was a solid mass of bodies. They wisely left the cars parked near the restaurant and walked to the bar. Luckily, it was a warm evening and, after making their way through the three or four main areas on the ground floor, they went upstairs to the roof patio, where they found a relatively uncrowded corner.

They'd been there less than ten minutes when Elliott heard a voice behind him call "Bruno!" Bruno, facing the caller, smiled and waved. A moment later, they were joined by a man they'd seen at Bruno's party, the one Button had identified as Rudy and described as the Heidi Fleiss of Boys Town.

Since they had not officially met at the party, there were introductions all around. Rudy was accompanied by an all-American college-boy type he introduced as Tim.

"I was hoping we might run into you," Rudy said, addressing Bruno jovially. "I was telling Tim about you, and he wanted to meet you. And I, of course, wanted to see if your nephew lived up to your glowing description." He smiled broadly at Cage. "I'm happy to see he exceeds it."

Elliott noted with some amusement that, while he and Steve were not being ignored, the dynamics of the group were clearly focused on Tim's predatory attention to Bruno and Rudy's only slightly more subtle attention to Cage. Elliott wondered if Rudy was thinking of adding Cage to his stable of "proteges," and what Bruno might think of the idea if he were.

⁂

"Interesting evening," Steve conceded as they drove back to his place a little after midnight.

"That it was."

"So, what conclusions did you draw about Cage and his intentions toward Bruno?"

"Hard to tell. The guy is an actor, after all, and if he has ulterior motives, he's playing his cards pretty close to the vest. You'll note he did drop several hints he's thinking about moving to Chicago, which might or might not imply his moving in with Bruno."

"Yeah, I sort of got that, too," Steve said. "Though he might ask you if you'd like a roommate if Bruno doesn't go along."

"And where did you get that idea?"

"Ever seen a lion eyeing a wildebeest?"

Elliott grinned. "Just what have you been smoking? But if that's the case, it might underscore that what he's really looking at is dollar signs."

"Bullshit. You're hot."

"May I write you a check?"

They both laughed.

"You're crazy, Smith."

⁂

When Elliott awoke Saturday morning, Steve was already up. He found him in his studio, working on a painting, wearing only a pair of paint-splattered sweatpants.

"Coffee's ready," Steve said without looking away from the canvas, which was facing away from Elliott.

"How long have you been up?" Elliott asked from the doorway. While he had never said so, the room was Steve's private space, and Elliott never entered without an invitation.

Steve shrugged, dipping his brush into one of the small cups of paint on the pallet in his left hand, still not looking at Elliott.

"Not long. I just had an idea and wanted to act on it before I lost it. I've almost got it. Pour me a cup while you're getting yours, okay? I'll be there in a minute."

"Sure."

He went into the kitchen. He'd been a little surprised to see how many finished canvases Steve had stacked against the wall. He usually showed them to Elliott as he finished them, but almost always, he brought them into the living room. Seeing them one at a time, Elliott had lost track of just how many there were.

He'd just put Steve's coffee down on a coaster on the table beside the couch when Steve came in, wiping the flat of his hands on his sweatpants.

"Sorry," he said, joining Elliott on the couch. "I didn't want to wake you."

"No problem. I hadn't realized how prolific you are. I'm impressed."

Steve nodded then took a sip of coffee.

"Yeah, there are quite a few. I wish Devereux had room to show more, but..."

Elliott knew Steve's paintings sold well through the gallery, which went out of its way to showcase newer artists. Steve met with the owner about once a month, showing him new works and exchanging those Devereaux selected for ones that hadn't sold. The meetings never took very long, so Elliott often accompanied him.

"I guess I never paid attention to how long it takes you to do a painting," Elliott admitted.

"It varies," Steve said, turning slightly to put his cup back on the table. "A lot depends on how much time I have to paint. Some only take a couple of days. Some I work on for months. But usually, they go pretty fast once I get started."

"Yeah, well, sometimes I think I should feel guilty for taking up so much of your time."

"Hey, what are you talking about? You aren't taking anything I'm not happy to give."

"You're speaking of time, I assume," Elliott teased, and Steve blushed.

"Now, about breakfast..." he said.

Chapter 3

They arrived at the Armitage building at 10:50, parking across the street. Elliott wanted to take a close-up look at the structure before meeting with Lamb, and Steve had brought his camera. He took a couple of shots as they got out of the car.

Elliott paid no attention to the ground floor's false front, since it would be the first thing to go if he decided to take the place. He did look carefully around it, though, noting evidence of all-but-hidden detail where the false front met the original building.

The main entrance was located in a triangular alcove under the turret at the alley-side corner of the building, and the corner itself was held up by a heavily painted-over metal Corinthian column. Crossing the alley to get a closer view of the turret, he was impressed by the extent of the obscured detailing. Garlands under the windows, arch-pieces above, and an elaborate cornice at the top of the turret were barely visible under the paint, but Steve took several more photos of what could be discerned.

Most of the width of the building at the ground-floor level had been enclosed during the conversion, but there was, on the far side from the original entrance, a small section of the original brickwork, into which was set a door Elliott had hardly noticed, since it was painted purple to match the rest. Obviously the entrance to the flats above, it, too, had an ornate lintel and outer frame.

Steve pointed out several other details Elliott either hadn't immediately noticed or hadn't fully appreciated.

"Ya gotta hand it to those Victorians," he said, smiling. "They never met a design element they didn't like."

As they walked down the alley, Elliott confirmed that, while the brick exterior walls were in need of tuck-pointing, there were no missing bricks and no large cracks that might indicate serious structural problems. The bay windows on the alley side of the second and third floors traditionally served the purpose of providing extra light for buildings separated by narrow spaces, but here they were more for appearance than utility.

A door near the rear of the building served as the back entrance for the converted apartment.

When they reached the garage, Elliott passed the side alley to get a better look at the back of the building. Directly over the center of the flat garage roof, on the second floor, was another, larger, bay window. The third floor had four evenly-spaced regular windows. There were fewer design elements on the back, though the bay window added character.

Although the garage was a relatively new addition, some care had been taken to match the bricks to those of the main building. The doors facing the rear alley were painted the same rust-brown as the turret. One of the three, Elliott noted, would definitely need replacing.

"Time," Steve said, and they returned to the front of the building.

Marvin Lamb proved to be, in Elliott's–and, he later learned, in Steve's–opinion, amazingly nondescript. Average height, weight, build, looks, age anywhere from forty to fifty-five. If he had a discernible personality, Elliott was unable to find it.

For someone supposedly eager to sell, he showed the building in a detached manner reminiscent of the guards who stood in each room of the Art Institute, looking mildly bored and answering questions without any particular enthusiasm or intonation. Still, Elliott sensed an underlying tension, and assumed the man was going overboard to avoid showing it.

The second- and third-floor flats were identical in layout and were, while in need of new fixtures and appliances, paint and minor repairs, in overall good shape. Since Lamb's ground-floor flat would be totally gutted and reconverted to retail space if he decided to buy the building, Elliott's only interest was in looking for any obvious structural flaws in the outer walls, floor and ceiling. He did take note of the pressed tin ceilings and wondered about the condition of the pressed tin Bruno had mentioned lay under the current paneling, and where interior walls had been connected to the ceiling.

Each of the upstairs apartments had crown molding in the living room and twelve-foot ceilings throughout. There were several other small architectural elements that indicated the hand of a builder who knew and cared about his craft.

The kitchen appliances and electric and bathroom fixtures dated from the 1950s, but the rooms themselves appeared not to have been structurally altered. The bay windows and the those in the turret allowed more light than was usual in similar buildings Elliott had seen.

At the end of a hallway running parallel to the stairway to the upper floors were two doors. The one on the left opened onto the basement stairs, the one on the right to the ground-floor apartment. The basement was basically an open space with three makeshift storage areas, apparently for the building's occupants. A washer and dryer sat under the stairway, and a variety of crates, boxes and stacks of unidentified material cluttered the rest of the space. Elliott inspected as much of the inner foundation as the obstructions would allow, checking for cracks or signs of leakage, and found none.

The furnace was relatively new, although he questioned whether the hot water heater was sufficient for three apartments. The presence of circuit breaker boxes indicated the wiring had been updated fairly recently.

As he followed Elliott and Steve out of the basement, Lamb said, "So, what do you think? It's a great building, right?"

"It's got possibilities," Elliott conceded, as always reluctant to appear too eager. Actually, he liked it a lot. "Have you come up with an asking price?"

"As a matter of fact, I've got a Realtor friend who'll be handling things for me. He did an assessment just the other day..." Probably immediately after Elliott called about the property. "...but he hasn't given me a figure yet."

They reached the front door and went out onto the sidewalk. Elliott took a business card from his shirt pocket and handed it to Lamb.

"Why don't you have him call me when he gets it?"

"I'll do that. I hope to hear from him today."

They shook hands, and Lamb went back to his flat as Elliott and Steve headed for the car.

"So, what did you think?" Steve asked as they got in.

"Nice. It's got a lot of potential, and obviously whoever designed and built it knew what they were doing. My only concern is that I've never done a commercial property before and I'm not sure of its practicality in this area. It's a little off the beaten track."

He glanced at Steve and could tell he was thinking.

"So, what did *you* think of it?" he prompted.

"I loved it. It's got class, charm, everything. You can turn it into a real gem."

"And?"

Steve looked at him.

"And what?"

"And what aren't you saying?"

"Nothing."

Elliott stared at him with a raised eyebrow.

"I mean, it's none of my business, and the last thing I want is to butt into yours. I was just doing a little fantasizing, I guess."

Elliott was sure he knew exactly what Steve was fantasizing about; he had thought about the same thing since the first time he'd seen the building.

"A gallery," he said.

Looking mildly uncomfortable, Steve said, "Well, yeah. Whatever the person you sell it to does with it would be up to them. But a gallery could be a logical option."

Elliott smiled to himself, started the car and moved out into traffic.

⁂

BJ's swim team won the meet, and it always pleased Elliott to see how proud Brad, Sr., was of his son. Since the parents of BJ's teammate who was supposed to ride with Brad and Cessy had been able to go to the meet after all, Elliott suggested he take the family out to an early dinner before heading home.

He was relieved that Cessy was the model of restraint when it came to probing the status of his relationship with Steve and pleased that the rest of the family and Steve seemed completely at ease with one another.

⁂

They returned to Elliott's condo shortly after seven to find a message from Bruno on the answering machine.

"Elliott...Bruno here. It's three o'clock Saturday afternoon, and I've decided to invite a few people in for drinks tonight to celebrate Cage's new job. Not a big do, but I hope you and Steve might be able to drop by for a bit, any time after eight. Later, I hope..."

Clearing the message, Elliott looked at Steve.

"Cage's new job? I wonder what that might be."

"One sure way to find out."

"Yeah, but I don't know if I'm up for a party tonight."

"Hey, we can have one drink and leave. I'm curious about Cage, too."

"I guess one drink won't hurt."

His cell phone rang, and he thought for a moment it was Bruno calling to see if he'd gotten the message, then remembered Bruno didn't have his cell number. He retrieved the phone from his pocket as quickly as he could.

"Mr. Smith?"

He didn't recognize the voice. "Yes?"

"This is Alex Freiburg. I'm a Realtor, and Marvin Lamb asked me to call you. I hope this isn't an inconvenient time."

"No problem. Have you come up with an asking price?"

"Yes, I have." He then proceeded to quote a price far higher than Elliott had anticipated.

While it was axiomatic that real estate agents and Realtors initially asked a higher price than they expect to get in order to allow themselves some wiggle room, the price Freiburg quoted was unrealistic, and Elliott did not hesitate to say so.

"I recently researched prices in that area for another project I was considering," he lied. He had, in fact, done only a cursory online check of roughly comparable properties in the area when Bruno had first mentioned the building. "And given the state of today's market..."

"Well, I'm sure he can be a little flexible. What figure did you have in mind?"

"It's a little premature to come up with an offer until I have my work crew do an inspection. Why don't you have a talk with Mr. Lamb and see if he can come up with a more realistic figure first? Then we can move on from there if it sounds reasonable."

"This is an exceptional building, as you know."

"I agree, it's a very nice building with a lot of potential. But realizing that potential will not be cheap."

"Well, I'll talk with Mr. Lamb, and get back to you."

"Good. I'll look forward to hearing from you."

Putting the phone back in his pocket, he looked at Steve.

"Lamb's real estate buddy."

"I gathered. Think he'll drop the asking price?"

Elliott grinned. "It's all part of the game. The question is whether he'll come down far enough."

They went up to Bruno's around nine. A lanky young cover-model type in a tanktop and Levi's answered the door.

"Come on in," he said. "I'm Chaz."

Elliott and Steve introduced themselves and followed Chaz into the living room, where Rudy and Cage were seated with a strikingly handsome mid-twenties hunk with an athlete's build and skin so flawless Elliott wondered at first if he were wearing makeup. Definite of oriental lineage, he decided. They exchanged waves with Bruno, who was at the kitchen breakfast bar, now lined with liquor bottles, mixes and a large bucket of ice.

"What can I get you?" Bruno asked as he finished pouring straight bourbon into an ice-filled tumbler.

"Bourbon-Seven," Elliott said.

"Same," Steve echoed.

"Have a seat. I'll be right with you."

Greetings were exchanged, and the hunk was introduced as Ralph. Rudy moved over on the couch, saying "Elliott, come sit by me." Steve took one of the dining room chairs, which someone had moved into the living room.

Bruno brought the tumbler to Rudy then returned to the bar for Steve and Elliott's drinks and, delivering them, took a seat.

"So, I hear you got a job," Elliott said, turning to Cage. "Here in town?"

"Yeah," Cage said. "I'll be driving for Rudy's limo service."

In other words, Elliott thought, Cage has joined Rudy's stud farm. He had little doubt that Rudy hired far more "drivers" than his limousine business could use, and he couldn't resist asking, "Full time?"

"No, the time is flexible, which is great, since I'll be able to keep on acting. Chicago's got a lot of good theater, and I'm sure I'll find something. As soon as I get my Equity card, I'll be doing an audition for the next production at the Goodman–I hear they may be casting soon."

"Well, I wish you luck." He wondered if that meant Bruno would be having a new roommate.

❧

The conversation wandered from topic to topic, with several discussions going on at once. Rudy seemed particularly interested in Elliott's background and family, and Elliott fielded his questions in his usual low-key and noncommittal manner. Rudy hinted of big plans for his limousine service and "other projects" he was contemplating, and Elliott recognized a fisherman dangling bait when he saw one.

Whenever he had the chance, he enjoyed observing the dynamics of the group and its splinter groupings. Ralph, he noted, alternated lavishing the bulk of his attention on Bruno and Steve, but most particularly on Steve. Elliott gathered, from what he could hear of their conversation, that Ralph was an aspiring artist and sculptor taking classes at the Evanston Art Center. Chaz divided his attention mainly between Bruno and Cage.

He assumed Bruno knew Cage's going to work for Rudy implied more than driving a limousine but would never bring it up unless Bruno did.

As they were getting ready to leave, Bruno called Elliott aside.

"I was telling you about my stamps," he said in a lowered voice, "and thought you might like to see my prize possession. I almost never show it, but I thought you would appreciate seeing it."

"Sure, I'd like that." Giving Steve a nod, he followed Bruno down the hall to the master bedroom.

It was furnished, he noted, in an odd mixture of styles. The sleigh bed and dresser were obviously quite old, but the rest of the furniture was modern and appeared new. The walls were covered with small paintings and photographs. Bruno pointed to a five-by-eight-inch frame in the center of an arrangement directly across from the bed. At first, Elliott assumed it was a painting, then noticed it was a block of four postage stamps. They looked oddly familiar, and he stepped closer, his eyes widening in recognition.

The stamps were of a World War One-era biplane flying upside down.

Turning to Bruno and still mildly incredulous, he said, "Are these real?"

Bruno nodded proudly. "Yes. Turn it over."

Taking the frame carefully off the wall, he turned it over to find what he assumed to be a certificate of authenticity.

"It's a PFC–a Philatelic Foundation Certificate, from the major stamp authentication organization in the US."

Without studying the certification but impressed nonetheless, Elliott replaced the frame on the wall and turned to Bruno.

"You have a block of four Inverted Jennys framed and hanging on your wall?"

Bruno nodded again. "I put them there so they're the first thing I see when I wake up in the morning."

Elliott's mental trivia file sprang open. The Jenny was one of the first airmail stamps, with a face value of twenty-four cents, at a time when regular stamps were three cents. It was printed in sheets of a hundred, but each sheet had to be fed through the printing press twice. One of the sheets was accidentally flipped on its second pass, and the plane came out upside down.

It was sold before the misprint was noticed, but the buyer soon realized the sheet was worth more broken up than in one unit. It became one of the most prized stamps in existence, and Elliott remembered reading that in 2005 a block of four Inverted Jennys was sold for $2.75 million.

"It's none of my business, Bruno, but shouldn't this be in a bank vault? Aren't you afraid someone will just walk off with it?"

Stepping beside Elliott to look more closely at the stamps, Bruno smiled.

"Why would I spend all that money only to put them in a bank vault? I want to be able to see them whenever I want. That's why I bought them. As for their being stolen, remember Edgar Alan Poe's 'The Purloined Letter?' No one ever thinks something so valuable would be left out in plain sight. Fewer than a handful of people even know I have them. Besides, I really don't have that many people coming through my bedroom."

"What about during your parties?"

"I keep the bedroom door closed, and the chance of anyone who might come in to use the bathroom seeing and recognizing what they are is infinitely remote."

Elliott definitely did not share Bruno's confidence.

"Well, it's none of my business, Bruno, but if I were you I definitely would not keep the stamps and the certificate together. If anyone ever did steal the stamps, they couldn't sell them without the certificate."

Bruno pursed his lips in thought.

"Good point." he said.

They returned to the living room, where Rudy immediately latched on to Bruno as Elliott returned to Steve. They finished their drinks, then excused themselves, pleading a busy day ahead.

As Elliott started to get up, Rudy suddenly appeared and said, "I'd like to talk with you about a business proposition. Can I have Bruno give me your number? I don't have a pen with me."

Though he wasn't overly eager at the prospect, Elliott found it hard to say no diplomatically, so reluctantly said, "Sure."

❧

"That was actually kind of nice," Steve said as the elevator doors closed and Elliott pressed the button." I had a nice talk with Ralph."

"Nice-looking kid."

"That he is," Steve agreed. "His mother is Taiwanese, and he's a painter and a sculptor. He's working for Rudy to earn enough money to get through school. He said he'd like to see my work."

Elliott grinned. "I'm sure he would!"

Returning the grin, Steve said, "Lechery does not become you. Oh, wait a minute. Yes, it does."

The elevator doors opened, and they headed down the hall.

"Where did you and Bruno wander off to?" Steve asked as Elliott opened the door to the kitchen.

Elliott told him about the Jennys, including their approximate value, and watched Steve's eyes open wide, as his own had.

"He's got two-point-seventy-five million dollars on his bedroom wall?"

Elliott shrugged. "I don't know what he paid for them, but it was a hell of a lot more than their ninety-six cents total face value."

"Wow!"

"Couldn't have said it better myself."

"And what about Rudy? What do you suppose he wants from you?"

"I'm not sure just what that's all about. I think he assumes I have money."

"Gee, I wonder where he got that idea?"

"Not from me, that's for sure. He says he wants to talk to me about some sort of business proposition."

"Odd he didn't hit Bruno up on it."

"I'm sure he did, and I'm kind of curious as to what Bruno's reaction was. He's a grown man, but when it comes to having money, he's on really unfamiliar ground. I don't want anything to happen to him. So, maybe I'll see what Rudy has in mind."

❧

As he was getting out of his car in the garage Monday night, his cell phone rang.

"Elliott Smith."

"Mr. Smith, this is Alex Freiburg. I had a chance to speak with Mr. Lamb, and he has agreed to reconsider his asking price."

Sunday afternoon, after taking Steve back to his apartment to paint, Elliott had spent some time carefully researching properties along Armitage and around Oz Park, so he felt he had a better grasp of what the property was worth in the current market.

"I'm glad to hear it," he said. "And what price did he settle on?"

The figure Freiburg quoted was still considerably above what Elliott thought reasonable, and he said so.

"Well, it took me a lot of time to convince him to come down this low," Freiburg said. "It *is* a great building in very good shape in an excellent location."

"I'm not disagreeing," Elliott said. "I'm merely stating what is practical for me. I buy buildings for renovation and resale. Restoration costs will be very high, and frankly, in today's market, I may have a problem reselling...as Mr. Lamb may have in selling."

There was a long pause, then: "So, what would you consider a reasonable figure?"

Elliott quoted a price lower than he was actually willing to pay, which again was all part of the ritual of the business. He knew it, and Freiburg knew it. The usual dicker-room was in the area of ten percent.

Again a pause. "I don't know if Mr. Lamb could possibly go that low. But of course, I'm obligated to present all offers..."

"We haven't reached the offer stage," Elliott pointed out. "We're in the 'would I consider making an offer if the price were practical' stage."

"Understood. Well, let me talk to Mr. Lamb and get back to you."

"I'll look forward to your call."

The evening news had just ended, and Elliott had gone into the kitchen to start dinner when the land-line phone rang.

"Elliott, it's Bruno. Sorry to bother you, but there were a couple of things I wanted to talk to you about, and I couldn't bring them up when you called yesterday."

Elliott had called Sunday morning to thank him for having them up Saturday night. He'd heard voices in the background and assumed either Bruno or Cage—or both—had had overnight guests. Bruno had sounded decidedly hung over.

"Sure. You prefer over the phone or in person?"

"Easier in person, I think, if you wouldn't mind. But I don't want to disturb your evening."

"No problem. I was just starting dinner, but if you'd like to come down around eight for coffee or a drink, that'd be fine."

"Why don't you come up here? Cage is going out for the evening. I've got an entire cake I forgot to put out at the party and hate to see it go to waste."

"Sure. That'll be fine."

"All right, then. I'll see you at eight."

No sooner had he hung up when the phone rang again.

"Elliott Smith."

"Hello, Elliott, it's Rudy. I hope I'm not interrupting your dinner."

"No, I was just sitting down for it now," he semi-lied, not wanting a long conversation. "What can I do for you, Rudy?"

There was only a slight pause before: "Ah, well, I won't keep you. But I mentioned to you at Bruno's Saturday that I had a business proposition you might find of interest."

"Yes? What kind of proposition?"

"I have the chance to buy one of the hottest bars in the city. The place is a gold mine, and I'm looking for one or two investors. Normally, I'd just do it all myself, but I've recently expanded my limousine service, and those stretch babies aren't cheap. So, I thought I'd approach you and Bruno to let you in on it. Bruno's definitely in, and since he speaks highly of you, I thought you'd like the chance to come in with him."

Elliott suspected that Rudy's main target was Bruno, and that getting Elliott to come along would be a means of assuaging any hesitation Bruno might have.

"Well, that's nice of you, Rudy, but I don't know if I'd be the right person for you. What bar, by the way?"

"I can't say at the moment–the current owners don't want it known they're considering selling, and I promised I wouldn't say anything until I had a chance to line up a few investors before making an offer. As I say, if I hadn't just placed an order for four new limos..."

Elliott's immediate thought was to wonder why the current owners would be selling if the place was a gold mine. But he didn't want to ask and possibly give Rudy the idea he was interested.

"Well, as I say, I'm not sure I'd be comfortable getting into the bar business."

"I understand, but this would only be as an investment–twenty-five, thirty thousand, tops. Bruno and I will put up the bulk of the cash. You can't go wrong."

Elliott paused. He wanted to give Rudy an immediate flat-out no but felt he should talk to Bruno first. He was sure Rudy's proposal was one of the things Bruno wanted to talk to him about.

"I'd need to know quite a bit more about everything involved before I could give it any sort of serious consideration."

"Of course. I'll work up some figures, and we can go over them. But promise me you won't just dismiss it out-of-hand before you have the facts, okay?"

"Okay," Elliott said, though he knew that even if the deal were totally legitimate, which he instinctively doubted, he had no interest in investing in a bar.

"Good! We'll talk soon, then."

They hung up, and Elliott returned to making his dinner.

⁂

He arrived at Bruno's at exactly eight o'clock, and as he followed him into the living room, Bruno asked, "Which do you prefer–coffee or a drink?"

"Whatever you're having."

"I think I'd better have coffee," Bruno said. "I've been drinking way too much lately. I'm a quick drunk, and the hangovers are deadly. I'm toying with the idea of stopping altogether before it kills me."

Elliott took a seat in the living room while Bruno went into the kitchen.

"Cream and sugar?"

"A little of both," Elliott replied, and a minute later, Bruno carried a tray with a coffee carafe, two mugs and two large slices of a very rich-looking cake to the dining room table.

"We might be a little more comfortable here," Bruno said, and Elliott got up to join him. "I'm glad you and Steve came up Saturday night," he continued after they'd sat down. "Ralph really enjoyed talking with Steve about art. He asked me if I could give Steve his phone number. I hope you don't mind."

Elliott smiled and shrugged.

"Of course, I don't mind," although he did have a small, quickly repressed twinge of concern.

Reaching into his shirt pocket, Bruno took out a folded piece of paper and handed it over.

"I'm sure he just wants to talk about art," he said, almost apologetically.

"Steve's a big boy," Elliott replied. "I trust him."

Bruno sighed.

"Good!" After taking another sip of coffee, he said, "But the main reason I wanted to talk to you is to get your advice."

"About Rudy's proposition," Elliott guessed, making it a statement rather than a question.

"Yes. He said he was going to talk to you about it, too."

"Yeah, I talked with him earlier tonight. Kind of short on detail, but he said he was pulling some information together on it, and that he'd present it to both of us." He didn't mention that the only reason he wanted to see it was to spot danger zones Bruno might not recognize.

"So, what do you think of the idea? I'd love to own a gay bar."

"Well, for one thing, I've made it a rule never to consider anything until I'm sure I have all the necessary facts, and even then I won't do it unless I'm positive all the Ts are crossed and the Is dotted. As for Rudy's proposal, I don't think I'd be interested in any event. The bar scene is a totally different world."

"But do you think I should consider it?"

"I can't tell you what to do, but I'd definitely suggest you don't make a commitment before you have all the information. I'd also strongly recommend you run it past your financial advisor."

"Oh, I definitely will. Cage is encouraging me to go for it, but I'm afraid he's hardly an impartial observer, especially now that he's working for Rudy. And of course, I'll mention it to Sensei."

"Cage has started already?" Elliott asked.

"Well, he has to apply for his chauffeur's license before he can officially start driving, but he's going out tonight with Rudy and Chaz to Lake Forest to meet one of Rudy's clients. I don't expect him back tonight."

Elliott suppressed a grin. "So, will he be staying with you permanently?"

"I'm sure not. He's really charming, but he's so much younger, and our interests aren't all that similar. Now that he's working, he'll be able to save enough money to get a place of his own. And he's hit it off quite well with Chaz, who I'm sure you remember from Saturday night. To be honest, I rather have this hope he and Chaz might end up getting a place together. But then, I'm an incurable romantic." He paused a moment then added, "With a strong streak of realism."

Elliott suppressed another smile and let the remark pass. Bruno, he decided, was nobody's fool. Perhaps he didn't need as much protecting as Elliott had first assumed.

As they finished their cake, Elliott said, "I'm curious as to how you came by your Inverted Jennys. I'd imagine they don't come on the market all that often."

Bruno washed down a piece of his cake with a swig of coffee.

"You're right, and it was a real stroke of luck. It was Sensei who put me onto them. I told you we met at a stamp show. He's a long-time collector with a lot of contacts in the stamp world.

"A couple of weeks after we met, he confided in me that one of his students, a very wealthy collector, was going through some serious financial difficulties, and was in desperate need of immediate cash. He told Sensei he was even considering selling his Jennys at far below market value. I immediately told him I'd be interested, and asked him to convey the message to the owner. He did, and the owner said what he wanted for them, and I agreed."

Elliott couldn't help but be suspicious.

"So, people just casually sell one another stamps worth millions of dollars?"

A quick look of what he interpreted as embarrassment flashed across Bruno's face.

"Of course, most sales of this magnitude go through dealers and brokers, but dealers sometimes engage in what are called 'private treaty sales,' whereby the dealer becomes the conduit through which one collector sells to another collector without going to auction or selling it outright to a dealer. The dealer makes a commission on the sale without having to expend any money himself."

"So, Clifford Blanton is a dealer?"

"Not technically, but he doesn't need to be. The owner was willing to sell, I was willing to buy, and Sensei was kind enough to act as the middle man."

"Do you know who the original owner is?"

"No, he wanted to remain anonymous. But I had the PFC, and I trust Sensei implicitly. I heard later that whatever financial problems the original owner was having that caused him to sell had been resolved, and he wanted to buy them back. I refused. He's been nagging poor Sensei ever since."

While Elliott did not share Bruno's sense of trust and wondered just how authentic the "certificate" might be, he realized that to pursue the subject any further might make Bruno feel he was being interrogated. And after all, whatever Bruno did was Bruno's business, not his.

They changed the subject and talked for another half-hour or so before Elliott headed back home.

❧

Alex Freiburg called Tuesday evening as Elliott was on his way from the garage to his mailbox.

"I've talked with Mr. Lamb," Freiburg began, "and while he was very reluctant to go much lower, I suggest you submit an offer and give me a chance to go over it with him."

"Please be sure Mr. Lamb understands that, while I do like the building and would like to have it, I don't need it. Considering the housing market's current condition, it's unrealistic to think in terms of prices as they were even two years ago. And my crew would have to go through the property first.

"Even then, I doubt I could go more than..." He paused for effect then stated a figure he knew was within ten percent of the property's real value.

"I'll see what I can do," Freiburg said.

He wasn't particularly concerned by the call. He'd been in the business too long to let the negotiation stage of any potential deal bother him. He did like the building–a lot–and he realized part of that was because of Steve's interest in it. Perhaps for that was the reason he was toying with the idea of adding it to the small collection of buildings he had bought, refurbished and kept as rental properties. That this one had commercial space, and that Steve had dreams of opening a gallery someday...

He tried not to let his mind go too far down that path, because it implied a level of commitment he kept telling himself he wasn't absolutely sure he was ready for. Whether he believed himself or not was another matter.

He hadn't finished dinner when the phone rang.

Freiburg got right to the point.

"I've spoken with Mr. Lamb, and he's agreed to a figure I think you'll find acceptable."

The figure he quoted was still high, but Elliott knew was at least entering realistic territory.

"I'll tell you what," he said. "Let's set up a time for my crew to go over the place to check for problems and to get an idea of what my costs will be. Then I'll be in a better position to talk offers. Late afternoon or a Saturday would be preferable."

"Fine. I'll set it up and get back to you as soon as possible."

"I'll look forward to hearing from you."

Knowing Steve would be curious as to what was going on, Elliott waited until he'd finished dinner and put the dishes in the dishwasher, then called to tell him.

"That's great, Ell! I really hope you get it!"

"I'll keep you posted." He didn't mention the possible gallery, though he'd not have been surprised if Steve were having similar thoughts.

Freiburg called early Wednesday to say Saturday morning would be fine, and agreed on ten o'clock as the time. Rudy called that evening to say he had more information on his proposed business deal and wanted to get together with both Elliott and Bruno Thursday to discuss it.

"I've got a meeting at eight near Roscoe's on Halsted, and thought we could meet there for a drink around six-thirty."

Again letting his concern for Bruno overcome the temptation to just say he wasn't interested, Elliott said, "Six-thirty might be cutting it a little close. I'll have to come home and change first, but I'll be there as close to then as I can make it. Have you talked with Bruno?"

"I'll do that as soon as we hang up here. If he can't make it, I'll let you know."

"Okay. I'll see you then."

Less than fifteen minutes later, Bruno called to verify he'd be there.

"Also, I wonder if you'd like to join me for dinner after our meeting with Rudy. There's someone I'd like you to meet."

"Someone?" Elliott asked, curious. "One of Rudy's...employees?"

Bruno laughed. "No, this is someone I met Sunday night on my own at the Lucky Horseshoe. His name is Ricky, and he's Puerto Rican and truly charming. He has the most beautiful skin! I know you'll love him. He's coming over later tonight, and if you're up for dinner tomorrow, I'll see if he can join us."

Curiosity prompted Elliott's reply. "Sure."

"Do you want to ride with me to Roscoe's?"

"I thought I'd just take the el to Belmont and walk from there. And as I told Rudy, I might be a little late. I'm never sure what time I'll get home from work, and I'll have to change, and..."

"Well, just call me when you're ready, and we'll take my car. Why walk all the way to the el stop and all the way from Belmont?"

"Okay. I'll call you when I'm ready."

"Good. See you then."

Rudy's proposal was long on promise but evasive in detail despite one impressively long spreadsheet, purportedly of the bar's current sales and expenses, and another he'd made of estimates of costs for improvements he had in mind, and projected sales after their implementation. Bruno was obviously impressed, Elliott considerably less so, especially when Rudy still would not name the bar, claiming the owners had sworn him to secrecy.

"I don't know," Elliott said. "I never buy anything I haven't seen first."

"I understand," Rudy replied, "but they won't allow me to say anything until they know there's serious interest. I can tell you this, though–it's on Halsted."

So were about twenty-five other gay bars.

"And the great thing is," Rudy said, "since they're anxious to sell, we can get the business for only fifty thou each, or the business and the building for one-point-seventy-five."

Elliott let Rudy's having assured him his investment would be "twenty-five, thirty thousand, tops" ride, and noticed Bruno's eyebrows rise when he realized Rudy meant one and three-quarter million dollars.

"I...I don't know," Bruno said. "That's an awful lot of money."

Rudy laughed and slapped him on the arm.

"For you? Come on, you've got that much behind the cushions in your couch."

Elliott didn't laugh.

Back-stepping with what Elliott was sure was practiced ease, Rudy said, "But we can just go with the business first, and talk about the building later."

When Elliott asked for a copy of the spreadsheets for closer study, Rudy said the one of current sales and expenses had to be returned to the owners, but that he could make a copy of his estimates for the projections and get one to both Elliott and Bruno. Elliott knew the projections without the current balance sheet were pointless, but he said nothing.

Rudy left at eight-fifteen, and he'd barely walked out the door before Bruno was asking Elliott what he thought.

"I'll be honest with you, Bruno, I'm more than a little skeptical. I personally can't see putting that much money into a business I'm not familiar with or interested in. And as far as the spreadsheets are concerned, they look great, but looking and being are two different things. I'd need to see some tax records before I could make any kind of final decision. And I strongly recommend you talk with your financial adviser."

"You're right, of course," Bruno said, although Elliott could tell from his expression the idea of owning a popular gay bar could easily outweigh logic.

Deciding a change of subject was in order, Elliott said, "So, what time are you meeting Ricky?"

Glancing at his watch, Bruno said, "I told him to meet us here at eight. He should be here at any minute." He'd no sooner said it than he looked toward the door and added, "And here he is!"

Elliott turned slightly to see a nice-looking Hispanic with black hair, dark eyes and skin the color of mocha enter the bar and look around. Spotting Bruno, he hurried over.

"I hope I'm not late," he said, addressing Bruno but giving Elliott a nice smile.

Bruno made the introductions, and Elliott was impressed by the strength of the younger man's handshake.

"Bruno's told me about you," Ricky said. "It's nice to meet you."

"Nice to meet you, too, Ricky." He noted that while Ricky was very attractive, he wasn't the pretty-boy type Elliott usually saw with Bruno. He was nicely and neatly dressed, although the clothes were more off-the-rack than designer, which Elliott took as a good sign.

"So," Bruno asked, "shall we have another drink here, or go on to dinner? It's getting a bit late."

"Dinner's fine with me," Elliott said, and Ricky nodded.

"I figured we could go to the Chicago Diner, if you don't mind vegetarian. The food's great, and it's right across the street."

Though he was a confirmed carnivore, Elliott always enjoyed the place and had long been enamored of one of the waiters who'd worked there for years, Then he learned, after making a discrete pass a couple months before meeting Steve, the man was in a long-term monogamous relationship.

❧

During dinner, Elliott paid close attention to the dynamics between Ricky and Bruno. He hated to be suspicious of Ricky's motives–or of anyone's, for that matter–but he realized he had set himself up as something of a protector of Bruno's interests, and was concerned lest anyone try to take advantage of him. With fifty-nine million dollars at stake, there were plenty of people out to do just that.

He was curious, but of course hesitated to ask, whether Ricky and Bruno had gotten together on a hustler/john level, or if Ricky, nearly twenty years Bruno's junior, just liked older men. He tried not to ask too many personal questions, but was able to piece together bits of information indicating Ricky had recently lost his job at a Chrysler dealership when the company went belly-up, that he was the eldest of five brothers–the youngest of whom was only six–and that both his parents were in poor health. Elliott's cynical side wondered how much of it was true, or whether Ricky might be laying the foundation for a scam.

He was no stranger to scam artists himself, which was one reason he never mentioned his wealth to anyone who wasn't already aware of it. But he'd dealt with it all his life; Bruno hadn't.

Still, Ricky did seem to be a nice kid, and deserved the benefit of the doubt–a decision subtly reinforced when, at dinner, he didn't order the most expensive thing on the menu, despite Bruno's insistence he get anything he wanted.

⁂

The rest of the week passed quickly and uneventfully, with phone calls to and from Steve, Cessy, various friends, and Jesse and Adam, who were getting anxious for the completion of the renovation on their house. There was no word from either Bruno or John.

After a Friday evening of pizza and movies, Elliott was getting ready to leave Saturday morning to meet Sam Brite, his plumber, Ted Swanson, his carpenter, and Arnie Echter, his electrician, for the Armitage place inspection when Steve said, "I've got something for you," and excused himself to go into his studio.

He came back a moment later with a large sketch pad, which he flipped through until he found what he was looking for. He then handed it to Elliott.

It was a pastel of the Armitage building as it might look after Elliott had finished it. Elliott was delighted to see the ground floor as it must have been when the building was new. The turret was burgundy, the garlands beneath the windows white, with shades of peach and light rose highlighting the cornice, base and other decorative elements. The color scheme was repeated on the side bay windows.

"This is fantastic!" he said. "When did you have the time to do it?"

"I've been playing with it several nights. I was looking at the photos I took when we went over to see the place, and I had a few ideas. I just thought you might like to see it."

"It's great! And if I do decide to take the place, this is how we'll do the outside, for sure. Keep it somewhere safe."

Clearly pleased, Steve took the pad, and closed it. "Will do."

"I'll be back by one. Maybe we can go grab lunch, if you can wait that long."

"I'll be here."

Sam and Arnie were already standing on the sidewalk across the alley from the building when Elliott arrived. He'd just exchanged greetings with them when Ted drove by looking for a parking space.

"We were gonna do a walk-around," Sam said, "but figured we'd wait until we could all do it together. At a quick first look, it seems to be in pretty good shape, but, jeezus–purple?"

Elliott laughed. "Hey, a paint sale's a paint sale. Maybe the guy who bought it was color-blind."

"Then I can imagine what the inside must be like," Arnie said.

Ted joined them, and they crossed the alley to the door to Lamb's ground-floor flat, where Elliott knocked. Ted was admiring the cast-iron Corinthian column directly under the turret when the door opened.

"Come on in," Lamb said, and the four men entered. Elliott quickly introduced his team, and Lamb began the tour.

Elliott and his crew had gone through the top-to-bottom inspection process so often they had it down pat. Sam pointed out minor water damage to the floor and baseboard near the toilet in the third-floor bathroom, but since there was no evidence of damage to the ceiling, walls or floor of the bathroom directly beneath it, he merely made a note of it. There was a small trapdoor to the roof located in the closet of the third-floor back bedroom, and Elliott and Ted climbed up to take a look. They found a couple areas that could use re-tarring, but otherwise no significant problems.

Elliott found the fire escape, accessed by windows in the kitchen of both upper apartments, to be in better shape than he'd anticipated. They needed wire-brushing to remove areas of rust and a good painting, but were otherwise fine.

While in the basement, Arnie subtly signaled to draw Elliott's attention to a stack of what proved to be ornate pressed-tin crown molding probably taken from the original store when it was converted to an apartment, and another stack of pressed-tin panels, probably from the covered-over walls. There were also a few original bathroom fixtures and a several other items that hinted of being possible treasures for the renovation.

After the inspection was completed, Elliott thanked Lamb and told him he'd give Freiburg a call on Monday. He'd already pretty well decided to make an offer but knew any show of enthusiasm in front of Lamb would be counterproductive when it came time for price negotiations.

As they left the building, he suggested they go up the street to a coffee shop for a quick discussion of their impressions and any potential problems they could foresee. Over coffee and pie, Sam and Arnie expressed minor concern about the age of the plumbing and electrical systems, but noted there were no immediately apparent problems. They felt the water damage in the top flat was minimal, and if necessary, the flooring and baseboards immediately around the affected area could be removed and replaced with relative ease.

"It's a crapshoot," Sam said. "But it always is in buildings this old. But overall, I think it's pretty solid."

"And whoever built it knew what they were doing," Ted added. "Even with all that paint, the detail work on the turret and around the bays is exceptional. And birds-eye maple floors–they really don't build 'em like that anymore. Sure wish we had the original blueprints."

Elliott looked at him, brows furrowed. "Unlikely on a building this old, but I can ask."

He had complete faith in his team and valued their opinions, and their confirmation of his own thoughts and impressions convinced him he was right in deciding to make an offer.

He made a call Sunday night to verify that Larry Fingerhood had returned from vacation.

"Sorry to bother you at home, Larry," he said, "but I want to act on this as soon as possible."

He explained what was going on–his contacts with Freiburg and Lamb, Lamb's asking price, the amount Elliott wanted to offer, and how much he was willing to go over the offer if he had to. He then gave Larry Freiburg's number and turned the matter over to him.

Normally, Larry would have been in on everything from the first contact, but they had worked together for so long each trusted the other to know what he was doing. Having Larry handle the detail work was expensive, but Elliott felt it was well worth the time and hassles it saved him.

As usual, he was right. Larry earned every penny he charged, and Elliott came close to backing out of the deal more than once in the course of the week-long negotiations. But finally, Lamb accepted Elliott's last offer, which included doubling the normal down payment, and the property went into escrow.

⁂

Between the negotiations for the property, which involved far more of his time than he'd planned, and putting the finishing touches on Jesse and Adam's renovation, Elliott had little time for anything else. He did talk to Steve, who was delighted when the deal finally went through, nearly every night, and to Cessy twice, and fielded a call from Rudy about his bar proposal, explaining he was just too busy to give thought to anything else at the moment.

Bruno called Wednesday just to chat, but Elliott was too distracted to give the conversation his full attention. Ricky, Bruno said, had not yet found a new job and was in danger of losing his apartment. Cage was so busy, both with his new job and his social life, that he was seldom home, and Bruno hoped he'd be getting his own place shortly.

So, it wasn't until the weekend that Elliott felt he could really relax, by which time he was more than ready to do so.

Chapter 4

The thirty days of escrow flew by. Work on Jesse's and Adam's house was completed to their satisfaction–and great relief, so Elliott and his team had a few weeks of welcome down-time. Arnie, Sam and Ted took short-term jobs and did maintenance work on Elliott's other properties in the meantime.

He hadn't yet discussed his plans for the ground floor with either his crew or Steve. He wanted to wait until he was absolutely sure the escrow wouldn't fall through, which, though rare, was not totally unheard-of in his experience.

The problem–or a potential problem–was that for him to offer Steve the ground-floor space was far more than a casual business proposal. It was a de facto acknowledgment their personal relationship had crossed the line into commitment.

It seemed to be Steve's nature to defer to him, which made it likely Steve was just waiting for Elliott to broach the subject. Yet for all of his confidence their feelings were mutual, he didn't like to consider the remotest possibility of Steve's not feeling the same way he did.

Of course, the rest of the world didn't stand still while Elliott's personal life evolved. He'd talked regularly with Cessy, as always, and had frequent–mostly phone–contacts with Bruno. Steve had talked several times to Ralph, the aspiring artist who'd invited him over to see his work, with which Steve was impressed. Though it didn't bother Elliott, he was pleased Steve went out of his way to assure him Ralph's interest wasn't personal, and that Ralph was aware Steve and Elliott were seeing each other.

Ricky had lost his apartment, and Bruno invited him to stay with him until he found a job and could get another place. Cage was still there, too, though Elliott could sense Bruno was beginning to feel more than a bit used where his nephew was concerned. Although Cage was apparently making good money, he had never offered to pay rent, or buy groceries, or pay any of the expenses of an evening out. He frequently borrowed money for new clothes or to take Chaz out for the evening.

"I feel kind of guilty about resenting it," Bruno said. "I mean, it's not that I need the money, but...well, it would be kind of nice if he'd at least offer."

Elliott understood completely and agreed.

Probably as a result of his new relationship with Ricky, the frequency of Bruno's Saturday night parties tapered off. He also was growing increasingly unhappy about his "friends," directly or indirectly, requesting money for one thing or another.

At one point, Elliott said, "Why don't you just refer all requests to Walter Means? He is your financial manager, after all."

"He doesn't want to be bothered. He says it's up to me to say no."

That struck Elliott as a pretty cavalier attitude for someone to whom Bruno was paying a lot of money to do just that.

"What about Rudy's proposal? That involves quite a chunk of change."

"I told Walter I'd already given Rudy ten thousand from my discretionary fund just to keep the door open, as it were, but that we hadn't done any formal paperwork yet. He all but called me an idiot."

Elliott gave a small mental sigh but said nothing.

"He says for me to make up my mind whether I want to do it or not, and if I do, to give him all the details and he'll look into it. His dismissive attitude really bothers me sometimes. I'm neither a kid nor an idiot, yet he treats me as though I were both."

"You can always find another financial manager."

"I know, and I've given it some thought, but there's just too much else going on right now."

Rudy had also called Elliott several times about the bar deal, until Elliott simply said he was too busy with current projects to have the time to worry about new ones. While he'd been a little disturbed to hear

Bruno had given Rudy $10,000, he was relieved to know nothing had been formalized; and he was willing to bet Means wouldn't go along with it. Bruno had also mentioned Rudy disapproved of Ricky and had implied he was only out for Bruno's money, which struck Elliott as ironic.

"I don't think it's fair of him," Bruno said. "Frankly, I'm more than a little hesitant to go into business with someone who thinks he has the right to run my private life."

Elliott again said nothing but agreed wholeheartedly.

❧

As the close of escrow approached, Elliott felt he couldn't put off having a talk with Steve about the potential gallery–and, by implication, the future of their relationship–any longer. His decision was prompted, in part, by one of John's infrequent-of-late visits.

–How long are you going to keep him hanging?

–Hanging?

–You don't do naive innocence very well, you know.

–You mean talking with Steve.

–I mean talking with Steve. You know he really wants that space, but he won't take it any further until you do.

–But he said he's not ready to open his own gallery just yet.

–Said, yes. But you're planning to keep the building. You don't have to rent out the ground floor immediately. And there are alternatives.

–Such as?

–A gallery always has more than one artist. Steve could take on new artists like Ralph, or talk with Devereux and maybe a couple of other downtown galleries and offer to display some of their work on commission–sort of a satellite gallery for them.

–Hmmm, I'd never thought of that. I suppose it's a possibility.

–And he wouldn't have to ask for much of a commission on anything he sold for them–the main idea is to display and sell his own work.

–Are these your ideas, or Steve's?

–I'm not saying a word. So, you will talk to him? Soon?

–I will talk to him. Soon.

❧

Elliott invited Steve to dinner the Friday before the closing. Even before his conversation with John, he was aware Steve had been very discreet in not asking too many questions on the progress of the escrow, or on Elliott's plans for the renovation. By way of laying the groundwork for broaching the subject, he asked him to bring the pastel he had made of the building.

As soon as he got home Friday night, he put a pork loin and baking potatoes in the oven. He'd decided to go all-out in the gourmet chef department and made a tray of one of their favorite hors d'oeuvres–bacon-wrapped pitted dates.

Steve arrived promptly at seven-fifteen, large sketch pad under one arm and a bottle of champagne wrapped in gold aluminum foil with a large red ribbon in his free hand.

"I figured you needed to celebrate," he said, handing over the wine.

"Thanks! Much appreciated. You want it before or with dinner?"

"Whichever you prefer."

"Well, let's have a drink first. I'll put this in the fridge. Go on into the living room, and I'll be right there."

While Steve took a seat, Elliott put the champagne in the refrigerator, took out the small cookie sheet with the bacon-wrapped dates and set it beside the toaster oven, then took ice out of the freezer compartment.

"Bourbon-Seven okay?" he asked.

"Sure."

Before he carried their drinks into the living room, he put the baking sheet into the toaster oven and turned it on high.

"Two minutes," he said, handing Steve his drink.

Steve looked puzzled, and Elliot jerked his head toward the kitchen.

"Hors d'oeuvres," he explained.

They had time for a toast to the new project and a sip of their drinks before Elliott got up and went back into the kitchen.

"So," he said, setting the plate on the coffee table in front of Steve and resuming his seat, "I have a proposal for you."

Steve cocked his head quizzically. "I'm listening."

"Your lease is coming up pretty soon, right?"

Still clearly puzzled, he nodded. "Yeah...three months. Why?"

"Would you consider a move?"

"A move? Where?"

"To the Armitage building. I figured since you want to open up your own gallery someday, what better place to live than right above it?"

Steve set his drink down on the table.

"I...I...wow! Talk about a surprise. I...I don't know what to say. Sure, I want a gallery someday, but I could never afford it now."

"Look," Elliott said, fearful he might somehow have spooked him, "the last thing I want is for you to feel like I'm putting a piece of cheese on the mousetrap. But it is sort of a fortunate convergence of several things.

"First, I'd already decided I was going to keep the building shortly after we went through it, so that part didn't have anything to do with you. Second, I do need to put some sort of business in there. Third, there are two apartments available. It's a lot closer to your work, and with the Brown Line only a short distance up the street, it's more convenient for getting around without a car than where you are now.

"Finally, I could really use your help in making the building everything I know it can be. I've already told you I'd like to use your color scheme for the outside, and I could definitely use your artist's eye on the rest of the place, particularly the first floor. I've never done a building quite like this one before."

Steve still looked mildly dazed. "I don't know, Ell. I'm really flattered, of course. And it's true that my lease is coming up. I could probably afford the rent on one of the apartments, but the retail space, too? I could never swing that, even if I were ready to have a gallery."

"Don't worry about that right now. We can always work something out."

Steve was quiet for a full minute.

"You know I've always wanted my own gallery, but let's face it, art galleries aren't exactly cash cows. I'm sure even some of the high-end galleries in River North have a tough time making it. I realize that for me to want my own, especially at this point, would be more a vanity thing than practical."

"But you still want it."

Steve gave him a small smile.

"Of course I do. And when you took me to see the building, I fell in love with it. It's got fantastic potential for a gallery, even though it is way off the beaten path for one.

"I know I don't have enough of my own work to fill a gallery, but if I ever did get one, I was thinking–well, more like fantasizing, but it doesn't hurt to dream–about maybe contacting Mr. Devereux and a couple of the other art dealers in River North and River East and maybe featuring new artists like Ralph, who's really talented."

So much for where John got his ideas, Elliott thought. That he had access to Steve's thoughts was more than a little disturbing.

"But for me to ever make any money at it..." Steve was saying.

"There's more to life than money," Elliott observed.

"Easy for you to say."

"Look, there's no rush, but this could work out well for both of us. I've been thinking for quite a while about getting an official office for my business, but I certainly don't need more than a fraction of the space available at Armitage. You'll need an office for the gallery, and we can just as easily put in two–one for the gallery and one for me. I won't be losing money on letting most of the space sit empty until you're ready to start your gallery. You'll be doing me a favor by using it."

Steve gave him a raised-eyebrow and a small grin.

"Riiiiight."

"Look, I know this is a lot to throw at you at one time, so let's take it one step at a time. Would you like to help me with ideas for the building?"

"Of course!"

"Okay. We'll leave it at that for the moment. The first thing I have to do is contact the sandblasters and the tuck-pointers. Then the painting contractor, and that's where you come in. Also, as soon as we can, we should do another walk-through of the place and talk about what to do in the apartments."

❧

–That went well.

–Better than expected, actually.

–And you both managed to tiptoe around the commitment issue very nicely.

–Back off, Cessy. So, how come you knew exactly what Steve was going to say about Devereux? What's going on between you two?

–Nothing's "going on" between us. Okay, so Steve is aware of me... peripherally. He can sense me a little–he's a pretty strong empath, don't forget–but he doesn't know who I am and I do not talk with him. I don't know that he's made any connection between me and you. But that's not to say he won't some day, with no help from me. You should think about that.

—Believe me, I have. But you knew exactly what Steve has been thinking about the gallery, and Devereux. I thought you said you didn't go rummaging around in other people's heads.

—Give me a break! I don't. The mind isn't like a sock drawer. Most people's are more like bank vaults, and I have no interest in finding the combination. But empaths often leave the door open a little bit, and sometimes I can't resist peeking inside. It's sort of like going to an art gallery.

But I never intrude or go places I know I shouldn't. Steve's mind is more open than most. The only reason I sometimes know what you—and, to a degree, Steve—are thinking is that you tend to leave your thoughts just lying around like toys in a kid's playroom. After all the time we've spent together, it's almost natural I'd know what you're thinking.

—Yeah, I suppose.

—So, are you going to tell Cessy about your...arrangement...with Steve?

—Right. And have her start calling caterers for the wedding? I don't think so. Besides, there's no arrangement. Steve's just going to help me with a few things on the building. The whole gallery/moving thing hasn't been decided yet.

—Of course, it hasn't. Come on, Elliott, I may be dead, but I'm not stupid.

—Say goodnight, Gracie.

—Goodnight, Gracie.

❧

If the thirty days prior to the close of escrow had gone by fast, the days following it seemed to pass in a blur. Having Steve in the renovation equation was a totally new experience, since Elliott was used to making all the decisions himself.

To keep things running as smoothly as possible, he worked independently with Steve and with his crew. Steve was never around during the day when Elliott was at work, and he didn't feel it necessary to mention Steve's involvement to Arnie, Sam and Ted, though he suspected they were aware of each other.

They had decided to make as few changes to the the apartments as possible. The only major structural change was to reinforce the roof of the garage to enable it to be used as a patio for the second-floor apartment, and to make the kitchen window looking out on the garage roof into a door to allow access to it.

The outside was the first priority, followed by the upstairs flats.

On closer inspection, the basement proved, as Elliott had suspected, to be a treasure trove. He was particularly happy to find, in an old built-in cabinet under the stairs, the building's original blueprints. He and his crew also found what appeared to be the original storefront exterior trim, which had been removed during the conversion, and the store's original front door.

When the previous owners renovated the bathrooms, they had not thrown out the original fixtures–pedestal sinks and wood-covered water tanks that hung suspended over the toilets, which were then flushed by pulling a chain hanging down from the tank. The original claw-foot bathtubs were also there, though in need of re-enameling.

The current bathrooms could be expanded by reducing the size of the large adjoining bedroom closets. The tubs would be replaced with the refinished originals with added shower capability.

Plans. Details. Meetings. Subcontractors. Painters. Tuck-pointers. Suppliers. Elliott was once again caught up in a blizzard of detail, and he loved every minute.

Away from work, things went on as usual, with a few minor ripples on the otherwise calm surface of his life. He talked sporadically with Bruno, who indicated his growing dissatisfaction with Walter Means's dismissive attitude and evasiveness in the answering of some of Bruno's questions on the dramatic losses in his investment portfolio, which Means blamed on the stock market plunge.

"I'm sorry, but frankly, I don't believe him," Bruno said at one point.

"You think he's stealing from you? Then you should report him."

"How? To whom? Based on what? I really don't have any proof and wouldn't know how to get it. Plus, I know nothing at all about finances, which is why I hired him in the first place. I certainly don't want to cause trouble for him if I'm wrong. I think I'll just keep a closer eye on things for now and demand he keep me better informed than he has been."

Elliott's own portfolio had suffered serious losses as a result of the plunge, but he'd gone through similar situations in the past and knew the market always bounced back and the losses recovered. Still, he could understand how Bruno, unaccustomed to both the financial markets and dealing with amounts of money he'd never dreamed of before, could be both confused and suspicious.

Bruno had also fallen quite hard for Ricky, to the point where Ricky had moved in permanently. Cage was dragging his feet on getting his own apartment, though he hadn't repaid any of the money Bruno had given him for the purpose of getting one. Bruno almost never saw him, but he was quite unhappy that Cage borrowed his car and got into an accident that earned him a DUI citation and did three thousand dollars'-worth of damage to the car. Cage didn't say a word about paying for it.

Calls to and from Cessy were so much a part of his life they went almost unnoticed, rather like breathing. Their parents came back to town briefly before heading off on another junket. He'd spoken to his mother once, shortly after their return, and was as always mildly amused that she never inquired into what was going on in his life. She thought his choice of career was beneath him, and he had no doubt she was well aware her only son was gay but felt the best way to avoid confronting those facts was to ignore his personal life altogether.

The broken garage door had been replaced. Tuck-pointing, sandblasting, scraping and repainting of the fire escape and the entire exterior of the building–utilizing Steve's suggested colors–were complete, and the ground floor exterior was restored, to Elliott's delight and Steve's barely concealed joy. Priority was then given to working on the apartments on the top two floors, leaving the interior of the first floor for last.

Butcher paper was taped to the inside of the new ground-floor windows to prevent passersby from staring in, though the work on the exterior was attracting a lot of attention, judging by the number of cars Elliott and his crew noticed slowing down as they passed, and the number of people who stopped to watch the progress being made. As he was coming to work one morning, a woman he assumed to be from the neighborhood asked him what was going into the downstairs space.

"I'm not sure yet," he had replied. "Maybe an art gallery."

Elliott and Steve spent an entire Saturday afternoon, most of it in the ground-floor flat, discussing possibilities and practicalities. In structural matters, Steve deferred completely to Elliott, but made several practical suggestions, which he carefully couched as observations, and which Elliott readily acceded to.

There were four central pillars spaced down the center of the ground space that couldn't be removed since they bore the weight of the upper floors, but Steve made suggestions on how they could be made to appear to be decorative elements rather than obstructions.

They'd have to wait until all the interior dividing walls were taken down before they could assess any damage done to the pressed tin ceilings, or to know the condition of what lay behind the paneling.

Both agreed on having the two offices–one for the gallery and one for Elliott's business–located in the rear adjacent to what had likely been the bathroom for the original store. Elliott was glad that during the conversion it had merely been expanded rather than moved into the apartment. It would be easy enough to reduce it to its original size.

Elliott envisioned an open space but knew it would probably need some sort of partitioning. Without his having mentioned it, Steve volunteered, "Movable wall units would provide maximum flexibility," and Elliott suppressed a smile. Though they'd not specifically talked more about a gallery since Elliott had first broached the subject, he was quite sure it had never been far from Steve's mind, and he increasingly wished Steve would say something about it.

It got to the point where, on one of John's visits, he casually asked if John might know what Steve was thinking about his proposal.

–You know that's not a fair question.

Elliott felt a wave of embarrassment.

–You're right, of course. I'm sorry. I have no right to ask you to tell me what's in someone else's mind. It won't happen again, I promise.

–That's okay. I know you want to know, and I understand. But we both know I'm not the person to ask.

❧

He became so wrapped up in the project that he frequently had to stop to think what day it was. Weekends were fairly easy, since he spent them with Steve, but workdays all tended to blend together. So, he wasn't quite sure whether it was a Tuesday or Wednesday when he got a call from Bruno.

"Are you and Steve free this Saturday night?" he asked. "It's Ricky's birthday, and I'm throwing him a party."

"Let me check with Steve, but I don't think we've made any other plans, so, thanks. What can we get him?"

"No, no gifts are necessary. Just bring yourselves."

"We wouldn't feel right about that. Can you think of something he'd like?"

"You don't have to, of course, but I think I mentioned that we share a love of stamps, and there's a book I've been meaning to get for him from the American Philatelic Foundation called *Stamp Collecting: a Definitive Book* by Michael DuBesso. I was planning to order it tomorrow, as a matter of fact."

"Well, why don't you let us get it for him?"

"That would be wonderful. I know he'd love it."

Jotting down the author's name and title, Elliott said, "Got it!"

There was a slight pause, then: "Actually, Ricky's birthday is only one of the reasons I'd like you here."

"Oh?'

"Yes. Rudy's really been getting pushy about my making a definite commitment to the bar project. I told him I'd mentioned it to Walter Means a couple weeks ago, and that Walter thought it was a bad idea but said he'd be willing to take a look at a detailed proposal. Rudy's been hedging on getting it to him, saying I could just use my discretionary fund, but I don't want to do that."

"I don't blame you. Don't let Rudy push you around. The fact that he won't produce the figures Means wants is a pretty good indication something's wrong."

"I know, but I do feel a little guilty, since Rudy's really depending on me."

"Which is exactly how he wants you to feel."

There was a pause before Bruno said, a little sheepishly, "I did give him a small loan last week out of my discretionary fund. He said he needed it to keep the deal open. But then yesterday he called asking for more. I'm planning to take him aside at the party and tell him I just can't keep lending him money until he starts repaying what he's already borrowed.

"Everything is smoke and mirrors and more money for this and more money for that up to now. I'm really beginning to think I never should have gotten involved with him in the first place. I'm sorry, but I'm not responsible for his financial problems.

"I so dread confrontations, and I figured that talking with him when there are other people around will forestall the possibility of a scene. I know he's not going to be happy. And I'll feel better if I know you're nearby for moral support."

"Well, let me call Steve right now to make sure he hasn't planned anything for Saturday, and get back to you."

Which he did.

"I really appreciate that, Elliott," Bruno said when Elliott called him back to confirm they'd be there. "About eight-thirty Saturday, then?"

"Sounds good. See you there."

❧

–You've really got to talk to Steve.

–I know. I know. And I will.

–When? You're really not being fair to him.

–What do you mean? There's nothing to stop him *from bringing it up.*

–Bullshit! You know he won't. It's your building, after all. You've got to let him know you want him to have his gallery. It's part of the reason you bought the building in the first place, and you know it.

–Yeah, I suppose you're right.

–You can leave out the "I suppose."

–It's just that...

–Okay, we're getting there. Spit it out.

–Shit! My wanting Steve to have the gallery and to live in one of the apartments–it's a huge step.

–They call it a commitment. And you're not thinking in terms of landlord-tenant.

–No, I guess I'm not. I'm just not sure Steve feels the same way.

–Good Lord, but you're dense! Steve has followed your lead since the first day you met.

–No, he hasn't.

–Look, while a rousing game of "has not/has too" is a lot of fun, I'm not going to play it with you. But I'm telling you, if you don't say something pretty soon...

–So, you have been in his head.

–I don't need to be in his head. I can sense what he's feeling just being within ten feet of him. For being as perceptive as you are, you have a blind spot the size of a Sherman tank when it comes to Steve.

–So, you're saying...
–I'm not saying anything. It's you who should be doing the saying.
–But...
–Goodnight, Elliott.

❧

The next day–definitely a Wednesday, Elliott determined–he called Unabridged Books to see if they had a copy of the book Bruno had suggested for Ricky. They didn't but put it on order, saying it might or might not arrive by Saturday. If it didn't, a gift card would have to do until the book arrived..

The call for the book was, however, only a momentary distraction. He found it uncharacteristically hard to give his full attention to his work. He knew John was right. He'd always had difficulty with the concept of love. It wasn't that he didn't know what it was, or that he wasn't sure that, if his feet were held to the fire, he would have to admit he loved Steve.

But love was not a word he had ever used lightly. He knew his parents loved him, although he couldn't remember either one of them ever having actually said so. As close as he was to Cessy, he couldn't recall any time he had said it to her, either. In his mind, love was far too complex to be encapsulated in just one four-letter word, and he sincerely believed that actions spoke far louder than words. He didn't have to tell Cessy he loved her, any more than she had to tell him she loved him. They just knew.

Likewise, he knew how he felt about Steve, and he was pretty sure Steve felt the same toward him. So, why did either one of them have to come right out and use a word that was far too often overused to the point of being worthless? He thought yet again of an observation a friend had made several years before: "The sooner somebody says 'I love you,' the sooner they forget your name."

It had certainly been true in Elliott's relationships. He realized he had never told anyone he was seeing that he loved him–which might, he reflected, partially account for why he'd only had one relationship of any duration.

And just what might he expect of a more formal relationship with Steve they didn't already have? That they live together? It would be nice to wake up together every morning, he admitted, but otherwise, their living arrangements were something of a non-issue. They both seemed comfortable with the way things were. He knew Steve needed a lot of time to himself to paint, and Elliott really liked his condo. He knew, too, that Steve would not, nor could Elliott expect him to, feel comfortable moving into Elliott's space, any more than Elliott would be comfortable moving in with Steve.

No, if that day did come, it would have to happen in someplace neither of them would feel was already-claimed territory. The Armitage building would qualify, and he hoped Steve might decide to move in there; but Elliott simply wasn't willing to give up his condo just yet. And once Steve moved into the apartment without him, it became his place.

All of which made perfect sense, until a sharp, clear thought appeared–whether originated by him or by John he couldn't be sure.

But you're not Steve.

⁂

"How about dinner here tomorrow?" he asked when he called Steve Thursday after work. "I kind of have a taste for meatloaf and thought I'd run out to the Boston Market on Ashland on my way home and pick us up something. What would you like?"

"Meatloaf's fine." There was a long pause, then: "You sound a little...odd. Everything okay?"

"Of course," he semi-lied. "I was just thinking we need to talk about a few things."

"Strange–I was thinking the same thing."

"No wonder we get along so well."

"Empaths of the world, unite!"

They both laughed, and when they hung up, Elliott felt a little better about the coming conversation...but not much.

⁂

"So," Steve said, smiling as he took the drink Elliott handed him, "what are we going to talk about?"

Elliott sat beside him on the couch.

"Care to make a guess?"

Steve set his glass on the coffee table and turned to face him.

"Oh, no, you don't! You're not handing the ball off to me on this one. It's yours. Run with it."

Closing his eyes and sighing, Elliott reopened them to find Steve staring at him intently, looking mildly amused.

"Okay. We've got to talk about the building, about whether you want to move into it, about whether you want the ground floor for a gallery, and..."

John, he knew, was nearby, and he sensed his immense enjoyment of Elliott's discomfort.

"And?"

"You're not going to make this easy, are you? And...about us."

There was what seemed to Elliott to be a very long silence.

"What about us?"

Elliott gave him a mock scowl.

"Jeezus, why the hell do I feel like I'm fifteen years old, sitting in the back seat of Tom Simmons's car drinking beer and trying to gather up the courage to put the make on him?"

Yet another silence during which Steve said nothing. Finally, Elliott threw up his hands.

"Look, are we officially together or not?"

"You silver-tongued devil, you," Steve said, laughing, then carefully composed himself. "I'm really kind of surprised you had to ask. We are as far as I'm concerned."

"Then why didn't you ever say anything?"

"Why didn't you? And what was there to say? Neither one of us is the gushy type. I just assumed you felt the same way. Was I wrong?"

"Of course, you weren't wrong. I just wanted to be sure we were on the same page."

"Chapter and verse. There's only one thing I'm kind of concerned about."

Elliott was puzzled. "And that is...?"

"Cessy. Please don't let her start planning a wedding. The very thought of some big ceremony with a cake and matching rings makes my toes curl."

Grinning, Elliott said, "We do make a good team."

"So, did you tell Cessy we were going to have this little talk?"

"Are you out of your mind? She'd be sitting on the arm of the couch with a video camera if she knew."

"Are you going to tell her?"

"Good question. Maybe next time we get together with the family we can wear matching shirts."

"Subtlety will do it every time."

They laughed again, then fell into a silence until Elliott finally said, "And the move? And the gallery?"

Steve pursed his lips and remained silent for another few seconds.

"Well, here's where it gets a little sticky. I really do like the second-floor apartment, especially since there'll be a door from the kitchen to the new patio so I wouldn't have to climb out the bedroom window to get to it. I'll have to give my current landlord notice that I won't be renewing my lease, but we need to talk about the rent to be sure I can afford it."

"Trust me, you can afford it."

Shaking his head, Steve said, "Which brings up another issue."

"Which is...?"

"Money. I know you have a lot more than I do–probably more than I can ever hope to earn in several lifetimes. So, I want it clear from the start that I pay my own way.

"I know perfectly well that one of the reasons you bought the building in the first place was because you knew I wanted a gallery. But I can't afford it right now, and I don't know when I'll be able to. I can't have you losing money on an empty retail space waiting for me."

Reaching out to lay his free hand on Steve's thigh, Elliott said, "Look, I know the money thing is an issue for you. It is for Brad, too, and I respect you both for it. But Brad and Cessy have worked it out, and we can, too.

"As for the rent on the apartment, I don't know what you're paying now, but I can't imagine the new place would be any more expensive, if at all. And if it is, I'd be happy to factor in a small 'sleeping with the landlord' deduction. And we've already talked about my only needing a very small area for an office. The rest of it can just sit empty until you're ready. I won't be losing any money on it."

They were both quiet for another moment or two until Steve took Elliott's hand and squeezed it.

"Well, as you said earlier, one step at a time."

"I'll drink to that!" Elliott grinned. "Now, how about dinner?"

–Congratulations! I'm really happy for both of you!

–Thanks, but actually nothing has really changed, other than we resolved the issues of Steve's taking the apartment and the gallery space.

–Horse-pucky. It was a big step. At least now each of you knows for sure how the other feels.

–We knew before.

–You knew, but I think Steve really needed to hear it from you. And you are going to tell Cessy, aren't you? You really should put the poor woman out of her misery.

–I know, and I will.

–And your folks?

–Uh, no. Like Steve said, "one step at a time," and that one's a couple of miles off. My parents live their lives and I live mine, and that's the way we all like it. I'm sure they know I'm gay, and they prefer to totally ignore it, and that's fine with me.

–And now your last big hurdle with Steve is telling him about me.

–Right. If you had lungs, I'd tell you not to hold your breath. And if you're talking to me now in hopes I'll wake Steve up again by talking in my sleep...

–The furthest thing from my mind.

–Riiight.

"Right what?"

With the sound of Steve's voice, Elliott was instantly awake.

"Oh, Jeezus, Steve, just shoot me. How in the hell can you put up with me constantly waking you up?"

"Hey, just think of all those guys out there who don't have someone to wake them up in the middle of the night."

"Point. But I am sorry. Go back to sleep."

Elliott turned on his side, facing away from Steve, and felt him turn, too–toward him, slipping his arm around Elliott's chest.

"By the way," Steve said, "I'm glad we had our talk."

Elliott took his hand, intertwining their fingers. "Me, too."

❧

After breakfast the next morning, Elliott drove Steve home to spend the day working on his latest painting. On the way back, he remembered to stop at Unabridged to see if the stamp book had arrived. It hadn't, but he got a card verifying it had been ordered, on which he wrote both his and Steve's names, then went next door to He Who Eats Mud, a card and gift shop he always patronized for its name if nothing else, for a birthday card.

Picking Steve up at the Thorndale el stop at six-fifteen, he drove the short distance to their favorite Chinese restaurant, after which they returned to his condo to relax and have a drink before heading to the party. As they were getting ready to leave, Elliott remembered the birthday card, which he had Steve sign.

"What do I owe you for the book?" Steve asked.

"Brunch."

They arrived at Bruno's at eight-forty-five. As usual, the kitchen door was slightly ajar and the front door partially open. They walked in to find about twenty people scattered around the living room, dining alcove, kitchen, and in the hallway leading to the den and bedrooms. Elliott immediately spotted Cage, Ralph, Chaz, Bruno's "sensei" Clifford Blanton and several other people he recognized as regulars at Bruno's parties. There were also several people he had never seen before, and he wondered where they'd come from.

Bruno and Ricky stood by the dining room table, which had several wrapped gifts on it, talking with Paul and the as-always impeccably dressed Button.

Walking over to greet them and to wish Ricky a happy birthday, Elliott casually laid the envelope next to the other gifts. He'd not seen Rudy but assumed he was coming, and knowing Bruno was probably already worried about a possible confrontation, he didn't want to ask.

"Please," Bruno said, "go get a drink and something to eat."

Rolling the ice cubes around in the bottom of his glass, Button drained it and said, "Allow me to show you the way. Excuse us, all."

He and Steve followed Button to the bar, pausing to exchange a few words with various other guests. Steve pointed out the large buffet spread out on a pair of tablecloth-covered card tables near the bar.

"My God, there's enough food there to feed the Sixth Fleet."

"We should be so lucky," Button observed. While they waited for the bartender to finish making drinks for the man in front of them, he said to Elliott, "It's none of my business, of course, but do I detect a hint of trouble in Paradise?"

"What do you mean?"

"Well, Bruno seems a little...on edge...tonight. Very unlike him. I really hope he and Ricky aren't having problems already. Bruno seems truly devoted to him, but you know how these young kids are."

"I'm sure it's nothing," Elliott said. "Everybody has an off day every now and then."

Button pursed his lips and looked from him to Steve.

"I'm sure you're right," he said, but he didn't sound totally convinced.

Paul joined them just as they were giving their drink orders to the bartender, and a moment later, Ricky came over. Glancing toward the dining alcove and the gift table, Elliott saw no sign of Bruno.

"A very nice party, Ricky," Steve said.

Ricky grinned. "It is, isn't it? This is my first real birthday party ever. Of course, I don't know very many of the people here, but it's still nice."

"Interesting centerpiece," Steve said, indicating the buffet table where a circular flower arrangement surrounded an empty champagne bottle with a lit white candle dripping small rivulets of different colors over the bottle as it melted.

Blushing, Ricky said "Bruno did that for me. It's the first bottle of champagne we shared, and I kept it. I love it with the candle!"

Elliott smiled to himself when he detected the distinct aroma of Old Spice. Bruno's influence, he assumed.

"Where did Bruno disappear to?" Button asked, scanning the room.

"Rudy came, and Bruno said he wanted to talk to him privately. I guess they went into the den."

That was quick, Elliott thought.

"Well, I wouldn't let you out of my sight for a second," Button said, resting his hand lightly on Ricky's arm. "A roving band of gypsies could come rushing in and just carry you off. Paul, where did we leave our gypsy costumes?"

⁂

Half an hour or so later, as a small circle of guests, including Ralph, Steve and Button, were talking about the Art Institute's new Modern Wing, Elliott noticed an angry-looking Rudy emerge from the hallway to Bruno's den. Motioning to an–of course–handsome young man with whom he had apparently come, he headed to the front door and left, his companion hurrying after him. A moment later, Bruno appeared, looking less than happy and, oblivious to Clifford Blanton's attempt to catch his attention as he passed, went directly to the bar.

Though Elliott hoped for a chance to talk privately with Bruno to learn what had happened during his meeting with Rudy, the opportunity did not present itself. Immediately after getting his drink and speaking briefly to Ricky, Bruno withdrew to one corner of the room with Clifford Blanton for a long and apparently earnest discussion.

Bruno returned to the main group for the opening of the presents and the cutting and serving of the birthday cake, after which the crowd began to thin out. At around eleven-thirty, Elliott and Steve sought out their hosts to express their thanks and say goodbye. Ricky thanked them profusely for the on-order book, and Bruno told Elliott he would call him soon. From the tone in his voice, Elliott gathered he meant very soon.

"So, how'd you sleep?" Elliott asked as they were getting out of bed. "You did a lot of tossing and turning."

"Sorry about that. I hope I didn't keep you awake."

"Not a problem. And it's not like I haven't woken you from a sound sleep more than a few times. Any particular reason?"

As he talked, Steve was stepping into his shorts, and Elliott opened a dresser drawer to pull out two pair of sweatpants. He tossed one to Steve and put on the other.

"Well, yeah, there's a reason," Steve said, hopping on one leg to pull the sweats over the other.

"Aha. Our Friday night talk." A wave of mild anxiety came over him.

"Right. Our Friday night talk. One hell of a lot of information to process all at once. I spent most of yesterday going over it, and I should have mentioned it before we went up to Bruno's last night."

Pulling the drawstring to tighten the waist and tying the string into a loop-knot, Elliott said, "And any conclusions? New thoughts? Change of mind?"

Steve grinned and ran his fingers through his hair.

"No, no, and no. Just thinking. I realized I was pretty pushy in assuming I could have the second-floor apartment. I know you could probably get a lot more rent for it, since it's got the patio, and..."

Elliott stepped over and put his hands on Steve's shoulders, holding him at arm's-length.

"Uh, did you miss the we're-a-couple part of our talk? I'm not just your landlord."

"I know. It's just a little hard to get a grip on everything, and I don't want to start presuming anything. It's your building, after all."

Releasing him and turning back toward the living room, Elliott said, "Look, if it helps, just pretend some guy named John owns the place. We're in this whole thing together."

Steve volunteered to make omelets while Elliott took charge of the toast, orange juice, and making a fresh pot of coffee. Realizing as they ate that Steve hadn't been to the building for a couple of weeks, Elliott said, "You want to take a run over to the building later to see how it's coming?"

"That'd be great! I didn't want to ask. Like I said, all this will take some getting used to."

"The blind leading the blind," Elliott said with a grin.

Chapter 5

Steve gave notice of his intent not to renew the lease on his Diversey apartment and began collecting boxes for his move. The interior of the ground floor space of the Armitage building was still largely untouched as Elliott and his crew concentrated on finishing the two upper floors and partitioning the basement to make a laundry room and storage areas.

Elliott had talked frequently with Bruno, whose problems appeared to be compounding faster than the interest on his lottery winnings. The day after the Ricky's birthday party, he'd called to report on his meeting with Rudy. It had turned into exactly the kind of confrontation Bruno had been dreading. Rudy, of course, played the injured party, claiming he never would have gone into the bar negotiations had he known Bruno was going to "pull the rug out from under him." He claimed that, as a result, he was going to to lose his entire investment in the project.

As for Bruno having the nerve to ask for evidence the money he had already loaned Rudy would be repaid...

It was at this point, Bruno said, that Rudy stormed out. Bruno felt terrible, but Elliott did his best to convince him it was all part of Rudy's game and his obsessive need to always keep the upper hand; he'd played the guilt card for all it was worth.

Cage had subsequently, and not surprisingly, lost his job as one of Rudy's limo-drivers-cum-escorts, Rudy citing a need to cut back because of Bruno's reneging on their deal. Cage blamed Bruno, even though he continued to live in Bruno's condo. Bruno was concerned because he felt Cage was trying to undermine his relationship with Ricky by implying Ricky was only out for his money–a point Elliott found ironic since it was increasingly clear to him that was exactly Cage's own motivation.

"It sounds like a bad soap opera," Steve observed when Elliott told him of the situation.

Elliott had heard very little from John, and while he still talked with Cessy several times a week, he had not yet mentioned his conversation with Steve or that Steve would be moving into the Armitage building. As the building neared completion and Steve's move-in date approached, however, he knew he couldn't put it off much longer.

So, when Cessy called to ask him to come to dinner the following day, he agreed. After hanging up, he called Steve to let him know.

"You want to come along? I'm sure she'll be happy to set another place."

Steve laughed. "Oh, sure. You show up with me in tow on a Thursday night, and she won't have a clue as to why? I appreciate the offer, but I think I'll let you handle this one on your own. I need to finish the painting I'm working on, anyway, and I've got some more packing to do. I know I've still got a month or so, but better early than late. Let me know how it goes."

"Yeah, like I wouldn't. See you Friday, then?"

"My place? You can help me pack. And if you see any empty boxes along the way, bring 'em."

It wasn't, Elliott told himself as he drove to Brad and Cessy's, that he was nervous about telling his sister her tireless efforts to get him paired off had finally succeeded. It was just that he didn't feel comfortable about having fusses made, and he knew she would undoubtedly do just that. She meant well, but he wished she would be able to accept it as calmly as Steve had.

Arriving at the Priebes's, he noted Brad's car wasn't in the driveway, so he took a just-vacated parking spot on the street a few doors down so Brad wouldn't have to move his car later to let him out.

He let himself in the side door, as always, to an empty kitchen. As he entered the living room, Cessy came down the stairs carrying their toddler, Sandy. They both smiled when they saw him.

Going over to take Sandy for an exaggerated hug and a baby-kiss, he followed Cessy into the kitchen.

"Brad called. He's running a few minutes late."

"Good," Elliott replied, setting Sandy in her highchair. "I wanted to talk to you about something."

His sister's eyes widened in a combination of curiosity and anticipation.

"Oh?"

"Yeah. I wanted to let you know Steve will be moving into the Armitage building."

She looked at him closely. "And does this mean...?"

He grinned. "Pretty much."

Shehurried over to him to kiss him on the cheek and give him a big hug.

"Oh, Elliott! I'm so happy for you. It's about time." She stepped back and said, "But why doesn't he just move in with you?"

"Because Steve wouldn't feel right moving into my territory, if you can call it that, any more than I'd feel right moving into his."

"But he's moving into one of your buildings," she pointed out.

"Which is fine. We can consider it something of a halfway point, or half-step, or whatever. Probably at some time down the road we'll consolidate, but for right now..."

"Well, I can't wait to tell Brad."

Elliott raised his hand in a "slow down" gesture.

"I really wish you wouldn't make a big deal out of this," he said. "You're far more interested in my love life than Brad is, I'm sure."

"You know I'll be discreet."

"Riiight."

He directed the conversation to other subjects until BJ bounded down the stairs from his room to ask when dinner would be ready. He and Elliott exchanged their usual cursory greetings.

"So, how's school?" Elliott asked.

"Same as always," the teenager replied. "School."

The sound of a car in the driveway announced Brad's arrival, and Cessy immediately went into what Elliott thought of as commander-in-chief mode as her husband came in.

"Go wash up and get your sister," Cessy directed BJ. Accepting Brad's peck on the cheek, she looked from him to Elliott and said, "You two can wait until after dinner for your beer. Elliott, would you bring Sandy's highchair into the dining room?"

❧

"So, how's your new project going?" Brad asked while passing BJ a bowl of mashed potatoes. "My partner and I drove down Armitage yesterday on our way to a case, and I wondered if that Painted Lady they've been working on might be yours. You've done a really great job on it. I remember it before, and it's like night and day."

"Thanks, Brad. I really do think it's a great building. I'd like you to see it when it's a little closer to being finished."

"We'd love to see it," Cessy said, then turned to Brad. "Steve's going to be living there," she observed with what Elliott knew was calculated casualness.

"Really?" Brad said, giving Elliott a very slightly raised eyebrow, into which Elliott read volumes. "I see there's retail space on the ground floor. Steve planning to open a gallery?"

Elliott was glad he'd just swallowed his coffee, or he might have had it spurting out his nose. As it was, he almost choked and had a violent coughing spell.

"Are you all right, Elliott?" Cessy asked solicitously.

"Sorry," he said when the coughing subsided. "Wrong drainpipe. You two make a great tag team."

Brad grinned, Jenny looked confused, and BJ reached for the gravy.

❧

"So, how did it go?" Steve asked when Elliott arrived at his place for dinner Friday with three cardboard boxes he'd picked up behind his condo nested one inside the other.

"Easier than I expected. It didn't seem to come as any great surprise. At least, I didn't have to scrape Cessy off the ceiling. And when the time comes for your move, I'm sure we can recruit Brad and BJ to help. Cessy wants to see the building, so I told her we'd have them come over to look at it soon." He found the ease with which he had used "we" more pleasant than surprising. "And she wants to have us over for dinner Sunday. I told her I'd check with you and get back to her."

"Sure. And maybe we could swing by the building sometime over the weekend? I want to take some measurements to get a better idea of what will go where."

"I can do you one better. You can take a look at the original blueprints–the room sizes haven't changed."

Driving back to Steve's after Sunday dinner, Elliott shook his head.

"I don't believe it," he said.

"What? I thought everything went really well. I had a good time. Didn't you?"

"Yes, I did. But this is the first time in living memory that Cessy didn't pump me about my love life or drop three thousand hints that it was time I settled down. It goes against nature, somehow. I can't wait to see what she'll come up with next." He pursed his lips and furrowed his brow. "Probably adoption."

Steve grinned. "As a matter of fact, when I was helping load the dishwasher, she did mention that all we needed now was a kid."

"See? I knew it! The woman's incorrigible."

He found an unusual number of calls on his answering machine when he got home, and saw four of them were from Bruno. He immediately called him. The phone rang four times, and he was about to hang up when Bruno answered.

"Elliott! Thanks for returning my call."

"Sorry I didn't do it earlier, Bruno, but I was with Steve all weekend. What's up?"

"I hate to bother you, but could I come down for a minute? I have a favor to ask you."

Puzzled, Elliott said, "Sure."

"I'll be there in a minute." And without saying goodbye, he hung up.

Elliott was still wondering what was going on when there was a knock at his door, and he opened it to find Bruno, a large envelope in his hand.

"Come on in," Elliott said, leading the way to the living room.

"I've only got a minute. Ricky ran to the store for some things, and he should be right back."

"Is there a problem?"

"I don't know, Elliott. I'm beginning to wish I'd never won that damned lottery! It was bad enough having everyone and his dog hitting me up for money like they think I owe them for something. They just never give up. I always have to check my caller ID now before I pick up–

if it says 'unknown caller' or I don't recognize the number, I don't answer. I've even gotten mail, with no return address, calling me a greedy, arrogant, selfish SOB and a lot worse. Arrogant? Me?

"I have no idea who's doing it, or why. I mean, what do they expect from me? What can I do about it? Friday night, Ricky and I went out to dinner, and when we got back to my car someone had left a really nasty note under my windshield wiper. I'm lucky they just left a note–imagine what they could have done to my car, and I just got it back from the body shop after Cage's accident. It's getting so I'm afraid to leave the building.

"My sessions with Sensei have helped, but I'm afraid not enough. Lately, I've been having trouble sleeping. I keep having these terrible dreams that I can never remember when I wake up, but they really bother me."

"I'm sorry, Bruno. I know you're under a lot of pressure. Have you talked to Walter about funneling all money requests through him? That might help a lot."

"Every time I try to talk to him, he makes me feel like I'm annoying him. I guess I'm just too intimidated by his attitude to say anything. And things with Cage have gotten so bad I'm thinking of asking him to leave. He blames me for losing his job with Rudy, he's increasingly demanding, and treats Ricky like crap. I won't have that, nephew or not. Life's far too short."

"I'm really sorry about all this, Bruno. Having money isn't all it's cracked up to be. Just try to ignore the notes and calls. Whoever it is will get tired and stop eventually. I know it isn't easy, but don't let it get to you. As for Cage, well, I don't know what to tell you there. It's one of those uncomfortable no-win situations, and I don't envy you. As you say, life's too short."

Bruno held up the sealed envelope he'd been holding.

"I wonder if I could ask you to hold this for me."

"Sure." He was hoping there might be some sort of explanation forthcoming, but there was none.

Handing it to him, Bruno said, "Well, I really appreciate your letting me cry on your shoulder, Elliott. I'm afraid I just don't have anyone else I feel I can talk to. Sensei says meditation and finding my inner self is the only answer. I wish it was. I don't want to burden Ricky, but it really does get to me no matter how hard I try not to let it."

"I understand, and I'm always willing to listen even if I can't offer much in the way of help or advice." He briefly thought of giving Bruno his cell-phone number but decided against it. While he was sincere in saying he was willing to listen, he didn't want to risk his offer leading to calls at work.

"Thank you! And now I'd better get back upstairs."

With that, he left.

Looking at the unmarked envelope in his hand, Elliott shook his head and carried it into his bedroom, where he put it beneath a stack of folded T-shirts in his underwear drawer.

Within two weeks, work on the building had progressed to the point Elliott felt he could invite Cessy and Brad to come take a look. The ground floor still hadn't been touched, other than replacing the false front with new showroom windows and the original trim; but work on it would begin as soon as the upstairs apartments were ready for occupancy.

Steve and he had, out of curiosity one Sunday afternoon, removed a small section of wall paneling and found the pressed tin he'd expected to be under it had been removed. He assumed the stacks of it in the basement had been salvaged during the removal.

Steve had been doing some sketches of how the ground floor space might look, which Elliott liked and had shown to his crew, who in turn agreed the ideas could be implemented fairly easily.

The following Monday evening, he got a call from Bruno, with whom he'd talked several times on the phone since their last meeting. It seemed easier for Bruno to talk when Ricky wasn't around, and Elliott agreed with Steve's earlier assessment that Bruno's life was becoming a soap opera, none of which Bruno was handling very well.

He learned there had been a confrontation with Cage, whom Bruno had asked to move out–he claimed Cage was seldom home, anyway, and apparently was trying to juggle dating two guys at the same time. Cage didn't take the news well. Even Bruno's offer to give him a couple hundred dollars a week until he found a job didn't seem to help–though, of course, Cage magnanimously agreed to accept the money.

"I don't know, Elliott, there's just so much going on I can't keep up with it. And now Sensei says the original owner of my Jennys has really been pressing him to buy them back, claiming he was under severe emotional distress brought on by the financial crash and a messy divorce. He says he only sold the Jennys to keep his wife from getting them. I told him no way. He wanted to sell them, I wanted to buy them, and I intend to keep them. I'm sure Sensei is unhappy with me, even if he didn't say so, because several of his students were referrals from the stamps' original owner, and he's afraid the man may cause trouble for him with his other students."

"Well, that really isn't any of your concern. You acted in good faith."

"I know, but I don't want Sensei to suffer for my refusal to sell them back."

"Again, that isn't your concern."

Bruno sighed deeply. "I know. You're right. Still..." He was silent a moment, then said, "Oh, and I finally talked with Walter Means and told him that from now on I'm going to refer all requests for money through him."

"I thought you'd said he didn't want to do it."

"He didn't, but I finally got tired of his attitude, and Sensei said I should let him know how I felt. He's done nothing but slough off my questions and suggestions, and...well, I know he knows far more about money than I ever will, but still...

"I finally decided he was working for me, and if he didn't want to do what I told him to do, I could easily find another financial manager, and I told him so. I'm really thinking seriously about doing it anyway. I'm just not happy with him. Sensei knows someone he says would do very well for me."

It occurred to Elliott that Clifford Blanton was exerting an increasing amount of influence on Bruno, and he didn't know if he thought that was a good idea. Then, he reminded himself Bruno's business wasn't his.

"Well," he nevertheless found himself saying, "if you ever decide on a change, I can put you in touch with the firm that handles my own investments. They could probably recommend someone you might feel more comfortable with."

"I just might do that, Elliott. Thanks. Sensei has suggested I invite everyone who's been dunning me for money to a party this Saturday and tell them all at the same time. I'm going to make it clear to everyone that any future requests for money will have to go through Means–whether he likes it or not–and end all this nonsense once and for all. If Means doesn't like it, I'll fire him. And I'm going to invite Rudy so he can see I wasn't singling him out or deliberately trying to sabotage his projects." There was another brief silence, and then Bruno said, almost as an afterthought, "You and Steve are welcome to come, but I'm afraid the air might be a little toxic."

"Well, thanks, but I think we'll pass. We're going to dinner and a movie, but should be home around eleven, so if you have any problems, just give me a call."

"Sensei will be there, just for moral support, and we'll have a session just before the party. I'll probably need it."

"That sounds like you're piling a lot on your plate for just one night."

"I know, but I'd rather do it all at once than drag it out. I really don't do confrontation well, but if I'm going to do it I might as well go for broke. I just want to tie up all these loose ends once and for all."

Though Elliott was firmly convinced a party wasn't the way to go on this, he didn't feel it was his place to interfere. Bruno was a grown man capable of making his own decisions, and he couldn't help but wonder if the man were finally starting to take more active control of his life, or if he were simply transferring his dependence onto Clifford Blanton.

⁂

Stopping for a drink after the movie Saturday night delayed their arrival home until just after eleven-thirty. Checking the answering machine for any calls from Bruno, he was relieved to see there were none.

They sat in the living room with a glass of strega, with only the hallway light for illumination, and stared out over the city.

"Cessy asked me why I hadn't asked you to move in here," Elliott said.

"You didn't because you knew I wouldn't."

"Right."

"And with a view like this I can see why you wouldn't consider moving."

"Also right. So, as I told Cessy when she asked, we're taking a half-step."

⁂

They got to sleep around one-thirty, and were awakened at three by the sound of sirens that stopped in front of the building. Elliott got up and looked out the bedroom window down onto Sheridan Road and saw nothing but reflections of lights flashing on the building across the street, indicating whatever was happening was on the living room side.

Curious, he went into the living room and out onto the balcony to look over the railing. He saw three squad cars, an ambulance, and a large number of people milling around something covered with a yellow tarp.

He felt the bottom fall out of his stomach, and he started when he felt Steve's hand on his shoulder.

"What's happening?" Steve asked.

"I think somebody fell," Elliott said. "And I'm afraid I know from where."

⁂

Leaving Steve on the balcony, Elliott hurried to the kitchen phone and called Bruno's number, a large knot in his stomach. The phone rang four times before being answered by a brusque voice he didn't recognize.

"Hello?"

"Hello, is Bruno there?"

A long pause before: "Who's calling?"

Elliott could hear other voices in the background.

"This is Elliott Smith in unit thirty-five-J. I'm a friend of his."

"Why are you calling?"

"I heard the sirens and looked over my balcony. Bruno was having a party tonight, and I was concerned someone might have fallen."

Another long pause. "You're in thirty-five-J?"

"Yes."

"Someone will be down to talk to you in a few minutes."

The phone disconnected.

Hanging up, Elliott discovered Steve standing directly beside him.

"We'd better get dressed," Elliott said. "Company's coming."

They went into the bedroom to throw on sweats. Steve was obviously upset.

"Do you think it might have been Bruno?" he asked.

Elliott was suddenly very much aware he and Steve weren't the only ones in the room.

"Yes."

⁂

Five minutes later, there was a knock at the door. Elliott opened it to find a burly plainclothes officer he would have spotted as a policeman a block away even if he weren't holding his badge in front of him like a priest with a crucifix confronting a vampire. Elliott thought he looked vaguely familiar.

"Come on in," he said, leading the way to the living room, where Steve sat on the couch.

Introductions made, Elliott offered the detective–Cabrera, he didn't give a first name–a seat, which he declined as Elliott joined Steve.

Looking from one of them to the other, Cabrera said, "Don't I know you?"

"You may have been at my brother-in-law's birthday party," Elliott explained. "Brad Priebe."

The officer gave a slow acknowledging nod. "Right. So, what can you tell me about Bruno Caesar?"

"So, it was him who fell?" Steve asked.

"Apparently so. Sorry. I assume he was a friend of yours?"

"He was," Elliott said. "How is his roommate holding up?"

"There were three guys in the apartment when we got there, all of them passed out. It took us a couple of minutes just to wake them up–it must have been some party. Two of the three claim to be Caesar's roommates–a Ricky Esperanza, and a Cage Caesar, who says he's the victim's nephew."

"Can I ask who the third guy was?"

Cabrera looked at Elliott with a slightly raised eyebrow then said, "One Chaz Conklin. You know him?"

"Yes, but not all that well. Did they tell you what happened?"

"They all claim they have no idea. They say they were all passed out when it happened. That's why I'm here. Did either of you see or hear anything unusual?"

"Nothing until the sirens woke us up."

"You weren't at the party?"

"We were invited but had other plans."

"So, you don't know who might have been there?"

Elliott shook his head. "Afraid not. Ricky or Cage should be able to help you."

"Well, Esperanza's pretty much of a basket case right now, and the other two are so drunk they could hardly tell us their names. We'll talk to them in the morning. Anything else you can tell me about the victim?"

"Yeah," Elliott said. "For one thing, he was terrified of heights. Being inside looking out didn't bother him, but he never set foot on his balcony, and I'm sure he never would, voluntarily."

"Well, you never know what people will do when they're drunk. But you're saying you think he might have had help going over the railing?"

"I wasn't there, so I have no idea." But even as he said it, Elliott realized he wasn't telling the whole truth.

"Well, we'll know more after we talk to the witnesses, and when the autopsy report comes in." He looked at his watch. "I'll let you get back to bed. If you think of anything–anything at all that might help–give me a call."

Reaching into his inside coat pocket, he pulled out two business cards, which he handed to Elliott and Steve individually.

Elliott showed the detective to the door and returned to Steve, who got up from the couch as he approached.

"We'd better try to get some sleep," Elliott said. "We're meeting Cessy and Brad at the building at three."

"You don't want to call and cancel? I mean, I'm sure they'd understand."

"Not unless you do. There's really nothing we can do to help Bruno at this point. It's probably best not to dwell on it."

"God, I feel so sorry for the poor guy. I just can't believe it."

As they walked down the hallway toward the bedroom, Steve stopped and looked at him strangely, then put his nose up against Elliott's neck. Pulling his head back, he looked puzzled.

"What?" Elliott asked.

"Nothing. I just wonder why I'm smelling Old Spice when I know you're not wearing it."

❧

Elliott wanted desperately to fall asleep, hoping John would be waiting for him, but he couldn't. It had taken Steve a good half-hour to return to sleep, but Elliott could tell by his breathing when he managed. He kept straining his mind for some awareness of John, but there was nothing. Finally, he just gave up.

–Sorry about your friend.

–Where have you been?

–Here. Waiting for you. You've just been too distracted to notice.

–What can you tell me about Bruno?

–I can't tell you anything about him except what I pick up from you. But there is something.

–Like what?

–It's hard to explain. Let's call it a disturbance–a large, swirling ball of confusion. I suspect it's your friend. This sort of thing happens a lot immediately after someone dies, especially if it's sudden and unexpected. It's sort of like what happens to the air in a balloon when someone pops it.

–So, dying is like popping a balloon?

–I said "sort of." Without going off on a philosophical tangent, let's just say it's what happens to the...I guess you'd call it the soul...when it's suddenly released from the body that's contained it.

–What happens to it?

–I'm hardly an expert, but from my experience, it usually just moves on to wherever it's headed. But sometimes, like with me, it coalesces and decides to stay around.

–And how long does that take?

–It varies. Usually it's almost instantaneous, but this one's been here for a couple of hours, now. Like I say, I assume it's your friend but can't be sure yet. Maybe he has a reason for staying around.

–I was afraid you were going to say that.

"Afraid I was going to say what?" Steve asked.

Instantly awake, Elliott turned toward him. "Why aren't you asleep? Did I wake you again? Damn!"

"No, I haven't really been fully asleep. I keep thinking of Bruno. I didn't know him as well as you did, but he seemed like a nice guy a little out of his league. That he should die like this..."

"I know. It's a real shame. What else was I saying?"

"Something about popping a balloon."

"Yeah, well, sounds like dream-talk to me," Elliott lied.

Steve's look dipped him in a large pool of guilt. He wondered how much longer he could keep lying, and how Steve would react when he found out the truth.

❧

The phone started ringing shortly after eight, by which time both Steve and Elliott had given up any pretense of trying to sleep. Several people from the building called to talk, gossip and speculate about Bruno's death. Elliott kept the conversations as short as politeness would allow and finally just disconnected the phone. He did call Bruno's number on his cell, hoping to talk with Ricky or Cage to offer his condolences, but the line was continually busy.

Morning coffee on the balcony, despite the relative coolness of the breeze from the lake, was a quiet affair, with neither saying much–the combined result of both still being a little groggy from lack of sleep and neither knowing exactly what to say. Finally, after their second cup, Elliott suggested they get dressed and walk up to the little diner under the Thorndale el station three blocks away for breakfast.

"We can shower when we get back," he said.

Steve borrowed a pair of jeans and a T-shirt, and Elliott threw on clothes he'd worn Thursday when he got home for work. The caffeine and the walk to the diner loosened their tongues.

"I can't stop thinking about Bruno," Steve said, shaking his head.

"I know. Me, either."

"Do you think it was an accident?"

"No."

"No? Why not?"

"Bruno would never have gone out on that balcony willingly. Never, not even drunk. And there were just too many people at that party who resented his not sharing his money with them. I'm glad we're seeing Brad today. I want to talk to him about it."

They were to meet Cessy and Brad at the building at three, but because Steve hadn't seen the progress on his apartment for some time, Elliott suggested they go early so he could see that first. The work was almost done, awaiting only the finishing of the floors and the installation of the new kitchen appliances. He hoped, too, that it would help to take both their minds off Bruno's death.

As they entered the garage and walked toward his car, Elliott experienced a familiar sensation he equated with a glass being filled with water. In this case, he was the glass, and the water was the growing awareness of John's presence. He had no idea what John was doing there until Steve looked at him, cocked his head, and said, "Are you sure you're not wearing Old Spice?" The scent was very subtle, but unmistakable, and Elliott immediately had his answer.

Despite his concern over Bruno's death, Steve was delighted with the way the apartment was shaping up, and especially with the patio.

"I can paint out here, and get some large pots for flowers and vegetables, though it's probably too late in the year for vegetables. And I'll have to start looking around for some patio furniture and maybe a barbecue grill, and..."

Elliott just grinned.

They went downstairs at about ten-to-three to await Brad and Cessy's arrival, and had just emerged onto the sidewalk when they saw the Priebes's SUV pull into a parking space across the street. As she got out of the car, Cessy stopped to survey the building before following the rest of her family as they joined Elliott and Steve.

"It's beautiful, Elliott," she said. "Really beautiful. I wish we'd brought the camera."

Brad exchanged handshakes with Steve and Elliott, and Elliott hugged Jenny and Sandy. BJ said his usual cursory "hi" and focused his attention on three teenage girls walking past on the other side of the street.

"We haven't done anything at all with the interior of the ground floor yet," Elliott explained, "and the front part is pretty much a shambles from putting in the new windows and restoring the original facade. So, unless you really want to see it..."

"Of course, we want to see it," Cessy said. "We seldom get a chance to see just what it is you do, and I'd like to get a before-and-after."

Leading them to the recessed corner front entrance, Elliott unlocked the door and let them in. The interior, with little light coming through the papered-over windows, was relatively dark and gloomy, but he was able to give them a rough idea of how it would look after the interior walls were removed and the paneling on the exterior walls had been replaced. Brad remarked on the pressed-tin ceiling, and Elliott expressed his concern for the condition of it where the interior walls met the ceiling.

"But I think we have enough extra panels to make it work," he said.

"It will be perfect for a gallery, Steve," Cessy said.

Steve looked mildly embarrassed.

"I don't know for sure that's what Elliott has in mind for it."

She looked at him with a mock scowl.

"Well, of course, that's what he has in mind for it. I knew that the moment he mentioned the ground floor had once been a storefront."

"You did?" Elliott asked. "May I ask how?"

"I'm your sister, Elliott."

"Well, that explains it."

Leaving the ground floor, they walked down the alley so Elliott could show off the details of the refinished side bay windows.

"I love the colors," Cessy said.

"They're Steve's idea."

"I could have guessed. Isn't it nice to have an artist in the family?"

Steve suppressed a grin, and Elliott said nothing.

Returning to the front, they went to the apartment entrance and climbed to the top floor. As Elliott placed the key in the lock, he caught a subtle whiff of Old Spice and, realizing this was Bruno's old apartment, felt the hair on his arms and neck rise.

He glanced at Steve, who was talking with Jenny and gave no indication he'd noticed anything.

Inside the apartment, there was no sign of anything at all out of the ordinary, and the hint of Old Spice faded and vanished. Nor was there any indication of John.

As they were getting ready to leave, Elliott handed the keys to Steve.

"Why don't you take Cessy and the kids down to your place? I need to talk to Brad for a second."

Brad, who had been carrying Sandy, looked at him with a slightly raised eyebrow but merely passed her to Cessy, who followed Steve, Jenny and BJ down the stairs.

"So, what's up?" Brad asked.

"There was an accident at my building last night," Elliott began. "A guy I knew–Bruno Caesar–he was the one who told me about this building, and he used to live in this apartment–fell from the fortieth floor at about three o'clock this morning."

"Sorry about that. He was a friend of yours?"

"I'd like to think so," Elliott replied. "I talked to one of the detectives who was there–Cabrera. We met him at your birthday party. I told him I don't think it was an accident."

"Based on what?"

"Mainly on the fact Bruno was terrified of heights. He was fine being inside and looking out, but to actually be on the edge of something high? He told me he had never set foot on his balcony. Never. So, for him to fall off it is incomprehensible."

"Do you know the details of how it happened?"

"No. Bruno had a big party last night–he threw a lot of parties. He won fifty-nine million in the lottery, and a lot of people resented his not sharing with them. He told me someone had been harassing him, and that he was inviting all the people who'd been hitting him up for money to tell them all future requests would have to go through his business manager. I'm sure that made some of them pretty unhappy."

"And you told all this to George...Detective Cabrera?"

"Only about the fear of heights. It was three a.m., and I wasn't thinking too clearly. That's why I wanted to talk to you about it."

Brad nodded. "Well, I appreciate that. I'll see what I can find out on Monday. I probably won't see George or Frank–his partner, Frank Guerdon–until our shifts overlap on Tuesday morning, but I'll try to talk to them then."

"I'd appreciate it. And now I suppose we'd better get downstairs."

❧

"I'm really glad Cessy and Brad liked the building," Steve said as they drove toward his apartment. "Cessy had some great ideas for the patio, and now I'm all hyped to get in there. I'm going to stop Monday after work and order the paint. Then, if it's okay with you, I can maybe go over this weekend and start painting, before you finish the floors."

In the course of all Elliott's renovation projects, all the rooms were routinely painted white, with the idea that whoever moved in could repaint to suit themselves. Elliott thought a moment before saying, "Tell you what–we're planning to start on the floors next week, so why don't I go with you to get the paint, and my crew and I can paint the day before we're ready to start on the floors."

"I don't feel right about having you do that," Steve said. "You've already got enough to do."

"Don't worry about it. We'd be painting in any event–it doesn't matter if it isn't white. It's just part of the job. We probably should have it ready for you to start moving in within two weeks–if you'd like to consider leaving your current place before the lease is fully up."

"Of course, I would!"

They had a drink and talked while waiting to go to dinner, and eventually, the conversation returned to Bruno's death.

"Brad didn't know anything about it, of course, since he hasn't been to work since it happened, but he said he'd check with Cabrera and his partner to see what they're planning to do about it."

"And you told him you think it wasn't an accident?"

"Yeah," Elliott said, his senses alert to any indication of John, or for any trace of Old Spice. "I just want to be sure the police don't just let it go as a suicide or an accident."

"Are you going to try to get in touch with Ricky or Cage?"

"Definitely. I don't really know what I can say to them, other than to offer condolences."

"Be sure to include mine."

"I will."

Suddenly, Steve's brows furrowed, and he looked at Elliott strangely.

"Do you smell it?"

He didn't smell anything, but he knew what Steve was referring to, and felt the goosebumps rise on his arms.

"Smell what?"

"Old Spice again! And I smelled it at the building, when we first went into the top floor apartment. That was Bruno's apartment, wasn't it?"

Elliott nodded. "Yeah."

"And you haven't smelled it?"

While Elliott really didn't want to go down the path to which Steve was pointing, he knew to lie would not only be unfair but could erode Steve's trust in him if he later found out.

So, reluctantly, he said, "Yeah. A couple of times."

Steve heaved a sigh of relief. "So, what do you think it means?"

Elliott was silent for a full ten seconds, trying to find the right words. He finally gave up.

"I'm not sure, other than that Bruno is still around. Maybe he's trying to tell us his death wasn't an accident, that he wants somebody to know it."

"But what can we do about it?"

Sighing, Elliott said, "I'm not sure. Maybe it's just because we both have this...whatever it is. And maybe he somehow knows we've helped someone in his position before. Maybe he thinks we can do it for him, too."

Steve said nothing for a full minute, then: "Does all this strike you as being just the slightest bit odd?"

Elliott grinned. "Yeah, that had occurred to me. But I think I'm getting used to it–which is pretty strange itself. Nice to know I'm not going through it alone, though."

He suddenly felt John nearby, and suppressed a smile.

❧

He tried calling Bruno's number as soon as he got home. There was no answer, and the answering machine didn't pick up. Elliott suspected it might be full. He decided to try after work the next day, and if he was unable to get through, he'd go up and leave a note on the door asking Ricky or Cage to call him.

In hopes of hearing from John, he went to bed early.

–Interesting.

–Glad you think so. What's going on?

–Well, the disturbance I was taking about is definitely your friend Bruno.

–What's with the Old Spice? Steve smells it, too. Is he trying to tell us something?

–At this point, I'm not sure. I think you're just feeling the ripples of the splash created when he didn't pass on through the gate. Why, I can't say, and whether or not he's reaching out to you or it's just your sensitivity to this still being around, I don't know. Even though I've been...here... for a while now, I still don't understand how everything works. I guess we're all different no matter which side of the fence we're on.

–But you're in contact with him.

–Again, I don't mean to be obstructive, but things are very different here. It's sort of like seeing someone talking across a crowded room–I'm aware of him, but he may or may not be aware of me. He's too preoccupied with adjusting to his...let's call it his change of circumstances...at the moment. But I'll see what I can do.

–Maybe you shouldn't be in any great hurry on that one.

–What do you mean?

—Well, the fact is I don't know for sure it wasn't some sort of freak accident, and from what you say, Bruno doesn't know, either. I've had enough of getting involved in dead people's lives unless I have to.

He felt the tingle of John's laughter.

—You know what I mean!

—Yes, I know. You'd better get some sleep now.

Of all the buildings Elliott had bought and renovated over the years, the Armitage building was a first in many ways. It was the first to have commercial space, the first he knew from the outset he intended to keep, and the first to be so directly linked to his personal life. As a result, the whole project felt somehow different, and his work routine was thrown slightly off-kilter.

Normally, each project was handled methodically as a whole—exterior to interior, top to bottom. Here, the exterior and the apartments were almost finished while work on the ground floor retail space had, other than the installation of the front windows and restoration of the facade, not even begun.

It was also the first time anyone other than his work crew was involved in the planning.

Still, he was pleased it was going so smoothly. Steve was, at Elliott's suggestion, doing sketches for the retail space. Elliott normally would have worked with Ted to draw up plans, but he wanted Steve to be a part of it; and Steve had made a few constructive suggestions that hadn't occurred to him. Basically, the entire space would be one very large room with two offices and a bathroom spanning the back. The gallery's office would open onto the main room, and Elliott's onto a short hallway to the exterior rear door.

About a quarter of the basement space would be partitioned to provide a small personal storage area for each of the apartments and a laundry room. The remainder would be divided into storage areas for the gallery and Elliott's business.

He went directly to Steve's from work Monday evening, arriving shortly before Steve did. They went up to the apartment for a drink then drove to the paint store. Elliott had calculated exactly how much would be needed for each room, and Steve already knew what colors he wanted.

Elliott didn't even consider offering to pay, although he could have gotten a contractor's discount, because he knew it was important for Steve to do it.

They made a stop at a hardware store to have keys made for Steve then had a quick dinner before Elliott headed home.

As soon as he walked in the door, he tried Bruno's number. The phone again rang four times and went silent. He was about ready to hang up when he heard the receiver being lifted.

"Hello?"

Not readily identifying the voice, he said, "Ricky? Cage? It's Elliott Smith, from downstairs."

There was only a slight pause before: "Oh, hello, Elliott. It's Ricky. Cage isn't here." He sounded exhausted.

"That's okay. I just wanted to check to see how you're holding up."

"Not well. I have to be out of here by the end of the month, and I still can't believe Bruno's dead. I really thought..."

His voice caught, and he didn't finish his sentence. Elliott felt his anguish, and empathized with it.

"Cage is kicking you out? On what grounds?"

"No, not Cage–he's got to get out, too. Mr. Means. He's the executor of Bruno's will, and he says we have to leave."

Elliott wasn't sure he'd heard right.

"Excuse me? Walter Means is executor of Bruno's estate?"

"Apparently so. He came this morning and told us we had to leave so he could put the condo up for sale. I mean, Bruno hasn't been dead two days yet!"

"That's bullshit! I'm not a lawyer, but I know that even if he is named in Bruno's will as executor, there's a whole string of legal paperwork that has to be gone through before he has the legal right to do a damned thing. Tell him when he comes up with the papers of authorization from the court, you'll listen to him. Otherwise, he can fuck off."

He wasn't sure just why he was so surprised–and angry. It was none of his business, but he couldn't help wondering exactly how or why Bruno had made his financial manager the executor in the first place. Why not a relative? It all struck him as being very strange.

Then he remembered that when Bruno first mentioned having hired Means, he said he'd drawn up a new will at Means's suggestion. It just hadn't occurred to Elliott Means would have been named executor, and he suspected that suggestion, too, may have come from Means himself. Added to the fact Bruno had been thinking of changing financial managers just prior to his death, it raised all sorts of questions.

None of which changed the fact Means had no legal right to do anything at all until the court said so.

"Have funeral arrangements been made yet, do you know?"

"Cage was here earlier. I heard him talking on the phone–I'm pretty sure it was to his parents–about shipping the body to Rockford for burial. If they do that, I won't be able to go to the funeral." There was a long pause. "I won't even be able to say goodbye!"

Elliott could tell Ricky was crying, and he grew more and more uncomfortable, wishing there were something he could do or say but knowing there wasn't.

"What will you do, Ricky?" he said finally, keeping his voice calm. "Do you have a place to go?"

There was the sound of nose-blowing and a few sniffles.

"I really haven't had time to even think about it. I've got a friend from where I used to work I can probably stay with for a few days, but I don't know for how long, and I really have to find a job."

Elliott remembered a conversation he'd had the week before with Jesse and Adam, who had mentioned they were thinking of hiring a houseboy. He had no idea if they'd done anything about it yet, or whether Ricky would be either qualified or interested, but it was worth at least a shot.

"I tell you what, Ricky, let me talk to a couple friends of mine. They might be looking for a houseboy, and if you'd be interested..."

"Of course, I would. That would be wonderful. Thank you, Elliott."

"Well, I can't guarantee anything, but I'll give them a call and see what's going on. In the meantime, just hang in there."

"I will. And thank you again."

As soon as they hung up, Elliott looked up Adam's and Jesse's new number and called. He recognized Jesse's voice immediately.

"Jesse, hi, it's Elliott. Remember last week when you said you might be looking for a houseboy?"

Chapter 6

Steve called within ten minutes after Elliot let Ricky know he had set up a meeting with Adam and Jesse for Tuesday evening. He was curious if Elliott had found out anything more about Bruno or his death, and Elliott told him about Ricky's predicament.

"Well, I hope it all works out for him," Steve said. "He seems like a good kid. I wonder if he might get any of Bruno's money?"

"I have no idea." He then told Steve about Walter Means being executor of Bruno's will.

"Isn't that a little strange? A business manager being executor of a will? What about one of Bruno's relatives?"

"I really don't know how it came about, but I'd love to get a look at that will."

Steve sighed. "It's such a shame that Bruno never really got a chance to enjoy life the way he should have."

"Yeah, but let's face it–life sucks sometimes."

Another sigh, then: "Anyway, I just wanted to tell you I've already got all those boxes you brought me packed, as well as several I picked up myself. I don't know where I got all this stuff!"

"Well, we can take over a few loads this weekend. We'll probably paint tomorrow, do the floors Wednesday and seal them Thursday. They should be ready to walk on by Friday night. So, if everything goes well, and if the weather's good, maybe we can bring your plants over and put them out on the patio."

"That'll be great. I can't wait to move. I..."

There was a pause so long Elliott wondered if they'd been cut off.

"Are you there?" he asked.

"Yeah, I'm here. Sorry."

"Is anything wrong?"

Another pause. "Not really. I just now got a really strong whiff of Old Spice."

—That's very interesting.

—What is?

—The Old Spice. I know you've both smelled it before, but I get the impression this time it was deliberate. And I'm starting to pick up a few things.

—Like what?

—Like an increasing concern about exactly what happened to him, although I can't tell if the possibility he might have been murdered has registered yet. There are definite feelings of sadness and loss—I'd imagine probably over his new friend...Ricky?

—So, he's not aware of what's going on on "this side of the fence," as you called it.

John laughed.

—I really can't tell exactly what he knows and what he doesn't. He's mainly been concerned with adjusting to this side. We still aren't conversing, which is why I'm not sure what's going on with him yet, and I haven't done much to find out, since you said you don't want to get involved.

—Well, I don't. But...

—Yeah, that "but" will get you every time.

—I mean, if we're just aware of him because of this whatever-it-is Steve and I have, that's one thing. But if he really is trying to get through to us...

—Fair enough. I'll try to get a little closer without getting in his way. It's not like we're sitting down over a cup of coffee, talking. Right now, our contacts are strictly non-verbal, like computers sending all those ones and zeroes back and forth. Hopefully, it will get easier. In the meantime, what are you planning to do, now that you know his death may not have been an accident?

—In the meantime? I think I'll just wait and see what the police do. Thank God Brad's on the force and is willing to keep me posted.

–And if they do nothing?
–We'll just have to play it by ear, I guess.

He went over his conversation with John both on his way to work the next morning and while driving back home. What might actually have happened to Bruno kept niggling at him. Despite Bruno's understandable confusion, he supposed it wasn't beyond the realm of possibility that, if he were really very drunk, he might have staggered out onto the balcony without realizing it and fallen over.

But Elliott couldn't ignore the equally valid possibility Bruno might have had help falling; and that if *he* didn't do something, a killer might never be caught.

He decided to call Brad to see if he knew–or could find out–what was happening on the investigation, and take his cue from that.

It wasn't until after dinner and a long call to Steve to report on the progress of the apartment painting, and to discuss other details of the impending move, that he had a chance to call Brad. Jenny answered the phone, and he spent several minutes with her as she related everything that had gone on in her young life since they'd last talked.

When he finally asked to speak with her dad, she said, "He's out working in the garage. I'll go get him," and before he had a chance to tell her not to bother, he heard the phone being set down and the sound of running feet, followed by the slamming of the screen door.

There was a moment of silence, then Cessy's voice. "Hello?"

"Hi, Sis."

"Elliott! I didn't know you were on the phone. I just came in and saw the receiver lying there, and I was about to hang it up."

"Jenny's out getting Brad in from the garage, though I tried to tell her he could just call me back when he gets time."

"That's all right–he'd spend the whole night out there tinkering if he didn't have a specific reason to come in. So, how are things going with the building? I imagine Steve's getting all excited about the move."

"He's looking forward to it, yeah."

"Well, remember, Brad and BJ will be glad to help when the time comes."

"I appreciate that, Sis, as I'm sure Steve does. We haven't set an exact date yet, but possibly a week from Saturday. We'll start moving some of the smaller things in the meantime."

"Well, just let us know."

He heard the screen door closing.

"Here's Brad," Cessy said. "We'll talk later."

"What's up, Elliott?"

"Sorry, Brad, I wasn't able to catch Jenny before she ran off to get you. It could have waited."

"No problem."

"I was wondering if you'd heard anything more on Bruno Caesar's death. I know how busy you are with your own cases, but..."

"Sorry, I haven't heard a thing. We've been swamped at work. I meant to catch George and Frank this morning before they left but didn't have the chance. If I don't see them tomorrow morning when I check in, I'll leave them a note." There was a slight pause. "How about you? You find out anything they should know?"

"I'm not sure, since I don't know what they've found out on their own. I'm going to try to get the names of everyone at the party from Ricky, though I'm sure he or Cage already gave that information to Cabrera and his partner. I told you before that people had really been nagging Bruno for money, and some of them were pretty unhappy when they didn't get it. That he died right after a party he threw specifically to let them know he'd had it with their hassling couldn't have been a coincidence."

"Yeah, I remember. That party sounds like a pretty dumb move."

"I agree, but I didn't think it was my place to tell him so. Maybe I should have."

There was a pause until Brad said, "I tell you what–I know George talked to you briefly right after the incident, but I'll suggest that he or Frank contact you again. You can probably give them a more objective view of what might be behind Caesar's death than they've gotten from most of the people at the party."

"I'll be glad to do whatever I can."

"Good. As I said, I really don't know what they're doing, and I can't tell them how to conduct their investigation, so I can't guarantee they'll call, but I can at least present them the option."

"Thanks, Brad. I appreciate it. You can give them my cell phone number, too, if you want."

"Well, just watch your step. If this wasn't a suicide..."

"Yeah, I know. And I will be careful." There was another pause until Elliott said, "I'd better let you go. Thanks again for everything."

"Like I said, no problem."

When he hung up, a hint of Old Spice hung in the air.

⁂

While he hoped for word from Cabrera or Guerdon Tuesday, there was none. He and his crew finished painting Steve's apartment, and he called before starting dinner to tell him. Steve sounded pleased by the description of how good it looked, and by the news the floor refinishing would start Wednesday.

He was watching TV and waiting for the ten o'clock news when Ricky called to say he'd gotten the job with Jesse and Adam.

"I can start right away, and I can't thank you enough, Elliott."

"I'm really glad to hear that, Ricky."

"Adam is coming over tomorrow to help me move my things. I don't have much, but I can't wait to get out of here. Every minute I stay, it just reminds me of Bruno, and the sooner I can get away from Cage, the better."

Elliott detected Old Spice, which caused him to shiver. Disregarding it, he said, "Any further word on the funeral plans?"

"Cage hasn't told me a thing, but there was a call on the answering machine for him yesterday from some funeral home in Rockford, so I guess Bruno's being sent there." There was a brief silence. "In a way, I'm glad I won't be able to go to the funeral. This way, I can remember Bruno the way I want to, and..."

Elliott was afraid Ricky was going to start crying, but he pulled himself together.

"I'm just glad Bruno didn't live long enough to know what a bastard Cage really is."

"What do you mean?"

"He's started stealing things before Bruno is even in the ground!"

"What things?"

"Well, Bruno had some reproductions of some classic stamps framed on the wall just opposite our bed, and it's gone. I have no idea why Cage would want them, other than he knew both Bruno and I loved stamps. Probably his way of taking a slap at me."

Feeling a rush of adrenaline, Elliott asked, "You're not talking about the Inverted Jennys, are you?"

"Yes. Had you seen them?"

"Bruno made a point of showing them to me. Did he tell you they were reproductions?"

"No, but they'd have to be. Nobody would just hang a block of real Inverted Jennys on a wall."

So much for hiding in plain sight, Elliott thought, but said nothing. To get his mind off further speculation for the moment, he said, "So, tell me about the party. How did everyone handle Bruno's announcement? Any big reaction?"

"Not really, and I think Bruno was really surprised–and relieved. I'm sure nobody was happy about it, but no one said anything."

"What about Rudy? I know Bruno was planning to have a private talk with him."

"He did. He talked to Rudy when he first came in. I stayed in the living room, so I don't know exactly what they talked about."

"But Bruno seemed okay with it?"

"Yes. Like I said, he seemed relieved afterwards. I think maybe that's why he drank too much, and..."

"I know this is painful for you, Ricky, and I don't mean to pry, but what do you remember about the last hour or so before you crashed?"

"It started thinning out around midnight. Sensei was one of the last to leave. There was just Bruno, me, Cage and Chaz. The last thing I remember is having a glass of champagne at around one-thirty. I didn't realize I'd had so much to drink. I don't usually drink all that much. I think I went into the bedroom to lie down, and I don't remember anything after that until the police woke me up."

"What time did the police leave?"

"I honestly don't know–I wasn't paying any attention to the time. But they came back again around eight the next morning to talk to us after we'd had a chance to sober up.

"They'd just left again when Sensei showed up. He said he heard about the fall on the news, and though they didn't mention Bruno's name, he said he knew it was Bruno, and came right over. He was really nice to me, and he insisted I go to back to bed, and sat there with me until I finally fell asleep. That was very kind of him, and I appreciated it. I know Bruno would have, too."

"Cage isn't there now, I assume?"

"No. I haven't seen him all day. We've hardly spoken to each other. For all I know, he went to Rockford for the funeral. I should go to the garage to see if Bruno's car is still there, but I really don't care."

"Could you leave him a note asking him to call me?"

"Sure."

"Well, it's getting late, so I should let you go. I'm really glad you got the job–Adam and Jesse are great guys."

"And thank you again for being so nice to me, Elliott. I know Bruno would appreciate it."

He was on his way to work Wednesday morning when his cell phone rang.

"This is Detective Guerdon," the voice said without preamble. "You'd spoken with my partner, Detective Cabrera, and your brother-in-law Detective Priebe said you might have some information on the death of Bruno Caesar?"

"I don't know what you've already learned from the others you've interviewed, but I think I probably have a broader and more objective idea of what was going on in Bruno's life than most, and some of it might help."

"Are you free this morning?"

"I'm on my way to work, but I'll be there in about ten minutes. If you want to stop by, I'll be happy to talk with you." He gave him the address.

"We'll meet you there in about fifteen minutes."

"Okay, I'll watch for you."

He assumed Guerdon and Cabrera had just finished their shift and were probably anxious to get home.

After making a quick run up to the apartments to check that everyone had what they needed for the day's work, Elliott went back downstairs to wait for the detectives. As he reached the bottom of the stairs, an unmarked car pulled into a vacant space directly in front of the building. He went outside just as Cabrera got out of the driver's side. The man opening the passenger's door, he assumed, was Guerdon.

Going over to meet them, he extended his hand to Guerdon and introduced himself, then shook hands with Cabrera.

"We can go inside if you'd like," he said, "but there's no place to sit other than on the stairs."

Cabrera gave a small wave of his hand.

"That's okay, we won't be that long. We can talk here." He paused only a moment before saying, "So, tell us what you know about Bruno Caesar."

Elliott gave them a rundown of everything he knew about Bruno's background and of the purpose of the party that had ended in Bruno's death.

"But I'm not positive as to who was there," he said, and wished he'd thought to ask Ricky.

"We compiled a list from the three guys who were in the apartment when we got there," Cabrera said, "but there were apparently a lot of people coming and going, and none of the three seemed to be able to agree on who was there when. We'll be checking everyone out. The tapes from the lobby security cameras will give us a good idea of when they all arrived and left."

Guerdon, who had not taken his eyes off Elliott since they arrived, said, "Do you have any idea who might have had a particularly strong grudge or a real or imagined score to settle with Caesar?"

Elliott shook his head. "I suppose just about everyone who was there had something of a reason, but I'd say the two with the strongest motivation would be Rudy, uh, Patterson and Bruno's nephew, Cage." He gave a brief explanation for his reasoning. He then reemphasized Bruno's dread of heights and his own firm belief he would never have willingly gone out onto his balcony, drunk or sober.

"Do you know if he had any problems sleeping, or if he took drugs?"

That caught Elliott by surprise.

"No. I never heard him mention problems sleeping, and I'd sincerely doubt he took drugs. Bruno struck me as a pretty average guy. I don't think he had the kind of personality that would have anything to do with drugs."

"Yeah, but not every average guy wins the lottery. A lot of people who do tend to go overboard when it comes to what they would or wouldn't do before the money came along. How about his friends? Any druggies among them that you know of?"

Elliott shook his head. "No idea. I never heard drugs mentioned, even at those of his parties I went to. Do you have any reason to think otherwise?"

"The autopsy found chloral hydrate in his system."

"Chloral hydrate?"

"Knockout drops. A Mickey Finn. Still pretty popular with hookers looking to rob johns."

"So, somebody drugged him?"

"Looks that way. But you don't have any idea who might have wanted to harm him?

"Other than what I've told you, no—but I'll bet I know why he was killed. He had a set of four very rare stamps, worth a couple of million dollars, that he kept in a picture frame on his bedroom wall, and Ricky told me someone's taken them."

Both detectives stared at him until Cabrera said, "He kept a couple million dollars'-worth of stamps on his bedroom wall? Are you serious?"

"Very. They're called Inverted Jennys, one of the first airmail stamps ever issued. One sheet of them was accidentally printed upside down, and they're worth a fortune. He kept them there so he could see them any time he wanted. He claims no one else even knew he had them other than the guy who arranged the sale, and that, even if anyone knew about the Inverted Jennys, they wouldn't imagine he'd just hang them on his wall."

"But other people did see them, if they were just hanging right out there."

"Yeah, but in the bedroom. There couldn't have been a lot of people wandering through there, I don't imagine. I suppose during his parties people might have gone in to use the master bathroom, but the chance that they'd see and recognize the Jennys, let alone realize they were real..."

Cabrera gave him a slightly raised eyebrow and the hint of a smile.

"Caesar was gay, right?"

The implication wasn't lost on Elliott. He nodded.

"And the roommates were just roommates?"

Elliott shrugged but said nothing.

"Any of them collect stamps, that you know of?"

While he would have preferred not to answer, knowing it could get Ricky into trouble, he was in something of a corner.

"Ricky collected stamps as a hobby as a teenager, and Bruno encouraged him to get back into it, but I doubt very much he's expert enough to know much about really rare stamps. I'm sure he had no idea the Jennys on the wall were real. And it's unlikely he'd tell anyone they were gone if he took them himself."

"Do you know where or how Caesar got them?"

Elliott nodded. "He bought them through a middle-man from the previous owner."

Guerdon took a notepad and pen out of his shirt pocket.

"Any idea who this 'middle man' might be?"

"Yeah. His name is Clifford Blanton. He was sort of Bruno's spiritual guru. I met him briefly a couple of times at Bruno's parties. No idea where he lives, though."

Writing the name down, Guerdon said, "I saw his name on the list we got from one of the guys who were there when Caesar died. We haven't talked to him yet, but we will."

It occurred to Elliott that exactly when the stamps went missing was the key to whether their theft was the motive for the murder. He also knew it would be nearly impossible to tell if they were there or gone when the police first showed up at the condo.

A sudden thought jarred him.

"Wait a minute. It wasn't until the Tuesday after Bruno died that Ricky told me the stamps were missing. But it's possible, given the shock of Bruno's death, he just didn't notice they were gone at first. He said Blanton came over as soon as he heard Bruno had died–apparently right after you'd left the second time–and that he sat with him–with Ricky–in the bedroom until Ricky fell asleep. *He* certainly knew the Jennys' value and could very easily have taken them then."

"Possible," Guerdon said noncommittally. "We'll check it out."

Elliott had another thought. "You said Ricky, Chaz and Cage were asleep when you got there. Were they just asleep, or had they been drugged, too?"

Cabrera, whose attention had momentarily been distracted by the sound of squealing tires, pulled himself back to the moment.

"Good question. Since we didn't know about the chloral hydrate at the time, we had no reason to assume anything but that they were all sleeping off the party. And by the time the autopsy found the chloral hydrate, it was too late to go back to check the others–it would have metabolized out of their systems by then. Still, I suppose it's not impossible they were all drugged to cover up what really happened."

"So, you're treating it as a murder?"

"All suicides are considered possible murders until it can be proven otherwise, so, yes. Chloral hydrate isn't exactly a recreational drug someone would be likely to take knowingly. We were already operating on the assumption the drugging was deliberate and the death therefore probably murder. But now with this stamp thing..."

"Where would someone get chloral hydrate? Can you trace who bought it?"

"Afraid not. Chloral hydrate's easy to make from readily available ingredients–hell, there are instructions on the internet. Takes fifteen to thirty minutes to work."

"Well, could you figure out how Bruno took it?"

"After we found out about it and realized the other three guys probably had taken it, too, we checked with them, and they all mentioned having had champagne shortly before they passed out. A couple of them had a drink after that, but the champagne was most likely the source. Of course, all evidence of the party was long gone by that time."

Elliott wanted to ask if they'd checked with the doorman to see if he'd noticed anything unusual but realized Guerdon and Cabrera undoubtedly had, and they'd said they'd be checking the building's surveillance tapes–they *were* experienced investigators, after all.

They talked for a few more minutes, then the two detectives left and Elliott returned to work.

—Well, we have Bruno's attention.

—How so?

—I get the impression he's aware of your conversation with the detectives—don't ask me how. He may finally be accepting the idea he could have been murdered. He is not happy, and I can sense these—I don't know what word to use. Vibes? Anyway, I can feel he's definitely directing them your way.

—What does he expect me to do?

—Other than find out exactly what happened to him, and if he was murdered, who did it? I don't know. I do know there's not much he can do about it himself from where he is now.

–Point. Look, if I'd wanted to be a detective, I'd have joined the police force. I don't. I just want to live my own life and not worry about other people's.

–I understand. But like it or not and for whatever reason, you've got a...well, a gift, for lack of a better word...and sometimes gifts come with implied obligations. Sort of noblesse oblige. If someone killed Bruno, how can you not help him find out who did it?

–That's what we have the police for.

–True, if they were as close to the situation as you are, which they're not.

Elliott felt himself rise toward the surface of consciousness, then drifted back down.

–Do you smell that? Old Spice.

–I think Bruno just sent you his regards.

⁂

He wanted to talk to Ricky but decided to hold off a day or so while he got settled into his new houseboy job. He tried calling Cage when he got home Thursday night, but there was no answer. Elliott had no idea if perhaps he was still in Rockford for Bruno's funeral, or just out.

After checking with Steve about taking most of his smaller items to Armitage by car over the weekend, he called Brad to verify that he and BJ would help with the main move the following week. They planned to rent a U-Haul and estimated the entire move would only take a few hours.

As he sat watching TV, his mind wandered to his latest conversation with John and his totally unasked-for awareness of...what? He didn't even know what to call it. The afterlife? The Other Side? Ghosts? Spirits? They all sounded far too melodramatic to fit into what he had always considered his well-ordered and practical life.

Each of his three encounters with...whatever it was...had been totally different. John, his first, had now become an accepted and even pleasant part of his life. Odd as it would have seemed to most people he knew–Steve being the notable exception–he even considered John a friend.

Aaron Styles, his second encounter, had been totally different. He'd had no direct contact with Aaron as he had with John. The only evidence Aaron gave of his presence was through rapping sounds, which Elliott had never experienced with John.

And now Bruno. No sleep conversations, no sounds. Just the scent of Old Spice to make Elliott—and Steve—aware of his presence.

John, from the moment he'd entered Elliott's life, was an active participant in the effort to find out who he was and who had killed him. They had worked so well as a team the relationship continued after the mystery was solved.

Aaron, though he never directly connected with Elliott, relayed information and clues as to what had happened to him, and why, through John.

But Bruno...

Other than the Old Spice, there was no indication of how aware he was of what was going on, or of his active participation in it. All Elliott knew was what little John was able to tell him. What, specifically, Bruno expected Elliott to do or how he expected him to do it were cyphers.

Elliott could understand that becoming suddenly non-corporeal must be an incomprehensibly traumatic experience, and that, based on his conversations with John, the period of adjustment from one state to the other varied widely from person/spirit to person/spirit. He hoped Bruno would make the full transition sooner rather than later, so he could get a better idea of what, if anything, was expected of him.

—You'll get brain freeze if you spend too much time thinking about it. Just go along.

Elliott awoke with a start, realizing he'd fallen asleep in his chair. Of course, the instant he woke up he lost contact with John, and though he went to bed shortly thereafter in hopes of picking up the conversation, there was nothing but dreams of lottery tickets and postage stamps.

❧

He was just finishing dinner when the phone rang.

"Elliott!" He immediately recognized Button's voice. "I hope I'm not catching you at a bad time."

Since he couldn't recall the last time he'd spoken with Button by phone, and hadn't seen him since the last party he and Steve had attended at Bruno's, he was puzzled.

"Not at all," he said. "How are things going?"

"I'm fine, really. I still haven't completely gotten over Bruno's death. I've known him since he first came to Chicago. Friends like him don't come around all that often. I'm just so sorry we didn't have nearly enough time to spend together ever since he won the lottery.

"It...well, all the things involved with coming into all that money put a definite distance between us. Certainly not his fault. There was just so much going on in his life–a new relationship, all those new people." He sighed. "I certainly don't blame him. It was unavoidable, but regrettable. I've tried calling Ricky to extend my condolences but haven't been able to reach him. I hope he's doing all right."

"He is," Elliott replied. "He has a new job and has moved."

"Well, if you see him or talk to him, please give him my best."

"I will. Thanks."

"The other reason I'm calling is to see if you might be able to help me with something."

His curiosity piqued, Elliott said, "What do you need?"

Another long sigh.

"I've just been notified the owners of my apartment building are tearing it down to put up another of those ungodly concrete-slab, rabbit-warren condominiums. Since I've lived here nine years now, they were kind enough to offer me first chance at buying one of them, but nice as some condos may be, I find most of them have all the warmth and charm of an operating room–no offense, of course. Your building is very nice, but to me a condo just isn't the same as an old-fashioned apartment.

"Since I knew you restore old buildings, I was hoping you might know where I might find one. I prefer the north side, and not too terribly far inland, but I'm open to anything, at this point. What I would really like is one like Bruno had before he bought the condo."

"Well, as a matter of fact..." He told him of the vacancy in the Armitage building.

"Bruno's old building?" Button's voice reflected his surprise. "He told me you'd bought it, but it didn't register until now. A wonderful building, if you can overlook the ghastly exterior paint job. And I loved Bruno's apartment."

"That's the one that's available."

"What a fantastic coincidence!"

Elliott couldn't help but wonder if it was, or if somehow Bruno was trying to do his friend a favor.

"When can I see it?"

Hanging up after making arrangements for Button to meet him and Steve at Armitage at ten-thirty Saturday morning, Elliott reflected on the apparent serendipity not only of Button's call but of how many by-chance events had brought him to where he was at the present moment. Had he not been hit by a car, John would not be a most intriguing part of his life. Had he stayed home instead of going out the night he met Steve...

He really liked Button, though he didn't know him all that well, and he knew Steve did, too, the few times he'd seen him at Bruno's parties. If Button took the other apartment, it would save the time and expense of having the rental agent find a tenant.

Steve, when Elliott called to tell him, was in favor of Button as a potential upstairs neighbor and commented on the luck of the timing. They agreed Elliott would go to Steve's from work Friday, and on Saturday morning they'd make one or two trips to Armitage with some of Steve's things before meeting Button.

–Nice idea.

–What's that?

–Button moving into Bruno's old apartment. I'm sure Bruno would be pleased.

–How is he doing? Getting anything more out of him?

–Not in so many words–and I mean that literally–but there's a definite change. He's getting himself together, and that's a good sign, but I'm still not really tuned into him enough to be able to pick up anything specific. There is *something I can't quite grasp yet, but apparently it's pretty important. I think it has something to do with you, and Ricky.*

–Maybe he knows about my having gotten Ricky the job with Adam and Jesse?

–Maybe, but there's a little too much of an edge of urgency for it to be that, I think.

–Interesting. See if you can zero in on it a little more. I don't have a clue of what it could be. Maybe if...

The conversation snapped like a dry twig, and Elliott was instantly fully awake. Someone must have spilled the bottle of Old Spice on his dresser. What the hell was going on?

He turned his head to look over at the dresser, which was exactly the way he'd last seen it. Not a thing out of place, no overturned bottle of

Old Spice, which in any case was in his medicine chest above the bathroom sink.

The smell quickly faded, but he got out of bed and moved to the dresser. The scent was gone.

He went into the bathroom, turned on the light, opened the medicine cabinet, and saw his bottle of Old Spice exactly where he'd put it after using it the last time.

Knowing that Bruno was responsible made him break out in goosebumps. What was going on? And then he knew, cursing himself for not having remembered earlier.

He returned to the bedroom and opened his sock drawer. There, in the back, under the pile of folded T-shirts, was the envelope Bruno had given him before the party with the request Elliott hold it for him. He debated on opening it but decided he was too groggy from his interrupted sleep. Laying it on top of the dresser for dealing with in the morning, he went back to bed.

❧

It wasn't until he was scrambling out of bed, the clock on the nightstand verifying he'd overslept, that he realized John hadn't resumed their broken-off conversation when he'd returned to sleep. He gave the envelope on the dresser only a cursory glance as he hurried into the shower.

When he returned to the bedroom to get dressed, he put the envelope back in the drawer beneath the T-shirts. It had waited this long; another day or two wouldn't matter. As soon as he'd completed the thought he detected the faintest whiff of Old Spice, which vanished as quickly as it had appeared.

As always, work absorbed him from the time he arrived until the time he left, focused on refinishing the stairwell, stairs and landings. It wasn't until he was driving to Steve's that he thought about the envelope.

Since there was no indication for whom it was intended, he didn't know if he should turn it over to Cage or Ricky or Walter Means. He thought about just opening it to see if whatever was inside might give him a clue. He could then put the contents in another envelope without anyone knowing he'd opened it.

Once he arrived at Steve's and they got on with their evening, he pushed thoughts of the envelope to the back of his mind.

❧

Though Elliott would have preferred to sleep a little later on Saturday morning, having once again not gotten to sleep before two a.m. thanks to their suppressed-through-the-week libidos, Steve was out of bed by seven, eager to get the move started. After a quick breakfast, they packed both cars and headed for Armitage.

They managed three trips, arriving with the third load at nine-thirty. Elliott taped a note for Button on the ground-level door leading to the apartments, telling him to come to the second floor. Leaving the door to Steve's apartment open, they put the labeled boxes in their respective rooms then went to the kitchen to put shelf paper in the cupboards and drawers.

"Hello?"

"In the kitchen, Button," Elliott called as he finished cutting a strip of shelf paper.

"Elliott, I can't tell you what a wonderful, wonderful job you've done with this building!" Button said as he appeared in the doorway. He was, as usual, dressed to the nines. "I've not been past here since Bruno moved to the condo, but I always avoided looking at that ungodly purple and tacky redone first floor."

Elliott grinned. "Thanks. Did you dress up just for us, or do you always wear a suit on Saturday mornings?"

"I'll be going to work when I leave here," he said, stepping across the room to shake hands first with Steve, then Elliott. "I just told my assistant manager I'd be in a bit late today." He went to the back door and looked out over the new patio, beaming. "This is beautiful! Really beautiful. I love it!"

"Well, let's take you upstairs to see Bruno's old apartment."

"Oh, I know it well. But I would like to see what you've done with it."

"You two go ahead," Steve said. "I want to finish this cupboard. I'll be up in a minute."

As they walked to the front door, Button reached out to touch Elliott's arm.

"I really had no idea you did this sort of thing for a living. I knew you were in contracting, but nothing like this. I'm truly impressed."

As they climbed the stairs to the third floor, Elliott was alert for the scent of Old Spice. There was none. Opening the door, he stood aside to let Button enter first. Button, after looking around carefully, went to the windows to look down on the street, and across to Oz park.

"I always told Bruno how lucky he was not to have nosy across-the-street neighbors looking right into his living room. I love it!"

They went from room to room, with Button commenting favorably and familiarly on each one, and on the new kitchen appliances. Steve joined them as they were returning to the living room.

"When can I move in?" Button asked.

Elliott grinned. "Don't you want to know what the rent will be?"

Button's happy expression dimmed just a little.

"Well, yes, I guess that would be nice to know. I just hope I can afford it after all your renovations."

When Elliott told him the price he had discussed with Steve, Button immediately brightened again.

"I'll take it!"

Suddenly, he paused, and a quick look of puzzlement tinged with sorrow crossed his face. Elliott was surprised when Steve gave him a strange look and a raised eyebrow.

Turning his attention to Button, he said, "Something wrong?"

Button shook his head quickly. "No, nothing. I just noticed your Old Spice and remembered how Bruno loved it."

Elliott, who had smelled nothing–and wasn't wearing Old Spice–felt a definite chill.

❧

After Button had left for work, with the agreement they would get together within the next few days to sign the lease, Elliott and Steve went back downstairs and resumed unpacking.

Steve had just opened a box of dishes when he said, "And what do you suppose Button's little observation means?"

"About the Old Spice? No idea, but I'm getting a little concerned this whole thing might be getting a little out of hand." Wadding up the piece of newspaper from which he'd just unwrapped a cup, he tossed it toward an empty box. It missed.

"It's one thing for you and me to know Bruno's around," Steve said, "but Button? Of course, I don't think he has a clue as to what's going on. He just smelled Old Spice."

"Yeah, well how come you smelled it and Button smelled it, and I didn't?"

"Maybe Bruno's cutting you off."

After placing the plate he'd just unwrapped in the cupboard, Steve picked up the paper from the counter, wadded it and gave it an overhand-arc pitch directly into the box.

"Nobody likes a wise-ass, Gutierrez."

❧

–A little jealous, are we?

–What the hell are you talking about?

–And testy, too!

*–You mean because Steve and Button...*Button...*knew Bruno was there and I didn't?*

–Yeah, something like that. But Button didn't know Bruno was there. He just smelled Old Spice.

–But I didn't*! Why?*

–Wish I could tell you, but I'm not the spokesman for everyone who's dead. Maybe he's unhappy because he wanted you to do something you didn't do.

–Great! I...The envelope he gave me! He never did tell me what I should do with it other than hold it for him.

–See? That wasn't so hard.

–I'll open it when I get home.

"Open what?" Steve was propped up on one elbow, looking at him.

"Shit! I did it again!"

"No problem. So, open what?"

Elliott sighed heavily. "Bruno gave me an envelope to hold for him right before he died. I've been meaning to do something with it but haven't had the chance. I'm sorry I woke you."

"And who are you talking to?"

"I'm talking to you. Who else is here?"

Steve grinned. "That's what I'd like to know."

"Can we talk about it in the morning? We really need to get some sleep. I'll try not to wake you again."

"Okay." Lying back down, Steve turned on his side away from Elliott. In a few moments, his breathing indicated he was asleep.

Elliott was not so lucky.

“Time?” Steve said, handing Elliott his morning coffee and sitting beside him with his own cup.

Taking a deep breath, Elliott said, “I suppose,” and began.

Chapter 7

When Elliott finished, Steve, who hadn't taken his eyes off him for an instant, said, "Well, that explains a lot. Do you think you'd ever have told me if I hadn't asked?"

Elliott hoped his flush of embarrassment didn't show.

"Of course. I just don't know when. It's not the kind of thing that comes up easily in conversation: 'Can you pass me the salt? And, oh, I've got a dead friend named John who talks to me in my sleep.' That'd go over big."

"It would have, actually. I knew damned well something was going on. And I gather John is behind that identical dream we had a while back–the one about the mansion on the lake?"

"Yep. He says he was experimenting."

"And I've been aware of–something–several times since we've been together. John?"

"Probably. I've told him not to bother you, though."

Steve grinned broadly. "Bother? I'd love to have a real conversation with a ghost!"

Elliott shook his head. "Be careful what you wish for," he said. "And John isn't a ghost. At least, not to me."

Steve cocked his head. "So, what is he?"

"John."

They finished their coffee in thoughtful silence, broken by an occasional question or observation by Steve and Elliott's response. Elliott was both relieved and pleased Steve seemed to take it all in stride, and apparently understood his earlier reticence about John.

"So, what about Bruno?" Steve asked as he got up to refill their cups. "Obviously, he wants something. Do you know what it is?"

"He gave me an envelope before he died and asked me to hold it for him, but there's no indication on the envelope what's in it or who it's for. I'm going to open it when I get home."

Returning to the living room, Steve said, "Bruno doesn't know how he died?"

Elliott took his cup and shrugged. "Apparently not."

"You aren't in direct contact with him, then?"

"No more than you are, with the Old Spice. All I know is what John can find out. I gather being dead takes some getting used to, let alone the idea you may have been murdered. But I'm sure it will."

"So, what will you do about it?"

Elliott sighed. "I don't really know what I *can* do about it, and you have no idea how I dread getting caught up in these things. As for Bruno, first and foremost, I trust the police are looking into it. If he was murdered, they'll find out who did it."

"And if they don't?"

"Oh, ye of little faith, We'll just have to take it one step at a time."

❧

–Congratulations! I'm proud of you!

–Thanks...I think.

–Come on, now. You feel better. Admit it.

–Well, at least I won't have to lie about talking in my sleep. What's going on with Bruno?

–It's really hard to tell. He's still adapting to his changed circumstances. And I can sense he's starting to wonder about the details of his death. Mainly, I gather he's concerned about something having to do with you.

–The envelope. I'm sorry about that. I should have opened it right away. I'll do it as soon as I get home.

–I'm sure he'll appreciate that.

❧

Because almost all of the easily portable things–dishes and most of his clothes–had already been moved Armitage, Elliott suggested Steve spend the week at the condo, bringing along anything he might need for work. Steve agreed, meeting him at the Armitage building after work Monday. Arriving home, Elliott found three calls from Cessy on his answering machine and realized he hadn't talked to her all weekend. He'd intended to get to Bruno's envelope as soon as he got in but decided he would call his sister first while Steve fixed them a drink.

"How come you didn't call my cell?" he asked when she answered the phone.

"I knew you were busy, and I didn't want to bother you."

Then why, he briefly wondered, had she called his land-line three times?

"So, what's up?"

Steve handed Elliott his drink and motioned he'd be in the den.

Included in Cessy's rundown of the family's activities since their last conversation was a report on their parents' travels–they were currently in Istanbul on yet another Middle East tour. Their mother wrote Cessy with fair frequency, but when they were traveling he received only an occasional postcard. Even when she asked how the weekend had gone, however, he didn't mention that Steve was spending the week.

Finally, he asked to talk to Brad, who agreed to help with the furniture the following Saturday.

After hanging up, he went into the bedroom to get Bruno's envelope from the dresser, pausing as he passed the den to tell Steve he'd be right with him. The 9 x 12 white envelope was sealed, but rather than go back to the den for a letter opener, he inserted his finger under a loose corner of the flap and ripped it open. Inside was a second sealed envelope, with "For Ricky" written on it in block letters. He was curious as to its contents but didn't want to open it.

It struck him as odd Bruno hadn't simply given it to Ricky directly.

Passing by the den again on his way to the kitchen phone, he said, "One more thing." Steve merely lifted his glass in acknowledgement without looking away from the TV.

When Adam's and Jesse's answering machine kicked in, he left a message to have Ricky give him a call and was just about to hang up when he heard the receiver lifted.

"Elliott, hi. This is Ricky. I don't normally answer the phone, but Adam and Jesse are out, and I was in the kitchen and heard your message. I was just getting ready to call you but wanted to be sure you were home from work first. The police came to see me today. They wanted to know about those stamps Cage took. They said they were real. How could they be real? They were in a picture frame hanging on the wall."

Elliott paused only a moment.

"Trust me, they were real. Did you tell them you thought Cage took them?"

"Well, yes. Who else could it have been?"

Deciding to let that ride for the moment, Elliott said, "I'm glad you talked with them. But the reason for my call is that Bruno left an envelope with me, and I didn't get a chance to open it until tonight. It's something for you."

There was a long pause, then: "Really? He left something for me?" The pleasure in his voice was mixed with sadness. "What is it?"

"I don't know. There was an envelope inside the envelope, and the inner one has your name on it. Would you like me to mail it to you, or..."

"Oh, no! Could I come over and get it? Tomorrow evening, maybe? Adam and Jesse are going out to dinner, so..."

"That'd be fine. Any time after five-thirty."

"I'll see you then."

As he hung up, Elliott detected just the slightest hint of Old Spice.

❧

He was awakened by Steve's suddenly sitting up in bed and exclaiming, "Whoa!" Glancing at the bedside clock, he saw it was just after one. He didn't have to ask the reason for the wake-up call. The room reeked of Old Spice.

He sat up, too, both of them looking around the room, although they knew it was pointless. The odor dissipated but didn't disappear.

Steve turned to Elliott.

"What the hell was that all about?" he asked.

"I have no idea." Elliott shook his head. "But I suggest we get back to sleep. Maybe I'll hear from John."

They both lay back down, and Elliott closed his eyes. As always, the harder he tried to fall asleep, the more difficult it was. He could tell Steve hadn't gone back to sleep, either, but he didn't want to start a conversation in the middle of the night.

Finally, after what seemed like hours...

—I think they call it an epiphany.

—It must have been one hell of an epiphany.

—Bruno knows for sure he was murdered.

—That'd do it. Does he know who did it?

—No. I get images and impressions of his being lifted up, going over the railing, then looking backwards and upside down at a pair of legs standing at the balcony. That's it. I gather he doesn't remember the rest of the fall.

—Thank God for that.

—Well, it really doesn't matter once you're dead.

—Now, there's an interesting if less than cheery thought.

—Sorry. Facts is facts.

—So, he doesn't know who did it?

—No. But I'm pretty sure he wants you to find out.

—I was afraid of that, but I don't think he'll need me. The police are treating it as a murder. They'll find out who did it.

—Hopefully. But I get the idea it may not be easy—there's one hell of a lot going on with all of this. I haven't a clue as to what it all is, or what it means, if anything. He may start focusing and come up with some specific information that will help, and you can pass it on to the police.

—Oh, sure. "My dead friends tell me..."

—You've done it before. You'll find a way.

—Let's see if I need to first.

Steve was in the shower when Elliott woke, so he first went to make coffee before using the guest bathroom shower. He was tempted to join Steve but knew, given their libidos, it probably wouldn't be a good idea if they wanted to make it to work on time.

As they had their toast and coffee, Elliott was curious as to whether he might have talked aloud during his conversation with John; but when Steve said nothing about it, he told him about Bruno's realization.

Steve gave an exaggeratedly slow nod. "Aha! Thus the Old Spice!"

After dropping Steve at the Armitage el stop, Elliott backtracked the few blocks to the building. He was nearly half an hour early, but just as he pulled into one of the garages, a truck drove into the alley with a large dumpster he had ordered for the ground-floor interior demolition. He directed them to put it as close to the building's side entrance as possible then went inside and started to work.

❧

As they approached the condo's driveway after work, they passed Ricky walking from the bus stop toward the building. Steve got out by the main entrance to wait for him while Elliott parked the car.

"Sorry if I'm too early," Ricky said as Elliott joined him and Steve in the lobby, "but I just couldn't wait, and I didn't want to interfere with your evening."

"No problem," Elliott said as they went to the elevators.

"I still can't believe Bruno actually left something for me. I never expected anything at all from him."

"Well, I have no idea what it might be," Elliott said. "All I know is that it's in an envelope with your name on it."

As soon as they were inside, Elliot retrieved the envelope from the bedroom while Steve fixed drinks. They were still in the kitchen when he returned and handed Ricky the envelope.

"Do you mind if I open it now? I'm just so...I don't even know what words to use."

"That's okay," Steve said. "We understand."

Ricky very carefully pried the envelope flap loose and opened it, extracting what appeared to be a small sheet of stationary wrapped around another folded piece of paper. He read a note written on the stationary first.

"It says, 'I want you to have something to remember me by.'" He then unfolded the second piece of paper, and his puzzlement was clear as he unfolded and read it. Elliott recognized it immediately but said nothing.

"It's a Philatelic Certificate of Authenticity," Ricky said, holding it so both Steve and Elliott could see. "For the stamps Cage stole. But why would he leave this for me? Do you think he knew he was going to die?"

Elliott felt a wave of relief that Bruno had taken his suggestion not to keep the certificate in the same frame with the stamps.

"I'm sure he didn't. But I'd assume he wanted you to have them just in case anything did happen. He really cared about you."

Ricky's eyes filled with tears, and he pursed his lips tightly. Elliott was afraid he was going to cry, but he recovered himself.

"But they're gone. Cage stole them."

"Let's go sit down," Elliott suggested.

Steve handed him and Ricky their drinks and, picking up his own, followed them into the living room.

"Exactly when did you notice the stamps were gone?" Elliott asked when they'd settled.

"Like I told the police, it was the Tuesday after Bruno died. All of a sudden, I just saw they weren't there. I called you almost right away."

Which meant they could have been taken any time after Bruno's death, including that same night.

"So, you don't know if they were there before or after Clifford Blanton sat with you while you fell asleep the morning after Bruno's death?"

"No. But I can't imagine Clifford taking them. He was Bruno's friend."

"Exactly what makes you think Cage took them? Had he ever expressed any interest at all in them? Is he even into stamp collecting that you know of?"

"No. Bruno really enjoyed sharing his love of stamps, and he told me he'd tried showing one of his albums to Cage one time, but that the only thing Cage wanted to know was how much each one of them was worth. He was really happy I was interested in stamps, though I hadn't done much about collecting since I was a kid, and I never really knew enough about them to be a serious collector. I wouldn't have had the money to be one, either."

"What about the rest of Bruno's stamps?" Steve asked. "Were any others taken?"

Ricky looked surprised. "I honestly don't know. Everything was going on at once, and it was all just too much. It never occurred to me to check his stamp collection. He kept it in a file cabinet in the front hall closet, but I didn't have any reason to think about it."

It occurred to Elliott that, unless the entire collection was missing, it would be a next to impossible to know if any others were gone.

"Do you know if he had some sort of...well, like a written catalog of what stamps he had?"

Ricky sighed. "Not that I know of, and I don't know how I could find out now. I haven't been back to the condo since I moved into Adam and

Jesse's." He paused, then said, "But what if Cage has sold them already?"

"Well, if he's tried to sell anything that belonged to Bruno, he'll be in serious trouble. Everything right now belongs to the estate. As for the Jennys, I don't imagine selling or buying a block of stolen stamps worth two million dollars without the proper paperwork is quite the same as fencing a stolen microwave.

"It's possible Cage might have taken the Jennys for spite, but I tend to doubt it. I'm pretty sure whoever took them knew they were real–and they're not going to let any harm come to them, you can be sure of that. It may take awhile, but they'll show up." He hoped he sounded more confident than he felt. "In the meantime, I'd suggest you put that certificate somewhere you know is safe. And I suggest you let the police know you have it. They might even be able to hold it for you as part of their evidence file. You'd get it back once everything's settled."

"Oh, I will!" Carefully replacing the certificate in the envelope, Ricky finished his drink and got up. "Thank you...both...for everything! You don't know how much this means to me. And even if the stamps are never found, just to know that Bruno...well, you know."

When the door had closed behind Ricky and they had returned to the living room, Steve said, "Do you buy that?"

"What?"

"That he'd be okay if the stamps were never found? I mean, a couple of million dollars..."

"...which he doesn't have now and never had any expectation of having. I wouldn't be surprised if the two million part of it hasn't really sunk in yet. But I think he meant it. He really cared for Bruno and, as he said, just knowing Bruno felt the same about him..."

Steve grinned. "Look, you let word get around you're a bleeding-heart liberal, you're dead in this town!"

Elliott returned the grin. "Right."

–Don't worry about the other stamps; they're all there. For the moment.

–How do you know?

–I don't. Bruno does. How he knows, I can't explain. He just does.

—So, who knew about the Jennys other than Blanton? My money's on him at the moment.

—I'm not sure; I'll try to find out.

—Yeah, well, I'm afraid it could be more people than he might think. He told me *about them. I suspect he was sort of like a little kid with a secret he couldn't resist sharing.*

❦

By Friday, the main floor of the Armitage building had been entirely gutted. While the damaged ceiling panels could be replaced by those they'd found in the basement, the walls were in very bad shape, and Elliott thought the best thing to do would be to just wallboard the entire space. However, on Steve's suggestion, it was determined there would be enough salvageable panels to do the first eight or ten feet of the side walls from the front of the building. It proved to be a long and laborious job, but everyone agreed it was worth it.

Button had come over to the condo Wednesday to sign the lease on his apartment, and said he'd be moving in the weekend after Steve. Elliott talked with Cessy a couple of times but heard nothing from Guerdon or Cabrera on how the case was going. Of course, there was no reason why he would or should. It was their investigation, not his.

There was no word from John until Friday night.

—Sorry it took so long to get back to you. Just remember your time isn't quite the same as Bruno's, and he and I still don't have what you'd call regular in-spoken-words conversations.

—What did you find out?

—You were right. Blanton knew, of course, since he was the one who put Bruno in touch with the guy Bruno bought the Jennys from in the first place. Walter Means knew in the course of his acting as financial manager; and Bruno thinks he may have mentioned them to Rudy.

—He might as well have put up a billboard on the side of the building. And Cage worked for Rudy, so it's not too much of a stretch to think Rudy would have asked Cage about them even if Bruno hadn't told Cage himself. Has Bruno remembered anything more about the party or his last moments?

—Not from what I can gather. Again, it's not like we're having a conversation where I can ask direct him questions. I have to sift through the dust clouds he's sending out. But I'll do what I can.

⁂

Moving Steve's furniture to the new apartment went without a hitch, thanks to Brad and BJ's help. Though Elliott knew Brad wouldn't accept any payment for his time and effort, both Steve and he each managed to slip BJ $20 when Brad wasn't looking.

They used the rest of Saturday unpacking and getting things in order, then spent the night in the new apartment, christening it with a champagne toast and, despite being tired from the day's work, a pleasantly extended period of what Steve referred to "horizontal recreation."

Elliott had just drifted off to sleep when he was aware of John.

–Bruno is getting restless.

–About anything in particular?

–About why he died, and who killed him.

–I can't say I blame him. Still no specifics?

–No. It's like watching laundry in a glass-doored dryer–several names keep churning past the window.

–Names like...?

–Cage, Rudy, Walter Means.

–The "usual suspects," in other words. How about Clifford Blanton?

–Not that I noticed.

–Well, then, my money's on him. It's always the guy no one suspects.

–Interesting! Uh, not about Blanton, but that Steve's close by.

–Yeah, like right next to me, in case you hadn't noticed.

–No, I don't mean physically.

–Oh, great! You mean he's listening in?

John laughed.

–No. I just sense he's out there on the perimeter. Not surprising, really, now that he knows about me. Link between you and me, link between him and you. I'm just the apex of the triangle.

–I don't know that I'm ready for a psychic three-way.

–Not to worry. We're nowhere close to that.

"A psychic three-way?"

Elliott opened his eyes to see Steve propped up on one elbow, grinning at him.

"Talking with John, I assume?"

"Yeah."

"Anything interesting?"

"It can wait until morning. We'd better get back to sleep."

A light rain was falling Sunday morning as Elliott joined Steve in the kitchen.

"I was hoping we could have our coffee on the patio," Steve said, gesturing toward his new deck with a tilt of his head as he poured coffee.

"You don't have any furniture out there yet," Elliott pointed out.

"Details, details!"

Taking their coffee into the living room, they sat on the couch among opened boxes and pictures leaning against the walls awaiting hanging.

"So," Steve said, "what was that about a psychic three-way? And what's up with John?"

Elliott told him.

"What now?" Steve asked when he'd finished.

"No idea. None. I'm not a cop. I'm not a detective. I don't have any authority to start questioning people and wouldn't even know what to ask if I did."

Steve moved aside a box on the coffee table to allow him to set his mug down and shrugged.

"Well, you can at least talk to the people Bruno's concerned about. You can get a feel for whether they're telling the truth or hiding something."

Elliott echoed the shrug. "I suppose it wouldn't hurt."

"And maybe John will be able to get some details from Bruno. He..." Steve leaned forward to pick up his coffee and stopped in mid-motion.

"What?" Elliott asked.

"Old Spice. Smell it?"

Elliott inhaled deeply. "Ah, yeah. Just a whiff. Looks like we have Bruno's attention."

"Too bad you can't communicate with him directly."

"Oohh, no! Having conversations with one dead guy–no offense to John–is more than enough, thanks.

"I really don't have any good reason to talk to Rudy, or Walter Means, for that matter, but I suppose I can *find* some reason to get in touch with them to see if I can learn anything. And I've never talked to Cage about what happened the night Bruno died."

"Well, if there's anything I can do, let me know."

"Have no doubt!"

Returning home Monday night, Elliott tried to figure out a good reason to call Cage. He didn't even know if Cage was in town, or whether he had moved from Bruno's condo as Means had insisted. If he had moved, it might be next to impossible to get in touch with him at all.

Luck was once again with him. As he was walking away from his mailbox, he saw Cage come in from the garage.

"Cage!" he called, hurrying to catch up with him.

"Hi, Elliott. How are things going?"

They crossed the lobby to the elevators.

"Fine with me, but how are you doing?"

"Okay, I guess. Bruno's death hit my mom pretty hard, and it's only made her sicker, so I've been running back and forth to Rockford a lot. When I'm not working for Rudy, Chaz and I are looking for a place to move to. Means tried to kick us out the minute Bruno died, but Rudy says he can't do anything until the court approves him as executor, so I told him to go fuck himself. Why Bruno ever chose him I'll never know. The guy's a first-class asshole."

The elevator doors opened, and they got on. Elliott decided to take advantage of the opportunity.

"If you've got a minute, how about stopping at my place for a drink? I haven't talked to you since Bruno died."

"Sure, I've got some time. Chaz is coming over around six-thirty. You still with Steve?"

Elliott thought that an odd question, but merely said, "Yeah."

"Hot guy."

"That he is."

When the elevator stopped at thirty-five, Cage followed Elliott to his unit.

"What'll it be?" Elliott asked, going immediately to the cupboards to take out two glasses.

"Scotch on the rocks."

"Sure. Why don't you go into the living room, and I'll be right with you." Going about the business of fixing their drinks–bourbon-Seven for himself–Elliott said, "So, where are you thinking of moving?"

"We looked at a little place–and I do mean little–on Roscoe just off Halsted. We can't afford anything more until the estate is settled."

"What are you going to do with all of Bruno's things?"

Cage laughed—a little bitterly, Elliott noted.

"Means warned me not to take anything I hadn't brought with me when I moved in. Everything belongs to the estate, he said, and until the estate's settled, nobody can touch a thing. He had the gall to go around taking pictures of everything. He said if I want any of Bruno's furniture, I can buy it from the estate. Did I mention the guy's a prick?"

Elliott brought their drinks into the living room, handed Cage his scotch, and took a seat in his favorite chair.

"Well, you should come out okay in the end, once the will is executed."

Cage merely shrugged and took a sip of his scotch.

"So, tell me about the night Bruno died. What happened?"

Shaking his head, Cage said, "I haven't a clue. The party was pretty much over, and everybody had gone home, and it was just Chaz and Ricky and me and Bruno. We'd all had a lot to drink, and I just conked out until the police woke us up."

Elliott didn't say anything for a moment. "Who was the last to leave the party? Do you remember?"

Cage thought about it,

"Yeah, Bruno's guru, Clifford Blanton. Talk about a phony! I tried to warn Bruno about that guy, but it didn't do any good."

"Warn him about what?"

"That he was just out to get as much of Bruno's money as he could. Do you know he was charging Bruno five hundred dollars for their little 'sessions'—sometimes three times a week?"

It occurred to Elliott it would be counterproductive for Blanton to kill Bruno and cut himself off from a lucrative source of income, until Cage added, "He wanted Bruno to go in with him on some resort in northern Wisconsin. He had this idea of creating some kind of 'Meditation Retreat.' I think I may have talked him out of that one, but I don't know. I know they had an argument at the party."

"Did you mention that to the police?"

"Sure."

"Did you say anything about Rudy?"

Cage looked up from his drink. "No. Why should I?"

"Well, Rudy wanted Bruno to go in with him to buy that bar."

"Yeah, but that was a legitimate business deal. Bruno could have made a lot of money—not that he needed it, but...Well, after the will's executed, Rudy and I might work something out."

Elliott assumed Cage was still working for Rudy, and wondered if he knew for sure he was in the will, but didn't want to ask. He wouldn't have been surprised to learn Rudy had rehired him so as not to let him—and the chance to get at any money Bruno might have left him—slip away.

❧

The door had no sooner closed behind Cage when Steve called, followed by Cessy; he wasn't able to start dinner until nearly seven. He went over his conversation with Cage, vacillating between putting him high or low on the list of Bruno's possible killers.

A lot depended, he decided, on whether or not Cage was mentioned in the will and had known it at the time. His comment about going into business with Rudy after the disbursement of the estate indicated he was pretty confident he'd be getting at least some of Bruno's money, which was a pretty strong motive.

But even if Cage weren't specifically mentioned in the will, his parents undoubtedly were as next-of-kin. Since Bruno had said both of them were in poor health, maybe Cage was counting on their not being around much longer, leaving him the primary beneficiary. Pretty calculating, but Cage struck Elliott as a man who knew what he wanted and wouldn't be too bothered with ethics in getting it.

He had wanted to talk to Walter Means since shortly after Bruno died but didn't know exactly how to go about approaching him. They'd had relatively few contacts other than the man's bids for Elliott's business several years previously. But after talking with Cage, it struck him that Means's intention to put Bruno's condo up for sale might provide an excuse. He made a mental note to call him and set up an appointment.

❧

—I suspect Cage isn't in it.

—In what? Bruno's will? How do you know that?

—Bruno's like a lot of people who die suddenly without having any idea of why or how they died. He's a lot like a hurricane. There's an "eye," which is him and everything that made him who he was—every thought, every memory he ever had—swirling around it. It usually all calms down in time, but some people take longer than others.

I did pick up some interesting nonverbal impressions of family background, though. There are strong positive feelings about his parents and his sister-in-law—I suspect they were probably the only members of his family he felt close to. There's almost nothing about his brother, and what there is, is pretty neutral. There's a little bit of anger and disappointment about Cage.

—But no specifics on the will?

—None. It would be a lot easier if I could communicate with him directly, but he's not to that point yet. All I have is the feeling Cage isn't in the will.

—Well, with both his parents being in ill health—he mentioned his mom wasn't doing well—he probably doesn't need to be. He'll end up with it all, eventually.

⁂

Having dinner at Steve's Tuesday night, Elliott related his most recent conversation with John.

"I'm really between a rock and a hard place here," he said. "There's no easy way of knowing what the police are doing, or what leads they may be following, or what they know that we don't. I can't pull the same sort of thing with them as I did with Brad—even he never fully bought the 'it's just a hunch' explanation, and God knows I don't want them to think of me as a possible suspect."

"All you can do is the best you can. At least you're getting some information, indirect as it may be, from Bruno. That's something the police can't say."

"True."

"So, what's next?"

"Walter Means, I think. I'll tell him Cessy and Brad might be interested in buying Bruno's place—or, better, that my parents are thinking of buying it for them. Since my folks are out of town, there's no way Means can check with them even if he wanted to."

During dinner, Steve said, "You know, since you have to be here to work every day anyway, you could just stay here until all the work's done."

Elliott could sense courtesy was the motivating factor behind the offer, and strongly felt that Steve really needed time to establish the sense the apartment was his.

"Tempting," he said, "but I need to be at the condo anyway for mail and to check for messages, not to mention that it's ground zero for most of what we need to do to get to the bottom of what happened to Bruno. But I won't mind being a frequent overnight guest."

Steve grinned. "I think that can be arranged."

~

At home Wednesday evening, Elliott located Walter Means's business card. Just as his mind collected trivia, he seemed incapable of throwing away business cards, which he kept in a special file, sorted alphabetically. Removing it, being careful to set the card behind it on end so he could easily locate the spot from which it had been taken, he went to the phone and dialed.

"Means residence," a female voice–probably Mrs. Means–said.

"Is Walter in?"

"Who's calling?"

"Elliott Smith, in thirty-five-J."

There was a moment of silence, then Means's voice.

"Can I help you?"

"Yes, I think you can. I understand you're to be the executor of Bruno Caesar's will?"

"That's correct."

"And I understand you'll be putting his condo up for sale?"

"Yes. Are you interested?"

"A member of my family might be, yes. Can we get together to talk about it?"

"Of course. When would be convenient for you?"

"Tomorrow evening would be good. Seven-thirty? At my unit? Thirty-five-J."

"That will be fine. I'll see you then."

As he finished dinner, Button called, verifying he planned to move in Saturday.

"Sure. Do you need any help?"

"That's very kind of you, Elliott, but Paul and a couple of friends from the Anvil have volunteered. I'll stop by tomorrow with the signed lease and the rest of the first and last month's rent. Will you be there around six?"

"Probably not–I have an appointment here. But I'm sure Steve will be there, and you can give it to him. I'll leave a receipt and a key with him."

"Thank you, Elliott. I am so looking forward to this move!"

They talked for a few more minutes, and after a quick call to Steve to make sure he'd be there when Button came by, Elliott retired to the den for a little TV before bed.

—An interesting bit of news on the will.

—Ah? And what is it?

—The bulk of everything goes to Bruno's sister-in-law.

—Not his brother?

—Nope. Or Cage. And I get a strong undercurrent of concern for her. I'd guess she's in pretty bad shape.

—Which means Cage might end up with the bulk, if not all, of Bruno's money.

—Seems likely.

—Anything at all on his "sensei," Clifford Blanton?

—Specifically on him? Oddly, no. But there are a couple of really dark areas swirling around he hasn't even come close to addressing yet. Maybe Blanton's in there somewhere.

—Interesting. I definitely should try to talk with Blanton, too.

A knock on Elliott's door at exactly seven-thirty Thursday evening announced Walter Means's arrival. He carried a glossy-covered prospectus with "Exclusive Realty" embossed on it. They shook hands, and Elliott escorted him into the living room, noting that Means made no effort to hide his inspection of the unit. Elliott did not offer him a drink.

Taking a seat on the couch, Means got right down to business.

"You're lucky you called when you did," he said. "I'll be putting the place on the market momentarily."

Elliott couldn't resist adding, "As soon as the court approves your executorship, you mean. You can't do it before."

Means face reflected his displeasure.

"Of course, but that will be any day now." Indicating the prospectus, he said, "I've already had an appraisal done, and even given current market conditions I'm sure there won't be any trouble selling it." He paused, then said, "You say your sister is interested in it?"

Elliott had said no such thing and didn't remember ever having even mentioned to Means that he had a sister.

"Her husband's a policeman, I understand."

Elliott found the fact he had obviously done some research into the family more than a little irritating. Unaware of–or unconcerned with–Elliott's reaction, Means continued.

"I'd thought this might be a little steep for him on a policeman's salary. But then, I'm sure your sister could easily afford it."

Elliott's irritation bloomed into anger, and he had to make a conscious effort not to let it show.

"They already own their own home. My parents are thinking of buying it as an investment."

Means nodded. "Aaah, I see. It would be an excellent investment. You know the J-units are the most desirable in the building, and Bruno's is in excellent condition."

Leaning forward, he offered the prospectus to Elliott, who took it and looked through it briefly.

"I don't see the suggested list price."

Means looked surprised.

"It's not there?" He took the folder and leafed through it quickly. "I must have left it downstairs. Sorry. We'll be listing it for three-fifty, but I'm sure if your parents are interested, money shouldn't be an object."

Elliott found the man's gall astonishing. He knew a newly renovated J-unit on a slightly lower floor had sold for $320,000 shortly before Bruno bought his, and while he had no idea how much Bruno had paid, he was sure it couldn't have been much more than $330,000.

"When do you think they'd like to take a look at it?" Means asked.

"They're currently overseas, but they've always liked this unit"–in truth, his parents had only been in it twice in all the time he'd lived there–"and when they heard of Bruno's death, they asked me to get them some information on it. I'll pass it on when they call next, and if they're interested, they can call you directly when they get back."

"Well, I hope they'll be back soon. It won't last long once we put it on the market."

Elliott resisted observing that at $350,000 it probably would. He didn't want to give Means an excuse to get away before he got some of the information he needed.

"So, tell me, how did you come to be named executor of Bruno's will? Isn't that a bit unusual, considering you were also his financial adviser?"

"Not unusual at all. When he saw how well I was doing for him, he insisted I agree to take care of his estate should something happen to him. I'd be surprised if he knew how to balance a checkbook before I came along."

"I gather he was very unhappy with his stock losses."

Means shrugged. "Wasn't everyone? And of course, he blamed me, a classic example of shoot the messenger. But I explained to him I was not responsible for his losses, and that in fact, it was only my astute management that kept him from losing a lot more.

"And his so-called friends were out for everything they could get. They would have bled him dry if I hadn't been there to prevent it. He wrote a very sizable check to his 'guru' or whatever he was supposed to be two days before he died. It was cashed–cashed, not deposited–the following morning. I find that very unusual."

So did Elliott, and the fact that piece of information was accompanied by the subtle but definite whiff of Old Spice caught him completely by surprise. Momentarily thrown off-balance, he surprised himself when he came up with a total non-sequitur.

"Were you aware of the value of his stamp collection?"

Means didn't bat an eye. "Of course, and I felt it a perfect example of his ignorance of finances. The money he spent on those...those...airmail stamps..."

"Inverted Jennys."

"Yes...could have been invested far more wisely. Unfortunately, he'd bought them before he came to me and refused my advice to sell them and reinvest the money in something worthwhile."

Elliott was very tempted to say the stamps were extremely worthwhile to Bruno.

"And did you know those stamps are missing?" he asked.

He couldn't tell whether Means's look of shock was real or feigned.

"Missing? How could that be? I instructed him to put them in a safe deposit box the minute I heard he had them."

"He didn't. He kept them in a frame on his bedroom wall where he could see them every morning."

Means shook his head. "I can't believe it! How could he have been so stupid?"

"I gather you didn't think too highly of him."

"How could I when he could do something so utterly irresponsible? That and his endless questioning and second-guessing. To be honest with you, it had gotten to the point where I was considering telling him to find another financial manager."

Elliott took that comment with a pound or two of salt.

Means glanced at his watch and got up from the couch.

"I really must be going. Please have your parents call me as soon as possible if they are interested. It won't be on the market long."

"I'll do that," Elliott said, rising to walk him to the door.

–Do you believe him?

–About whether he knew about the Jennys? Hard to say. If he's as big a con artist as I think he is, that bit about not knowing their name was a nice touch, and of course, he'd look surprised to hear they're missing. The one thing that stood out other than the obvious bullshit was that he's an arrogant son of a bitch.

–Being an arrogant son of a bitch is hardly motive for murder.

–True. But playing coy about the Jennys could be. That thing about Blanton cashing a "sizable" check from Bruno two days before Bruno died set off some bells, as maybe Means knew it would. A classic example of "Oh! Look over there!" I think I can guess what the the check was for, and why he was in such a rush to cash it. So, Blanton's next on my list, if I can figure out how to reach him. Bruno told me he had a website, so I'll check there.

–Good luck.

–I'll need it!

Friday was too full of work details–replacing damaged pressed-tin ceiling panels, paneling the front eight feet on either side of the to-be-showroom area with the remaining panels, reducing the size of the bathroom and starting the framing-in of the two back offices–for Elliott to have even a chance to think about Clifford Blanton. He'd brought a change of clothes, since Steve had suggested dinner and a movie, so there was no time to do an internet check on Blanton.

They had their morning coffee on Steve's new patio, using folding chairs and TV trays since Steve hadn't had a chance to pick up any outdoor furniture for it yet. Elliott suggested they go by Target later that morning to see what was available.

"I probably won't be able to buy anything until at least next payday," Steve said, "but we can get an idea."

Elliott knew better than to suggest he get it and Steve could pay him back.

He had just gone into the kitchen to refill their coffees when sounds in the hallway announced the arrival of Button and his moving team. Going to the door, he opened it to the passing of a large, muscular man carrying an upside-down wingback chair, the seat balanced on his head and the arms resting on his shoulders. Behind him, struggling with a slab of thick glass–likely the top of a coffee table–was Paul.

"Good morning, Elliott," he said brightly.

"Need some help?"

"No, I'm fine, thanks. I hope we aren't making too much noise."

"Not at all."

"Button wanted us to start at six-thirty, but I told him that would be a sure way to get evicted before he even moved in."

"Don't listen to him, Elliott," Button said, squeezing past the guy with the chair and heading down the stairs. "He's just in a snit because I told him he'd have to carry more than two throw pillows at a time."

Elliott grinned. "Well, if you need anything, just let us know."

With that, he went back into the apartment to get the coffee and rejoin Steve on the patio.

Chapter 8

He'd planned to return to his condo Saturday afternoon to give Steve some time to paint, but they went looking for patio furniture at Target as intended and ended up going to a couple other places as well. They had lunch, and on returning to Steve's, ran into Button and Paul, who had just dropped off the rental truck, and who invited them up to see the apartment.

"It'll take a couple of days to get things in order," Button said as he showed them in.

Elliott was impressed by how much had already been done. The furniture was arranged, boxes awaiting unpacking were stacked neatly in one corner, and paintings leaned against the walls where they would be hung. Steve was impressed by some of the original pieces, including a signed Bernard Buffet print.

"I was hoping you were in," Button said. "I was going to stop on the way up to invite you for a glass of champagne to celebrate. I'm so glad we caught you."

"The place looks great already," Steve said with admiration. "I really appreciate your taste in art."

Button smiled. "Thank you. I hope to have a Gutierrez among my collection one of these days." He paused only a moment before saying, "Please, sit down. Paul, why don't you keep these lovely people entertained while I go see to the champagne?"

"You really got a lot done in a very short time," Elliott observed to Paul as Button went into the kitchen.

"The joys of OCD," Paul replied with a grin. "A place for everything, and everything in its place. Or else! But he was so lucky to have found this place. He loves it. Too bad this isn't a three-flat–I'd jump at it."

"Paul," Button called from the kitchen, "could you give me a hand?"

Excusing himself, Paul got up and hurried away, to return almost immediately carrying two glasses of champagne, which he handed to Steve and Elliott, followed by Button with his and Paul's.

"A toast," Button said, raising his glass, and both Steve and Elliott stood to echo his gesture. "To friends old and new."

They clicked their glasses and sat down.

"Sorry not to have hors d'oeuvres," Button said, "but it's the butler's day off."

"I had the day off?" Paul said. "You could have fooled me."

They talked and laughed and took their time drinking their champagne. After Button refilled their glasses, the conversation got around to Bruno, and immediately Elliott detected a very subtle hint of Old Spice. Steve's sideways glance said he'd noted it, too.

"So, tell me about Bruno before he won the lottery," Elliott said.

Button's expression softened to one of reflection.

"Ah, dear, sweet Bruno. I forget exactly how we met." He paused. "Oh, yes. At the Caribou on Broadway and Aldine. All the tables were taken, and I asked Bruno if I could join him. We met there a couple more times and gradually became friends.

"He didn't have many friends, I'm afraid. He was really very shy and withdrawn. Winning the lottery was a real shock for him, and I don't know that he really got over it, even though having all that money made him far more outgoing on the surface. But he was much too trusting, and he drew predators like a wounded antelope attracts lions. I warned him time and again. Rudy, his nephew, that phony 'sensei,' and all the others."

"What do you know about 'Dr.' Blanton?"

"The graduate of the University of Metaphysics? Please! He probably got his degree out of a Cracker Jack box. But he had Bruno thoroughly fooled. However, I noticed a slight change in his utter devotion toward the end. I have no idea what the cause may have been, but I know

Blanton had been trying to convince him to invest in some sort of metaphysical retreat in Wisconsin."

"You do know the police are treating Bruno's death as a homicide?"

Button shook his head slowly and sighed.

"I got that impression when they talked to me, but they didn't come right out and say they were investigating a murder, so I hoped my impression was wrong."

"Afraid not. Can you think of anyone else who might have had a motive to see him dead?"

A long pause before: "Not really. A lot of people 'borrowed' a lot of money from him and, I'm sure, never intended to pay back a nickel. But I understand the night of his last party–neither Paul nor I were there–he intended to tell everyone he wasn't going to be a patsy anymore, and the loans had to be repaid. He didn't like his financial manager very much, and I don't think he trusted him, but his insistence that Bruno lay down the law to them was good advice." Button stopped abruptly, and the fingertips of his free hand rose to his chest. "Unless it got him killed!"

Actually, Elliott knew it had been Blanton who suggested the party, but he merely shrugged and said nothing.

"If you can think of anything or anyone the police should be taking a look at, please let me know. I can pass it on to my brother-in-law, who's a cop, and he can give it to the detectives on the case."

"I certainly will."

As if by mutual agreement, the conversation moved on to other topics, and Elliott and Steve left about twenty minutes later.

"Too late for me to get any painting done," Steve observed as they got back to his apartment, "so why don't you spend the night, and I'll get to it tomorrow? We can have dinner and..."

"You talked me into it," Elliott replied, grinning. "I especially liked the 'and' part."

❧

He didn't get home until shortly after noon on Sunday and immediately spent half an hour catching up on phone messages and talking at length with Cessy. He then spent another forty-five minutes going through piled-up emails.

Finally, he did a web search for Clifford Blanton and came up with a number of entries, all making reference to the "Center for Metaphysical

Growth." He hadn't a clue as to what that might mean, but it sounded impressive, which he was sure was its sole purpose.

He went through them until he found a phone number for a "Clifford Blanton, Ph.D., Director." Being fairly certain any reputable non-retail business would not be open on a Sunday, he called. He wasn't particularly surprised to hear the phone being picked up on the third ring.

"This is Dr. Blanton. How can I help you?"

"Clifford, hello." He was taking a risk of alienating him by using his first name instead of addressing him as "Doctor" but wanted to make it clear from the start he wasn't willing to play games. "This is Elliott Smith, Bruno Caesar's neighbor. We met a couple of times at his parties."

There was only a slight pause before: "Ah, yes, Mr. Smith." Blanton was obviously no slouch at playing the upper-hand game. "What can I do for you?"

"I had a few questions about Bruno you might be able to help me with."

Another pause. "What kind of questions? I'm sure I covered everything with the police when I talked to them. May I ask just why you're curious?"

"Well, first of all, did the police tell you they're operating on the belief that Bruno was murdered?"

"When I spoke with them immediately after Bruno's tragic death, they said they could not rule out the possibility, and I hastened to dissuade them of that idea. I really can't discuss my specific reasons, other than to say that Bruno had some serious issues not apparent to his friends...or neighbors."

"I understand. And are you aware his Inverted Jennys are missing?"

"Yes, the police contacted me again after they learned of it, since they heard it was I who had acted as middle-man in their acquisition. They asked if I had any idea what might have happened to them. Of course, I didn't. Bruno had a very active social life, and there were people coming and going constantly, some of whom I fear were quite capable of theft. Now, if you'll excuse me, I have a seminar to prepare for."

"Of course. One more question, though. I understand you wanted Bruno to fund some sort of a resort or retreat you're planning in Wisconsin."

Blanton laughed. "I offered him the opportunity to become one of the many investors in the project, yes. Bruno believed fully in it, and he was looking forward to participating."

"So, the check he gave you two days before he died was for the project?"

"I'm afraid I really must go, Mr. Smith. Thank you for calling." The phone went dead.

❧

On a whim, he called Adam's and Jesse's number, hoping to talk to Ricky. It had occurred to him he hadn't asked how much Bruno had confided in Ricky about his dealings with Blanton—or Rudy or Cage or any of the other people who might have had a good motive for murder.

When the answering machine kicked in, he left a message saying "hi" to Adam and Jesse and asking Ricky to call him, then spent an hour or so opening his accumulated mail and paying bills.

Ricky returned his call just as he was fixing his before-dinner drink.

"Hi, Elliott, I just got home. What's up?"

"A couple of questions. Bruno talked with Rudy privately at the party, right?"

"Yes."

"Any idea how it went?"

"No, there was so much going on, and I'd already had a little too much to drink. I know he stayed for quite a while after their talk, though."

"Thanks. And I was wondering what you might know about Bruno and his relationship with Clifford Blanton, and especially about Blanton's trying to get him to invest in some project."

There was a pause on the other end of the line.

"Bruno didn't talk to me much about financial stuff. I did know Sensei was talking with him about a TV show of his meditation seminars, and he was really enthused about starting some kind of metaphysical retreat. The day before he died, Bruno got a call from a real estate office. He wasn't home, so I took the call."

"You wouldn't remember which office, or where it was, by any chance?"

"Yeah, I remember the name of the place—Superior Realty. I remember because I thought it was a pretty la-di-dah name."

"Do you remember where they were located?"

"Iron Falls...Iron Lake...Iron something-to-do-with-water. It was in Wisconsin, I know."

"Iron River?"

"Yeah, Iron River. I think so."

"Do you know if Bruno called them back?"

"Yeah, he did. I don't know what they said, but Bruno was pretty unhappy afterwards, and said he was definitely going to have a talk with Sensei at the party."

"Did he, do you know?"

"Yes, he spent some time alone in the den with several people, and Sensei was one of them."

"Did he tell you what he was going to talk to each of them about?"

"No. I knew it had something to do with things he wasn't happy about, but he didn't go into detail. I did notice most of them left right after he talked to them."

"But not Blanton?"

"No, he stayed."

"Did you mentioned the talks to the police?"

"No. It didn't even occur to me at the time. There was always something going on, and I couldn't remember everything that happened. I never even would have thought of that call from the real estate place if you hadn't mentioned Sensei and a resort. Do you think one of the people he talked to might have been responsible for his death? Should I call the police and tell them? I don't want to interfere with what they're doing."

"I'd hold off," Elliott said. "Let me try to call the real estate office and see if I can find out what the call was all about. I'll let you know if I think you should talk to the police."

"Okay."

After hanging up, and making a mental note to track down Superior Realty on Monday, he went into the kitchen to fix dinner.

⁂

–You like this, don't you?

–Like what?

–Playing detective.

–I like finding out what's going on, and since Brad isn't involved in this case, I don't have any real link with the police to know what they're doing or not doing. There are so many...details...they can't possibly be aware of that might be a clue to what happened to Bruno. Like Ricky said, nobody can be expected to remember everything. And speaking of remembering, how's Bruno doing?

–He's making real progress, I think. He's calming down, pulling himself together. I think we're pretty close to actually being able to communicate one-on-one. I do know he's aware of what you're doing, and I can tell he appreciates it.

–Well, I hope he can start the direct communication thing with you pretty soon. There's a hell of a lot I don't know that he can tell you.

–Yeah, but keep in mind there's also a lot he doesn't *know.*

He called Steve first thing Monday morning before he knew he'd be leaving for work to ask if it would be all right to take his laptop up during lunch to hook into Steve's internet connection to look for Superior Realty and a phone number for them.

Steve laughed. "You don't need my permission. You have a key–use it whenever you want."

"Thanks, but I'm still walking a fine line here. It's your apartment and your space, and I don't want to come in unannounced."

"Well, you're a lot more concerned about it than I am. Just come on up when you're ready."

Finding Superior Realty in Iron River, Wisconsin, proved relatively easy, thanks to Google. Noting that their webpage included a listing of their available properties, he went through and found the resort he was sure Blanton had in mind–ten lakeside cabins plus a central lodge. The asking price was very reasonable by Chicago standards, but this was in northern Wisconsin, a good seven-hour drive north with no convenient public transportation access.

He called.

"Superior Realty," a decidedly male voice said.

"Yes, I was looking at your website and noticed a resort for sale. Is it still available, by any chance?"

"As a matter of fact, it is," the man said.

"Has it been on the market long?"

"Only a month or two. I must tell you we have one party extremely interested in it. We've sent him a complete packet of information, and we're expecting an offer, but first come, first served. If you act quickly, it can be yours. Could I fax you some information on it?"

"Well, I just now came across it and haven't discussed it with my business partner yet. Let me check with him and get back to you. I appreciate your help." He hung up before the agent had a chance to say anything more.

Returning to the ground floor, he finished his lunch with his team and resumed work. He kept working after the others had left, waiting for Steve to get home. Steve already had a key for the ground floor front door, and Elliott knew he stopped in every night to check on the progress made during the day.

Around five-thirty, as he pulled electrical wire through holes drilled in the wall studs of what would be his office, he heard Steve call his name.

"Back here."

"Wow! Lookin' good."

"We're getting there."

"Kind of surprised you're still here."

"I wanted to fill you in on what I found out when I called the real estate agency in Wisconsin, and thought I'd tell you in person."

Steve had been looking around the newly created office spaces while Elliott talked.

"Glad you did. Why don't we go upstairs and have a drink?"

Laying the roll of wire on the floor, Elliott said, "Good idea," and followed him out, pausing to lock the door.

"So, what do you think happened?" Steve asked as they settled down on the sofa.

"Strictly conjecture, but from what Ricky told me and considering the timeline, it sounds like despite what Blanton said about Bruno only being 'one of the investors,' he was counting on him to come up with all or most of the money."

"I wonder why the agent called Bruno rather than Blanton."

"Just a guess, but maybe he wanted some earnest money immediately, which I doubt Blanton has. He probably mentioned Bruno and his money to stall for time. He might even have given the agent Bruno's number, or the guy found it somehow and called to check if Blanton was telling the truth. Bruno probably—and rightly—became suspicious.

"That Blanton cashed rather than deposited the check Bruno gave him shortly before Bruno died could mean he was afraid Bruno was going to stop payment on it. And Blanton was one of the people he took aside to talk to the night he died."

"I wonder how much of this the police know?"

"I don't have a clue, and that's really frustrating. I can't just ask them—well, I could, but they wouldn't tell me, since it's not really any of my business, and I don't want them to think I'm butting in on their investigation, or that I think my brother-in-law's being a policeman gives me any special privileges. The last thing I want is to get Brad in any kind of trouble with anyone on the force."

"Which leaves you where?"

"Good question. I'll just try to check in with Brad from time to time to see if he knows anything, and if we find out anything the police might not be aware of, I'll have to figure some way to let them know."

"What's next?"

"Rudy, I think. I really don't like the idea of contacting him, because sure as hell he'll take it as an invitation to hook me into one of his scams."

They finished their drinks, and Elliott declined the offer of another.

"I'd better head on home—I might as well bite the bullet and see if I can get in touch with Rudy tonight."

It took him a moment to find Rudy's number after he got home, and while he had both cell phone and land-line numbers, his reluctance to talk with the man at all made him opt for the land line. He was frankly relieved to get an answering machine. He left a message and went into the kitchen to fix dinner.

He was just getting ready for bed when Rudy returned his call.

"Sorry I'm so late getting back to you, Elliott. I was meeting with a group of investors on a project that immediately made me think of you. I'd intended to call you earlier, but things have been moving so quickly. I'd really like to get together with you to discuss it."

"Well, I want to talk to you, too—about Bruno."

"Bruno? Ah, I still haven't gotten over the shock of his death. I knew he had several serious problems, but I'd never have imagined he'd take his own life."

This was the second time someone had suggested Bruno might deliberately have gone off the balcony, and wondered how Rudy had come up with the idea.

"He didn't. And that's what we need to talk about. When can we meet?"

"Are you saying he was murdered? You can't be serious!"

"I'm afraid I am. We can talk about it when we meet."

"How about tomorrow, then? Seven-thirty at Roscoe's?"

"I'll see you there."

Rudy was at the bar when Elliott walked in at seven-twenty-five.

"There's a table over there," Rudy said, gesturing with his head before Elliott reached him. "I'll go grab it while you order." He laid a twenty on the bar. "On me," he added and moved off before Elliott could say anything.

Elliott ordered, left a tip with his own money and joined Rudy at the table, placing the change from the drink in front of him.

"Thanks," he said.

"Now, what's this about Bruno being murdered?" Rudy asked, leaning forward. "The police said nothing about it...well, now that I think of it, I'd have to add 'directly.' They did ask about anyone Bruno may have been concerned about. I've talked with them twice."

"Did they mention anyone in particular?"

"Cage, Ricky, his financial manager...Means?...that phony 'doctor,' Blanton, a couple other people."

"And what did you tell them?"

Rudy took a sip of his drink and shrugged.

"The truth. I frankly think every one of them contributed to Bruno's death–I still can't imagine it being murder. I'm very fond of Cage, but he's young and can be very insensitive at times. They all were out to get whatever they could from Bruno. Don't get me wrong, I really liked the man, but let's face it–what would a sexy little hustler like Ricky really see in a forty-something chunk of total vanilla like Bruno, other than dollar signs? His financial manager was robbing him blind, and that Blanton character might as well have 'con artist' stamped across his forehead. And the others...well, again, they were all after Bruno's money."

"Are you saying Ricky was a hustler?"

"I don't know it for a fact, but the town's crawling with guys with pretty faces and hot bodies looking for a sugar daddy. I sure wouldn't be surprised."

Elliott chalked that comment up to cynicism and moved on. He knew he was risking jeopardizing the chance to get any other information out of Rudy, but he couldn't resist saying, "Well, your own interest in Bruno wasn't exactly altruistic."

"Of course not. But I wasn't out to screw him. I had a legitimate business proposition that could have added to his financial stability, not knocked the pins out from under it. And I have to say, you didn't do him any favors by turning him off to my proposal."

"Bruno was a big boy," Elliott observed, "and he made his own decisions. I just told him, as I told you, that it wasn't something I was interested in. The fact you were pretty evasive about the details I'm sure had a larger influence on his decision than I did."

Rudy swirled the ice around in his glass for a minute.

"Yeah, I'll have to give you that. But the owners really tied my hands by not letting me mention the name of the bar. I still think we could have made a fortune with the place if Bruno had been a little more trusting."

Elliott had to fight to keep a straight face and say nothing, but he managed.

"I appreciate honest skepticism," Rudy said. "It's the mark of a good businessman. But a good businessman recognizes the line between caution and opportunity.

"Which is why I wanted to talk to you about a project I'm lining up, a gay senior retirement complex. We'll start off with one building–I've got my eye on a six-story twenty-four-unit. It needs a lot of work, but I know that's your area of expertise. And here's the kicker–you wouldn't have to invest a dime. I'm lining up several investors, and we'll all put in an equal amount of money. You just handle the reconstruction up to that amount. If it can be done for less, you're still in for a full share. I don't know much about construction costs, but I can't see it being anything other than a win-win situation for everybody."

That he actually might consider such a proposal caught Elliott completely by surprise, but he recognized it as a knee-jerk reaction.

"Well, I have to admit, it sounds like a worthwhile project. And I agree that gays and lesbians having their own retirement housing complex is an idea whose time has come. Still, there are a lot of factors to consider, not the least of which is the potential profitability of such a venture–I assume you're intending to make a profit.

"And as for me handling the reconstruction, I work with a small team, and we've never taken on a building with more than twelve units, and never wanted to. I concentrate on smaller, older apartment buildings with historical interest. If they don't have character or something that sets them apart from their neighbors, I'm just not interested. A twenty-four-unit building would really be more than I'd be comfortable dealing with."

Rudy said nothing for several moments, lips pursed.

"I see. And I understand. But what if we were to decide on a series of smaller buildings. Would that interest you?"

"The problem there would be that, depending on the number of people involved in the project, while the contribution of each would be considerably smaller the cost of renovations would undoubtedly far exceed the equivalent of my share of the purchase price. It could all get pretty complicated."

Rudy stared at him, his face frozen into a pursed-lips mask.

"Well, let me think about it and see what we come up with."

"To get back to Bruno for a moment," Elliott continued, "I'm curious about why he invited you to the party the night he died. I'd understood you and he had already talked about his limiting his spending."

"We had, and he asked me to the party to show me his decision wasn't personal. I never thought it was."

"I know Bruno took several guys into the den to talk to them. If you already knew what the party was all about, why did he call you in for a talk?"

"To let me know he was reconsidering his position on the bar deal, and that he thought Means was wrong in not letting him in on it. I was going to see if I could get the other investors back in, and set up a meeting with everyone that following week. But when he died, the whole deal pretty much fell apart again. I lost a potential fortune."

Elliott was sure Rudy couldn't actually think he was dumb enough to believe that, but the story couldn't hurt if Rudy were constructing a scenario to deflect being considered a suspect.

"I do know he took Clifford Blanton in for a talk because he finally realized Blanton was screwing him on that so-called retreat, plus Blanton wanted Bruno to back a series of TV infomercials. I tried to warn him from the minute I heard about the deal.

"I mean, why would he invest in a glorified infomercial that would air at three in the morning and a 'retreat' eight thousand miles from nowhere that might be used once a month in the summer when he could get in on one of the hottest bars in Chicago that's packed every night of the week? It was a no-brainer, as far as I was concerned, and I think I finally convinced Bruno."

"I'm surprised, actually, that he was considering either option. Walter Means was very much against the bar idea, and I can't imagine he'd be any more enthused about the retreat."

"Like I said, Bruno realized Means didn't have his best interests at heart, and was on his way out. I kept telling him it was his money and he could do whatever he damned well pleased with it."

Elliott resisted pointing out that people sometimes hired financial managers to protect them from themselves.

"And you know, I've been thinking about what you said about Bruno's maybe having been murdered, and the more I think about it, the more I think Means might have done it. Maybe he knew Bruno was going to dump him, and he'd lose that hefty monthly billing and control of all of Bruno's money. If not him, Blanton. Take your pick."

Elliott mentally noted Rudy did not include either Cage or himself in the list of suspects–himself for obvious reasons and Cage because he probably assumed Cage would get control of Bruno's money and thereby leave the door open for him to step in.

"What about Cage? He had a lot to gain by Bruno's death."

"Cage? No, I sincerely doubt it. He's a nice kid, but strictly between you and me, he's not the spiciest gingersnap in the tin. Frankly, I can't imagine his having the balls to kill anyone. Besides, Bruno left all his money to his sister-in-law, nothing at all to Cage."

Elliott didn't have to ask how Rudy might have come by that information, and why he had omitted mentioning the obvious fact that Cage's parents' health would likely put most of Bruno's money directly or indirectly into his hands before too long.

Finishing his drink, he said, "Well, I've got to be getting home. It was nice talking with you, Rudy."

"Same here," Rudy replied, reaching across the table to shake hands. "I'll be in touch about the seniors' project. I'm sure it could be a really profitable venture. There are a lot of well-to-do older gays and lesbians out there. A virtually untapped market."

Elliott got up, smiled, said, "Later," and left.

–One step forward, two steps back.

–Meaning?

–I told you Bruno was pulling himself together–figuratively speaking–but that there were some dark areas involving Clifford Blanton. I gather he knows what you've been doing and what you've found out about the retreat idea. He's regressed to his cyclone stage, and there's really a lot of unambiguous anger directed at Blanton. There's a strong sense of betrayal, and some of his anger seems directed at himself, probably for having trusted Blanton in the first place.

–Have you tried to calm him down?

–There's really not much I can do. We were making progress toward establishing a more direct communication, but that's been overwhelmed for now. All I can do is wait.

–Well, I hope it isn't too long. There's a lot I need to know only he can provide.

–I know, and I'll keep trying to get that through to him.

One definite advantage to Steve's knowing about John, Elliott decided, was that he didn't have to keep everything to himself, and could bounce ideas off someone with a pulse. He felt he really needed some idea-bouncing to try to sort out the pile of bits and pieces of information and conjecture that had been piling up over the past several days. He called Steve early Wednesday morning before work and suggested dinner, to which Steve readily agreed.

"I'll make a quick stop at the store and pick up a couple of steaks on my way home," he volunteered.

"No, don't go to all that bother. We can either go out or order in."

"You sure?"

"I'm sure. I'll see you when you get home."

By Wednesday night, both offices and the bathroom had been wired and wallboarded and wiring of the main space had begun. Elliott was very pleased with the results, as was Steve when he came in after work.

They spent a few minutes walking around the space with the schematic Arnie had drawn up showing Steve's suggested placement of electric outlets and track lighting, then went up to Steve's apartment.

"So, in or out for dinner?" Steve asked as they climbed the stairs.

"How about Thai take-out?"

"Sounds good," Steve said, opening his door. "I'll fix us a drink, then we can order. I got a flier in the mail from a new place that looks interesting, and they deliver."

⁂

They were halfway through dinner before Elliott said, "Had a talk with John last night."

Steve took another crab rangoon from the container. "I was curious as to whether you'd heard from him, but figured you'd tell me when you did."

"Yeah, well, I did."

He proceeded to tell Steve everything he'd not had a chance to mention before about his meeting with Rudy, John's report on Bruno's situation, and his various speculations on just who might have been responsible for Bruno's death.

"I knew before I even met with him he was going to try to con me into something, which he did. I noted that, while he was pretty quick to point a finger at Blanton–even at Ricky–he dismissed the idea that Cage might have done it. Rudy's no dummy, and if he thought he might be a suspect, it would be natural for him to also promote Cage as a suspect. But he didn't.

"Which got me wondering whether he and Cage might be in cahoots, and that maybe both of them were responsible for Bruno's death. Rudy made it clear he doesn't think much of Cage, but with as much money as Cage will probably be coming into, I'm sure he's plotting just how he can get to it. I don't know if Cage is smart enough to plan and carry out a murder, but I don't doubt Rudy is. I'm just wondering if Rudy might not have convinced Cage the shortest route to Bruno's money would be over the balcony."

He paused for a moment and took a hearty swallow from his drink.

"But then, he might just be avoiding trying to implicate Cage because he knows that if Cage were convicted of killing Bruno, he couldn't get to the money. Damn, I hate having all these questions and no way to find out the answers."

Steve shrugged. "Well, that's not exactly true. There are ways–just not easy ones."

"Yeah, you're right. If Bruno would just get his act together and start working with John, it would be a hell of a lot easier."

They finished eating in relative silence, and as they were taking the empty cartons and their plates into the kitchen, Steve said, "This may be a big stretch, but as long as you're considering people, what about Ricky?"

Pausing in the act of dropping the cartons into the trash, Elliott looked at him.

"Right. You've got to be kidding."

"Hey, I said it was a stretch. I like Ricky, and think he's a sweet kid, but what do you really know about him? What did Bruno really know about him? They were together, what...a couple of months? Isn't it possible Bruno could have told him about the stamps...or that he figured it out for himself? He had no way of knowing Bruno was going to give them to him. Or maybe he did and just wanted to hasten the process."

"But Ricky is the one who called attention to the stamps being missing. He wouldn't have done that if he'd taken them himself."

"Hmmm. True."

They returned to the living room and sat on the couch, Elliott largely lost in thought until he felt Steve's hand on his thigh. Pulling himself back into the moment, he said, "Sorry, my mind wandered off. I'd better be getting home."

Steve's hand began a slow movement toward Elliott's crotch. "Did I ever mention thinking makes me horny?"

Elliott grinned. "Me, too, now that you mention it."

They got up from the couch and headed for the bedroom.

–For somebody who was so laid-back in life, your friend Bruno sure is pretty volatile on this side of the fence.

–He still hasn't started to calm down?

–Yeah, he starts, then something comes along to stir him all up again.

–What this time?

–You can't guess? I'd imagine Steve's suggesting the possibility Ricky might have been involved really got him going. Lots of Ricky impressions and images, though I did manage to get "Phelps Chrysler" out of it, for whatever that's worth.

–Thanks! That was probably where Ricky was working when he lost his job. If they're out of business I don't know how I can verify he worked there, but it's a start. Still...well, Bruno did say he first met Ricky at the Lucky Horseshoe, and hustlers aren't unheard-of there. Damn, I hate being cynical!

–There's a pretty thin line between a cynic and a realist at times.

–Thanks. That helps. Not a lot, but it helps.

Steve's alarm did not go off in the morning, and Steve had to scramble to get ready for work and leave on time. Elliott didn't have a chance to tell him of his conversation with John.

But something John had said kept niggling at him all morning–Phelps Chrysler. He knew the name, and remembered its being on Western, but something wasn't right. And then he remembered–Phelps Chrysler had gone out of business two years before. Which meant that if that's where Ricky told Bruno he had worked until just before they met, he'd lied. And if there were one lie...

He made up his mind to have a talk with Ricky then pushed everything aside to concentrate on work.

He'd told Steve he'd be going directly home Thursday. It was much too easy to wait around until Steve got home then spend the night with him, and he wanted to resist the temptation to move too quickly toward what he accepted was their inevitable moving-in together. But he called as soon as he knew Steve was home to tell him about Phelps Chrysler and his intention to talk to Ricky.

"Well, it's possible Ricky really did work for Phelps," Steve said.

"Yeah, but nearly two years before he met Bruno? What was he doing in the meantime?"

"Good question. Maybe he couldn't find a job and was hustling. I don't know. And if he had worked for Phelps, then it wasn't totally a lie."

"So, it's possible Bruno might not have met Ricky quite as casually as he first told me. Maybe that's why John says Bruno went off into another one of his cyclones when you suggested Ricky might be involved."

"Possible. Has John ever told you how he—how Bruno—manages to know what he knows about what's going on with everybody and everything?"

"No, and I probably wouldn't be able to understand it if he did. But with John, at least, it seems to be pretty selective. If he wants to know what's going on, he just knows."

"Then why doesn't Bruno know who killed him?"

"Good question. Obviously, there are limitations to what even a spirit can do."

He waited until after dinner to call Ricky, and Jesse answered the phone. They talked a few minutes, catching up on what had been happening in their respective lives, and Jesse announced he and Adam were leaving for Europe on Saturday morning.

"A long-overdue vacation," he explained. "Sort of a spur-of-the-moment thing. We'd been putting it off until we knew just how we'd stand after the house remodeling but decided we could manage it."

"How long will you be gone?"

"Only ten days—that's all the time Adam can spare from work. Ricky will look after everything while we're away. And as soon as we get back, we'll have to have you and your friend over for dinner."

"We'd like that. Have a great time and take lots of pictures. And give Adam my best."

"Will do. And if you'll hold, I'll go get Ricky for you."

After a minute's wait, Ricky picked up the phone.

"Hi, Elliott, how have you been? How's Steve?"

"We're both fine, thanks. Look, Ricky, there are some things I'd like to talk to you about, and was wondering if we could get together."

"Sure. Any time."

"How about this weekend? Maybe Saturday afternoon?"

"Sure. You want to come over here and see where I live? I don't think you've seen the house at all since Jesse and Adam moved in. I know they wouldn't mind."

"Fine. How about two-thirty?"

"That'll be great. I mow the lawn every Saturday afternoon, but as you know it isn't a very big yard, and I'll be sure to be through by then."

Friday night was, by mutual agreement, a movie/dinner/bar night, ending at Elliott's condo. They talked over dinner of Elliott's pending visit with Ricky, and what might be gained from it. They also talked of the nearing-completion gallery space, though neither of them speculated on when the gallery might actually open.

Elliott was mildly relieved when Steve said, "While you're over with Ricky, I think I'll spend some time online checking out what's available in movable wall panels. There's plenty of time, but it's good to plan ahead." He really wanted to talk to Ricky one-on-one without making him feel he was being ganged up on but didn't want Steve to feel he was being left out. He suspected Steve realized it and wanted to let him know he didn't expect to be invited to go along.

"Good idea. And maybe you can take a look at commercial flooring, too. We'll need to order it as early as next week. I've got a couple of catalogs around here somewhere–I'll be glad to have the office done so I'll have somewhere to put all this stuff–but see if you can find something you like to give us an idea."

Declining Elliott's offer to drive him home Saturday after breakfast–"The el's a straight shot, no problem"–Steve suggested they get together for brunch Sunday.

"I've really been neglecting my painting, and I'd like to spend as much of today as I can catching up. But I'll be ready for a break tomorrow."

"We can skip brunch if you want. I feel guilty for taking up so much of your time."

"Hey, you're not taking anything I'm not willing to give. So, twelve-thirty tomorrow?"

Chapter 9

He'd only driven past Jesse's and Adam's place since he'd finished the renovation, but seeing it again, from a more objective perspective, Elliott was impressed. It really stood out from its neighbors, and they'd done a great job landscaping the small front yard. The tiny square of grass had just been mowed, and remembering there was a slightly larger back yard he was curious to see what they'd done with it.

His knock at the front door was answered almost immediately by Ricky, who welcomed him in.

"I told Jesse and Adam you were coming by," he said, "and they said to be sure to show you around."

"They got off all right this morning?"

"Their plane left at noon, but Adam insisted they get to the airport by ten, so they left at eight-thirty. Come on, let me give you the tour."

He remembered the layout of the rooms and the changes he and his crew had made, but it was the finishing touches Jesse and Adam had added that had turned it into a real home. Ricky's room was in what was originally the attic, a large, comfortable space with its own bathroom.

He couldn't help but notice a framed photo of Ricky and Bruno on the dresser, next to a champagne bottle with a half-burnt drip candle. There was nothing else he recognized as having come from Bruno's condo.

Returning to the living room, Ricky gestured him to a seat.

"Would you like some coffee?"

"No, thanks, I'm fine."

Taking a seat himself, Ricky said, "So, what did you want to talk to me about? I did talk to the police about the certificate, by the way. They suggested I get a safe deposit box for it, and I told them I would. I haven't had a chance yet, though."

Elliott didn't ask where it was at the moment but hoped Ricky would take the detectives' advice.

"I was curious about a couple of things you might be able to help me with."

"Sure, if I can."

"Bruno told me you met at the Lucky Horseshoe."

Ricky's quickly suppressed look of embarrassment didn't escape Elliott's notice.

"Yes."

"And he said you'd just lost your job at Phelps Chrysler."

"I worked there for two years."

"But they closed at least two years before you met Bruno."

Ricky stared at the floor, and he nodded.

"I lied. I didn't want to let him know I'd been out of a job as long as I had. I really tried to find work, but..."

"Were you hustling?"

He nodded slowly. "But I didn't hustle Bruno. Honest. After we got to talking, and he was so really nice to me, I couldn't tell him I was hustling. The only reason I ever hustled was to make money. I never told my folks I'd lost my job, and I'd always sent money home to them, and when I lost my job and my unemployment was running out, one of the guys I worked with suggested I hustle, which is what he was doing. So, I did. And then, when I met Bruno, I was so afraid he'd find out."

Elliott detected a hint of Old Spice in the air.

He was tempted to ask Ricky why he hadn't looked for a job after he got together with Bruno but was fairly sure, knowing Bruno, that he wouldn't have wanted him to.

"I wasn't being critical, Ricky, but I was curious. I appreciate your being honest with me."

"So, did they find out who took the stamps? I still say it had to have been Cage."

"Not that I know of. But I'm sure they're working on it."

It suddenly occurred to Elliott the police might never have told Ricky Bruno's death hadn't been an accident, that he had been murdered. He had no intention of asking.

He did have one question that rose to the surface of his mind from something John had said about Bruno having looked up as he was falling and seen someone wearing a pair of pants.

"This is an odd question, but when the police arrived and woke everybody up after Bruno fell, was everybody fully dressed?"

Ricky's puzzlement showed clearly on his face. "Yeah. Why?"

"So, everybody was wearing pants?"

The puzzlement deepened. "Yeah. Well, Chaz had spilled a drink all over his and had put on a pair of Cage's cut-offs, but yeah."

"When was this?"

"About an hour before everybody went home. What do pants have to do with anything?"

Elliott shrugged. "They don't, really. I was just curious."

Though Ricky said nothing, it was clear he thought that was a pretty weird thing to be curious about.

Changing the subject, they talked for another half-hour or so, but other than learning Chaz wasn't wearing pants and therefore wasn't the person in Bruno's flashback of going over the balcony, Elliott didn't find out anything he didn't already know. He did come away with the impression Ricky had told him the truth as he knew it. That he didn't know more about how Bruno was dealing with his other problems could be chalked up to Bruno's trying to shield Ricky from them.

Driving home, the small swirling cloud of frustration of which he'd been aware ever since Bruno's death grew noticeably. Though it was in his own mind, it was probably, he thought, not unlike John's description of the cyclones surrounding Bruno's present state. So much he did not know, and without access to knowledge of what the police were doing, and with no real authority to do anything on his own, he felt basically powerless.

For him to call Cabrera or Guerdon would undoubtedly be considered unwelcome meddling or interfering with police business, and might cast a bad light on Brad for having a nosy brother-in-law. But, he thought, he *could* call Brad to see if he knew anything at all, or could find out without stirring up suspicion.

But that had its own, closer-to-home dangers. Brad was already more than a little suspicious of how Elliott had come by the details that had helped catch two killers in the past. For it to happen again was risky, at best. Still, he felt he had little real choice.

He had just parked in the garage and was walking toward the elevators when his cell phone rang.

"Elliott, it's Cessy."

"I thought I recognized the voice from somewhere."

"I've left a couple messages on your machine. I didn't want to bother you if you and Steve were busy. Is he with you now?"

"No, I'm just getting home. What's up?"

"Well, Brad got the urge for chili, and we made a huge pot, and we haven't had you over for dinner in such a long while, we thought maybe you and Steve might like to come by, if it's not too short notice."

"Steve's spending the weekend working on his painting, but I'm game, if I can come without him."

"Well, of course, you can. Five-thirty? That way you and Brad can have time for your beer before we eat."

"Anything I can bring?"

"Just yourself."

"Five-thirty, then."

Giving a silent thank-you to the gods of serendipity, Elliott picked up his mail and went upstairs. He thought of calling Steve but decided not to interrupt him and to wait until they got together to fill him in.

"So, how's the building coming," Brad asked as they went into the living room with their beer.

"Really well. Cessy probably told you the top-floor apartment's been rented, and we're pretty well along in finishing the ground floor. It'll be nice to have a real office for the business, and there'll be plenty of room in the basement for storage. We've always had to rent storage space before if we didn't have room to put things at the worksite."

Brad had a ball game on the TV, but knowing Elliott had little interest in it, he kept the sound turned low. They drank their beer in silence for a while until Elliott decided to take the plunge.

"I've got a favor to ask."

Brad, eyes on the TV, grinned. "Let me guess–Bruno Caesar."

"Well, yeah. It's not that I don't think Cabrera and Guerdon are doing everything they can, but since they didn't know Bruno personally, there's no way they could be as aware of everything that was going on in his life as someone who knew him."

"Like you."

"I didn't know him as well as some of the other people around him, of course, but I do think I had a better general overview than most. Those closest to him may have been too close. I was maybe at just the right distance."

"So, what do you want me to do?"

Taking a swig of his beer before replying, Elliott said, "I really don't know. I thought maybe we could kick it around and come up with something. I've said it before and I'll say it again–I am not a cop, and I have no interest in being one. I don't want to step on any toes in the department, and the last thing in the world I want is to get you in any kind of trouble. But on the positive side, I've had something to do with a couple of murderers ending up behind bars who might otherwise not be there."

"I remember. Your hunches. What hunches do you have on Caesar?"

"Very few, at the moment. But I have been checking a bunch of things out and getting some insights Cabrera and Guerdon might not have gotten simply because they're the police and I'm not. I can ask questions without spooking people the way a cop asking the same questions might. I'm not a threat."

"Unless you ask the wrong questions of the wrong people, and then you could be dead."

Brad was right, and Elliott knew it.

"Tell you what I'll do. George and Frank switched shifts from eleven-to-seven to seven-to-three. I'll see if I can talk to them individually, and I'll tell them about the help you gave us on the John Doe and Stiles cases, and ask them if you and they can pool some information. I can't promise anything, and even if they're willing, you know there are some things they won't be able to tell you. But having the three of you on the same page, even if some of the pages have marked-out passages, can't hurt in finding out who killed Caesar."

"That'd be great, Brad, thanks. I really appreciate it."

They'd just finished their beers and were watching the game when Cessy came in to call the Jennie and BJ downstairs for dinner.

⁂

–It ain't easy being dead.

–Let me wake up and get a pencil for that one. It ain't easy being alive, either, in case you don't remember. What, specifically, are you talking about?

–Ricky's having been a hustler. That was a shocker to Bruno.

–How do you know? Are you actually talking, finally?

–No, but it came through as clearly as a lightning bolt. Still, it was just an initial reaction, and there was no follow-up thunder, so I think that, while he was shocked, it didn't change the way he feels about Ricky.

–Well, that's good to know.

–And he was touched by the fact Ricky has his photo on his dresser. Again, images, not words.

–He didn't know that before?

–No. We're getting into another one of those existential philosophical mumbo-jumbo things I hate because it's nearly impossible to explain so it makes any sense.

For people like Bruno–and me, and Aaron, if you'll remember–who don't just go straight on through the gate, arriving on this side of the fence is like finding yourself in an impenetrable fog. It's the trauma of the transition, I suppose, and for most of us, the fog dissipates over time. For some it takes longer than others. And if we're lucky, we can make a connection with someone–like you, for instance–who has the ability to sense us, and who we depend on to help us get the answers we need.

But usually we don't know any more dead than we knew alive. Death doesn't bestow omniscience; we don't automatically know anything we didn't know before. It's up to people like you to find out for us. Everything you're learning about Bruno he didn't know before he died is news to him.

–You're right, it's nearly impossible to understand.

–Yeah, I guess you gotta be here.

–I'll take my time, thanks.

⁂

When he picked him up for brunch, Steve was carrying a large envelope.

"Walls and flooring," he said, noting Elliott's attention to the envelope. "I printed up some possibilities in case you want to run any of them by your guys. Oh, and I also looked at some pedestals for holding sculpture. Hey, if I'm gonna dream, I might as well dream big."

As they sat at the bar awaiting their table, Elliott told Steve of his meeting with Ricky, his talk with Brad, and his conversation with John.

"You've been busy."

Taking a sip of his drink, Elliott nodded.

"Some progress," he conceded, "but not nearly enough."

"But you believe Ricky."

"Yeah, I do. He might have known the stamps were real, but I can't see him stealing them. The only things I could see he took from the condo when he left were a picture of him with Bruno and an empty champagne bottle with a candle in it. He could have gotten away with a lot more if he'd wanted to."

"So, he's out as a suspect."

"You disagree?"

"Not at all. I always got good vibes between them."

"Well, we can't rule anybody out totally, but I think we can move Ricky to the outer perimeter of the suspects circle–and Chaz, too."

"Chaz?"

Elliott realized he hadn't told Steve about John's report of Bruno's looking up and seeing a pair of pants as he went off the balcony, so he did.

"Interesting!" Steve said, then grinned. "The suspects' circle! Wow, you really do like playing detective!"

"I'm not about to quit my day job. But John's right–if we don't help Bruno, who will?"

"Uh, the police, maybe?"

"Of course, the police. But they can't possibly know everything they really need to know, and they don't have access to the one person who could help them the most–Bruno. We do...sort of."

"But Brad said he'd put in a good word for you with the detectives on the case?"

"Cabrera and Guerdon. Yes. But whether they'll be willing to talk to somebody they might consider to be just a nosy amateur detective is another matter. I couldn't really blame them if they aren't."

"Think positive."

"May I quote you on that?"

They both grinned, and the bartender informed them their table was ready.

⁂

Before Elliott realized, it was Wednesday. Both offices and the bathroom were done, electrical work completed, and wallboarding of the main space was well underway. He had dinner at Steve's Tuesday night and went over the pricing and specs of the flooring choices from Steve's research. They came up with two they agreed on, which Elliott presented to his crew Wednesday morning for comment. Ted pointed out some potential problems with one of them, so they opted for the other; and Elliott called his flooring subcontractor to set up a meeting.

He'd had a brief conversation with John Monday night—basically just an update on Bruno's progress, which appeared to be getting back on track, with no new revelations.

Just after his lunch break, his cell phone rang.

"Mr. Smith? This is Detective Guerdon. Your brother-in-law, Detective Priebe, suggested we should get together again to go over some things about Bruno Caesar's death. Any chance you might come by the station around two-thirty?"

"Sure. I'll see you then."

The station—the 23rd, on Halsted and Addison—was the one Brad also worked out of, a classic old gem right out of a 1950s TV cop show, and it was slated for demolition when the newer, larger one just to the west of it was finished. Brad was looking forward to moving, but Elliott thought it a shame to lose another piece of the city's history.

Not wanting to bother Steve at work, he left a note on the door for him saying he'd call later.

⁂

Climbing the worn wooden steps leading from the entrance to the officer-on-duty's desk on the main floor was like stepping back in time. He stopped to ask for Detectives Cabrera and Guerdon, and was directed down a short hall to a small office with an old wooden table in the center, surrounded by eight solid, no-nonsense wooden chairs of the same vintage. He went in, and a moment later, Detective Guerdon entered.

"Have a seat," Guerdon said after they'd shaken hands. "Want some coffee?"

"No, thanks."

They both sat down as Cabrera appeared in the doorway carrying a notepad and an official-looking file. Because the width of the table and the fact Elliott was seated facing the door made shaking hands difficult, they merely exchanged nods of greeting.

"Oh-kay," Cabrera said, sitting down heavily and placing the file and notepad on the table in front of him. "I have to tell you, this isn't the way we usually do things around here, but Detective Priebe says you were a big help in the solving of a couple of previous cases. What are you, psychic?"

Elliott cringed but managed a small smile.

"Hardly. Let's just say I'm lucky, and that I pick up on things. As I told you the first time we talked, I figure that because I know most of the people you're probably looking into in your investigation, without having any vested interest in any of them, I likely have a perspective you can to use. I've been in touch with most of them since we first talked, and learned some things you might want to check out.

"But first, can you tell me if you've found out anything about the missing stamps?"

Receiving a barely perceptible nod from Cabrera, Guerdon said, "After you told us about Blanton's being in Caesar's bedroom Sunday morning, we had a long talk with him, and he swears he knows nothing about who might have taken them. He said a lot of people were going in and out of the bathroom in the master bedroom during the party, so it could have been any of them.

"He said he knew Caesar had hung them on the wall, and that he'd done everything he could to urge him to put them in a safe deposit box, but Caesar had refused. And he claims he was too concerned with looking after the boyfriend when he was there after Caesar died to notice whether the stamps were still on the wall or not.

"We took that one with a grain of salt, and we're keeping a close eye on him. We've also alerted all the leading stamp dealers in the city, who'd be pretty sure to know when stamps this valuable show up anywhere on the market, and there's been nothing so far.

"The bottom line is that finding the stamps might or might not lead to the murderer, and finding the murderer might or might not lead to finding the stamps. But for right now, our main concern is who threw Caesar off the balcony."

Elliott shook his head. "I sure don't envy you your jobs."

Guerdon leaned forward in his chair.

"So, what, specifically, do you suggest we check out?"

"I don't know everything you've done so far, and the only way to avoid going over ground you've already covered thoroughly is for me to know as much as you're willing to tell me before I start. Brad can verify I don't repeat things I hear in confidence."

The partners exchanged a glance that wasn't lost on him.

"Look, guys, I don't have any horses in this race. I'm not trying to play detective, but I don't like the idea of letting someone get away with murder, and I don't go around broadcasting things I shouldn't. It would really save us all time if we're on the same page with what we know."

Another glance, then Cabrera said, "Rudy Patterson's been on our radar for a number of years. He's definitely a con man, and he runs a couple shady operations, but he's never officially crossed the line. He claims he and Caesar were good friends and were planning a couple of joint business deals, but that was it. We tracked down some checks Caesar made out to him, but Patterson claims they were for a deal that was in progress when Caesar died. What do you know we don't?"

"I know he's lying, for one thing. Bruno was fed up with his scams, and had tried to cut him off several times, but Rudy wouldn't let go. Bruno told me he was going to have a private talk with him the night he died."

"Yeah, we knew about the talk, but Patterson says it was a business meeting."

"That's what he told me, too. But a business meeting at a party Bruno gave specifically to tell everyone who'd been dunning him for money that he was turning off the tap? Not likely. And I assume you knew Cage worked for Rudy, got fired when Rudy and Bruno had a falling out, and apparently is back in his good graces now that Bruno is dead.

"Rudy clearly still has his eye on Bruno's money, and doesn't care whether he got it from Bruno or gets it from Cage. He might consider Cage an easier mark than Bruno. I wouldn't put it past him to have made some sort of arrangement with Cage."

"Are you suggesting they might have conspired to kill Caesar?" Cabrera asked, looking up from scribbling notes.

"I'm not suggesting anything. Just throwing things out."

Cabrera nodded and resumed scribbling.

"So, how about Blanton?" Guerdon asked. "Anything on him?"

"Again, I don't want to waste your time telling you things you already know."

Guerdon leaned back in his chair. "Like with Patterson, we don't have anything specific on him. There's a pending civil lawsuit from one of his former clients for repayment of a loan. We looked into his having put Caesar in touch with the guy he bought the missing stamps from, and it was apparently legit.

"Blanton lives pretty far above his means, and from what we can tell, he's barely hanging on with his seminars and what he calls counseling. His credit cards are maxed out, but the only real motive we can come up with is the check he cashed two days before Caesar died. The jury's still out on whether it's a strong enough motive for murder. People have killed for less. But we're watching him."

Elliott realized he didn't have anything specifically incriminating on Blanton, but he told them about the resort project and the proposed infomercials, both of which depended on Bruno's backing.

"Bruno thought the sun rose and set on this guy," he said, "and for him to realize, probably after getting that phone call from the real estate agent for the resort, that Blanton was pretty much on the same level as Rudy could have sparked a confrontation. Blanton told me he was at the party for moral support, but I wonder if Bruno wasn't cutting him off, too.

"And if Bruno tried to stop payment on that last check he wrote to Blanton only to find out it had already been cashed, and demanded the money back, that would have painted Blanton into a pretty tight corner."

"What about the boyfriend?" Guerdon asked. "Anything on him you think we should know? He stands to come out of this with a couple million dollars."

Elliott nodded. "True, but I had a talk with him the other day, and he really comes across as a good kid. He seemed genuinely surprised when Bruno gave him the certificate for the stamps. He told you about it, right?"

Both detectives nodded.

"We told him to put it in a safe deposit box," Cabrera said. "I still can't imagine that anybody would just leave two million dollars hanging on his wall. I hope to hell his boyfriend has a little more sense, frankly."

"And as for his being surprised when you handed him the certificate, that doesn't mean he didn't take the stamps," Guerdon added.

"You're right, of course, but his reaction didn't strike me as the kind of 'now-I've-got-it-all' surprise he might have shown if he already had the stamps. And even though Bruno gave him the certificate, I'd imagine Cage could and will contest it. So, whether or not Ricky will ever benefit from the stamps is still way up in the air. But I really do think he cared for Bruno and wasn't out to rip him off."

The detectives remained silent, so Elliott moved on.

"What do you know about Walter Means, Bruno's financial manager?"

"We checked him out and he seems legit. He's lost a number of clients lately, but claims it was due to the economy's tanking. He claimed everything was fine between him and Caesar, though he admitted they had a couple strong disagreements over Caesar's unwillingness to follow his advice."

"Well, that isn't exactly true. Bruno was getting ready to fire the guy. And I assume you knew Means is the executor of Bruno's will?"

"He didn't volunteer the information, but we check the will out with the Clerk of Courts as a matter of routine in cases like this. It looks like it was pulled off the internet–about as basic as it could get. Names one beneficiary and specifies Means as executor.

"We called Means on that, and he says Caesar didn't have a will when he was hired, so Means had him make a basic one out practically on the spot, telling him he could amend it later. He claims that, since controlling a client's money while the client is alive is what financial managers do, his being the executor of the will isn't unusual. And since he's not named in the will and doesn't benefit directly from it, we let it go."

"*Directly* is the operative word here," Elliott pointed out, "Plus, he controls all the money until the estate is closed, and I wouldn't put it past him to do a little sleight-of-hand. Bruno suspected he was doing just that, though I don't know how he might have proved it, and I know he was seriously considering firing Means. The possibility of losing control of all that money would seem like a pretty good motive to me."

Cabrera nodded. "Well, the bottom line is that having a motive is not the same as committing murder. We just have to keep working at it until we get the right answer. Anything else you can think of at the moment?"

"Not at the moment, but if I run into these guys on a casual basis and I find out anything, I assume you want to know about it?"

"Of course. Just keep in mind that running into someone casually is one thing. Actively playing detective is another. We'll be happy to hear anything you might come across, but we strongly suggest you leave the police work to us."

"Not a problem. I appreciate your hearing me out."

"Like you said, no problem."

As if on cue, both Cabrera and Guerdon got up, and Elliott followed suit.

"Thanks for coming in," Guerdon said as Elliott walked around the table to shake hands with both detectives. They then escorted him to the main desk, where they turned to go back the way they'd come and Elliott headed for the door and the street.

❧

He'd gone into the meeting hoping, but not expecting, to learn something that might indicate where they were on the case and where he might look. However, other than the reassurance they were actively working on it, he didn't come away with much. They were playing their cards close to the vest, as he'd expected, but he did hope they might have found something in what he said that could be of help.

He debated going back to Armitage then decided against it and headed home. Going over the meeting on his way, he realized that, for all practical purposes, unless he could find out something new about Bruno's possible murderer himself, he was pretty much at a standstill.

He was also mildly concerned that what he might have expected to be mounting frustration was, instead, resignation. He didn't want to be resigned. Somebody had killed Bruno, and that somebody had to be found. He was just less and less confident he would be the one to do it.

He called Steve before beginning dinner to tell him about the meeting, and the conclusions he had drawn on the way home.

"Don't give up just yet," Steve urged. "Something will turn up that will point you in the right direction. I'm sure of it."

Elliott sighed. "Maybe. I hope so. But to be honest, I'm not very confident at the moment."

They talked for a few more minutes then hung up, and Elliott went into the kitchen. He wasn't in the mood to cook, so he took a frozen dinner from the freezer and put it in the microwave.

As he did so, he remembered he hadn't picked up his mail and decided to run down to the lobby to get it. As he passed the doorman's desk, he noted a FedEx van in front of the building, just forward of the revolving doors. It was parked directly over the spot where Bruno's body had landed, and he felt a very odd sense of sadness.

He went to the mailbox, pulled out the contents and, without looking through it, went back to the lobby just as the delivery man, pushing a dolly stacked with four boxes marked "Fillion Fils," said "Thanks" to Marco and headed for the elevators.

"A little late for a delivery, isn't it?" Elliott asked, pausing at the desk and indicating the delivery man with a tilt of his head. "And I thought all deliveries had to come in the back."

"They do, for most people. But it's the Means's anniversary this Saturday, and Mrs. Means insisted the champagne for the party be delivered today. The service entrance is locked at five o'clock, so he came around here. I wasn't about to risk getting the wife of the president of the board mad at me by telling him he had to come back tomorrow."

⁂

After dinner, Elliott called Brad to tell him of his meeting with Cabrera and Guerdon. Cessy, as usual, answered the phone.

"I'm glad you called, Elliott," she said before he had a chance to ask to speak to Brad. "I've had an idea I'd like to mention to Steve, now that you're almost done with the ground floor."

"What's that, Sis?"

"I know you've both said he won't be opening a gallery for some time yet, but every time I look at that painting of the rose he did for me, I've envied him his talent and wished I could do something like that. So, I was wondering if he might consider giving painting lessons–or maybe teaching a painting class. I know I'd love to learn how to paint, and when I mentioned to some of my friends that Steve was an artist and that maybe I might talk him into giving me lessons, several of them said it sounded like a wonderful idea and they'd be interested, too."

"Well, I don't know, Sis. You certainly could talk to him about it. Whether or not he'd be willing to do it I can't say."

"The only way to know is to ask. I'll do that, then. I just wanted to check with you before I called. Thank you!"

"You're welcome. Is Brad around?"

"Of course. Just a minute."

There was the usual thirty seconds or so of silence before: "Elliott. How did it go?"

"Ah, you knew I was getting together with Cabrera and Guerdon today?"

"They said they were going to call you."

"And they did. I just wanted to thank you for putting in a word for me. I know it was an imposition, and you went beyond the call of duty to do it."

"It wasn't that hard to convince them. From what I gather, they need all the help they can get, and as I told them, you do have more of an in with the people involved than they do."

"Exactly the point I tried to make."

"So, how did it go?"

"Okay, I guess. They listened to everything I had to say, asked a few questions, and that was that. I don't know if anything I told them might help, or even if any of it was news to them, but at least I tried, and that's all I wanted."

"I'll keep you posted if I hear anything," Brad said.

After hanging up, Elliott went into the den to watch TV until it was time to go to bed. He didn't remember falling asleep, but it seemed his head had barely hit the pillow before:

–Something's going on.

–With Bruno? What?

–I have no idea, and I can't tell whether he even knows for sure himself. I can't get anything at all specific. But whatever it is, it's big.

–Then how can he not know what it is?

–You keep expecting things to make sense on your level. Sense and logic are the glue that hold the living's world together. They don't necessarily work the same way for those of us on this side. All I know is that, because of the timing, it must have something to do with today.

–My meeting with Cabrera and Guerdon? Bruno knows about that?

–I can't be positive, but I'd suspect so. I get the impression he's pretty much tuned in to you, which isn't surprising, I suppose. He's counting on you for help.

–I wish I could give him more. But I can't imagine what it might be. Is there any way at all you could find out what triggered this latest reaction?

–Like I said, I don't know if he knows himself. But I'll keep trying.

Chapter 10

He met with his flooring subcontractor Thursday, who said he could get exactly what Elliott wanted, and that the flooring could start the next week. He also, during his lunch break, called Larry Fingerhood to tell him to start looking at potential properties for the next project.

By the end of the workday, the two offices were all but finished, with lighting fixtures, including a circle of small adjustable ceiling light spots around each of the center support posts, installed throughout the main floor. Elliott would buy the paint Monday, and they'd start painting Tuesday.

Steve called to ask whether Elliott would be going directly home from work.

"No, I wanted to talk to you about a couple of things. I'll be here when you get home."

"Good. I wanted to tell you about a call I got from Cessy last night."

Elliott smiled. "Can't wait to hear about it."

They were walking to the door upstairs, having spent some time talking about the progress and the painting, when they saw Button coming from the direction of the el. He waved and hastened to join them.

"Amazing," he said. "We live one floor apart, and we never see one another. How does that happen?"

Both Elliott and Steve grinned.

"Life's strange," Steve observed.

"Indeed, it is. Well, can I ask you two up for a drink now that we've finally run into one another?"

Exchanging a quick glance of confirmation with Steve, Elliott said, "Sure."

"Normally, I run out to the Anvil for a drink after work–I know it's miles and miles out of my way, but I am a creature of habit."

As they took a seat, Elliott glanced around the apartment, noting that Paul's comment about Button's OCD seemed to have some merit. The place was immaculate.

Moving to the stereo, Button quickly ran his index finger across a long row of CDs and chose one. He slipped it into the player, and the opening notes of the *Cabaret* overture filled the room.

Smiling broadly, he said, "Nothing like a little Liza Minnelli after a long day's work. Now, how about some champagne?"

"What's the occasion?" Steve asked.

With a wide-eyed look of surprise, Button said, "Thursday," and, excusing himself, went to the kitchen. Elliott and Steve looked at one another and grinned.

"I do hope you'll be taking the paper off the windows downstairs soon," Button called to them. "I'm dying to see what you've done with it."

"We'll be painting and putting in the new flooring next week," Elliott replied, raising his voice so it would carry into the kitchen, "then we'll have you down to look at it."

A muffled *pop!* was followed by "I'd like that. Have you decided yet what you're going to do with it?"

Elliott was a little surprised to realize they'd never told Button about the gallery.

"Steve's going to open a gallery."

"Eventually," Steve hastened to add.

Button reentered the room with a large silver tray on which were a silver ice bucket containing a bottle of champagne, three crystal flutes, a plate of cocktail crackers, and a small crystal bowl of what appeared to be caviar.

"See?" he said, setting the tray on the glass-and-chrome coffee table, "I knew we had a reason to celebrate!" He poured the wine and handed Elliott and Steve theirs. "To success," he said, raising his glass.

Steve and Elliott stood up for the clicking of the glasses. When they were reseated, Button took a sip then said, "A gallery! How wonderful! I can't wait!"

"Do you have champagne and caviar every Thursday?" Steve asked, reaching for a cracker and the small spoon in the center of the bowl.

"Unfortunately, no, but I look for any excuse. I never drink champagne alone. One of my long-time customers is an importer, and he gives me a great price on both the champagne and the caviar. I give him a discount on his suits." Taking another sip, he said, "So, have you heard anything new on who killed Bruno?"

Elliott took the spoon from Steve and moved forward to take a cracker.

"I know the police are still investigating. I'm sure they'll find whoever was responsible."

"Well, I certainly hope so. I still can't grasp the idea that Bruno is dead, let alone that he was murdered!"

Recognizing an opportunity when he saw one, Elliott said, "Did Bruno mention having any specific difficulty with anyone before he died?"

Leaning to reach the coffee table, Button placed a small spoonful of caviar on a cracker.

"Other than the witches from Macbeth I'd mentioned before? Rudy, Cage, and 'Sensei' Blanton?"

"Yeah. And did he talk to you about his financial manager, Walter Means?"

"Other than that he didn't trust him farther than he could throw him? No, but that was a continuing theme. He did say you had offered to help him find another manager, and he was thinking seriously of taking you up on it."

"You weren't at the party the night he died, you said."

"No. I do know Bruno was dreading it–he hated confrontation, which is one of the reasons people thought they could walk all over him. He said he was planning to have a private chat with those who had 'borrowed' money promising to pay it back and never did. And then he was going to make a general announcement that any future requests for money would have to go through his financial manager. He didn't trust Means, but he figured Means should start earning his keep, and that turning the requests for money over to him would take some of the pressure off. He knew Means would automatically say no to any request.

"He originally told me he was inviting Clifford to the party for moral support, but when we talked the day before, he said he was going to talk to him, too, which puzzled me. When I asked him why, he said he'd given him a check a couple of days before, and that something had happened and he wanted his money back. Though he didn't say what the problem was, it must have been pretty serious, because I'd never known him to be even mildly upset with Clifford before."

Button's expression momentarily changed to one of sadness, and he stopped talking for a moment, staring into his glass. Then, as though he'd flipped a mental switch, his face brightened, and he lifted his head, smiling.

"So, enough of that. Tell me all about your plans for the gallery."

"It's Steve's baby," Elliott said, tossing the conversational ball to Steve, who was obviously a little hesitant to catch it.

"We haven't made any detailed plans just yet, but I'm mulling a lot of things over in my head."

"Well, I'm sure it will be absolutely wonderful, and I'll insist all my friends come by with their checkbooks."

They talked for another fifteen minutes, and then, declining Button's offer to open another bottle of champagne, Steve and Elliott thanked him for his hospitality and headed downstairs.

"Shall we just run out to grab something for dinner?" Elliott asked. "I don't want you to have to cook."

"I don't mind cooking. I think I've got some frozen enchiladas from that last batch I made a while ago. I'd almost forgotten about them, and they really should be used before long."

"Who am I to argue with your enchiladas? Sounds good. Want me to run to the convenience store for some chips and salsa or anything else you might need?"

"Some beer, maybe. And sour cream, if they have any."

"Done. See you in a minute."

"Forget the gallery," Elliott said, scooping a large dollop of sour cream onto his enchilada. "You should open a Mexican restaurant. I keep forgetting how good these are!"

"Well, maybe we could combine the two. A Mexican restaurant and an art gallery. Maybe knock a hole in the wall to the alley so we could have a drive-through."

Returning from a trip to the refrigerator for two more beers, Elliott said, "So, you still sure on the colors?"

"Cream for the ceiling, burgundy for the walls. Yep. They'll look great with the grey wall panels. Why? You having second thoughts?"

"No. I like the idea of carrying some of the exterior colors inside. I plan to pick the paint up during the day Monday, unless you want me to wait until you get home so you can go with me."

"I trust you."

"Good to know. So, what about your conversation with Cessy?"

"She called last night and asked if I might consider teaching a painting class. She said she's always wanted to try painting and had a couple of friends she thought would also be interested."

"And what did you say?"

"I told her I'd never really thought about it. I don't know how qualified I am to be a teacher. I mean, painting's so subjective."

"Exactly. No textbooks, no grading, no lectures. All you'd be doing is sharing your enthusiasm for art and giving them some basic advice on different techniques and what works and what doesn't, and why. And you've got all this space just sitting here until you're ready to open."

"Hmmm. Well, on the one hand, it might be fun, and a good way to promote the gallery, especially when we're first starting out. But there are always a ton of problems you never see until you're too far in to back out."

"That's true with every business."

"Point. And this might at least bring in a little money. I still feel bad about your just sitting on this big, empty space without any money coming in." He sighed. "The problem is that I don't have nearly enough time to work on my own things–nothing at all to do with you, it's just a fact of life."

"I understand. But nothing has to be done this minute. Take some time to think it over. Cessy won't be upset if you say no."

"She already told you about this, didn't she?"

"She mentioned she wanted to talk to you but didn't want to bother you if I thought you wouldn't be interested. I told her the only way to find out was to ask. She didn't tell me she'd be calling the same night, before I had a chance to tell you."

"A lot going on."

"For sure. And I'll be one happy camper when we put this Bruno thing behind us."

"And so will Bruno, I'm sure."

Realizing he hadn't yet told Steve about his most recent talk with John, he said, "Speaking of Bruno…"

When he'd finished, Steve said, "Did you figure out what it was all about?"

"No. It has to be about something Cabrera, Guerdon and I talked about during our meeting, but I've gone over and over it and can't figure out what it could have been. I hope I might have given them a few things to think about, but if Bruno has some idea of what we're doing–and John seems to think he does–nothing we said should have come as any great surprise. So, I honestly don't know what set him off. But John's sure that whatever it was is important."

As he was lifting his beer to take a drink, Elliott detected the faint scent of Old Spice. He glanced at Steve, who said nothing but gave him a small smile and a raised eyebrow.

❧

Though he was home by ten and went to bed shortly thereafter, Elliott not only couldn't fall asleep but had no idea what was keeping him awake. He was still thinking about what could have caused Bruno's most recent outburst, although no more intently than he had been since it occurred, and he'd had no problem getting to sleep on previous nights.

He lay there, trying to block out any thought that would set off a chain reaction of frets and conjectures, and–with equal lack of success–not to look at the clock every five minutes. He would begin to drift off only to be yanked back awake.

Finally, at 2:26 a.m., it occurred to him to see if the boredom of late-late-night TV might do the trick. He couldn't remember the last time he'd awakened in the middle of the night to turn the TV on.

He began flipping through the channels, almost immediately bored. He was just about to give it up as an exercise in futility when a delayed reaction made him suddenly flip back to the channel he had just passed.

There, in front of a lectern and a banner proclaiming "Inner Peace Institute," stood one Clifford Blanton, earnestly extolling the necessity and virtues of harmony between body and soul to a rapt group of apparently enthralled listeners. Elliott noticed that, as in most of the infomercials he had seen, the camera never used a wide angle when focusing on the audience, to give the impression it was considerably larger than it was.

Blanton? Doing an infomercial? Rudy had told him Blanton was trying to convince Bruno to back him in making some but hadn't mentioned Blanton was already on TV. He probably hadn't been then, and Elliott immediately wondered where the money had come from, and when. He made a mental note of the station, and determined to call them to see just how long the program had been running.

He flipped off the TV and soon fell asleep.

⁂

He checked the Yellow Pages before leaving for work Friday morning, found the station's phone number and wrote it down. During the morning break, he called and asked to speak to the advertising manager.

"This is Alexia Reynolds. How can I help you?"

"I happened to catch a program on your channel this morning at two-thirty–about the Inner Peace Institute. I was wondering how I might find earlier episodes, or if you'll be doing reruns of previous shows."

He heard the soft click of a computer keyboard, then: "It began airing two nights ago, but they're scheduled to run regularly for the next three months. And I'm sure a contact number appears at the end of the program so you can reach the sponsor directly."

"Ah, I must have missed it. Thank you. I'll watch for it."

⁂

He and Steve had earlier planned a dinner-out, movies-at-Elliott's evening, so as soon as Steve got home he told him about his discovery.

"Doesn't that strike you as a little odd?" Steve asked as they had a drink at his place before going for dinner.

"What's that?"

"You never have trouble sleeping. And then you to wake up at just the right time and turn on just the right channel–are you sure John didn't tell you to do it?"

Elliott shook his head. "I didn't go directly to the right channel. And no John. I never forget a conversation with him, and we didn't have one last night. And there was no scent of Old Spice, if that was your next question."

Steve grinned. "It was. So, how do you suppose...?"

Pausing to take a sip of his drink before answering, Elliott said, "I have no idea. And I'm not sure I want to know."

"So, what are you going to do?"

"I can call Guerdon and Cabrera and maybe suggest they take another look at Blanton's finances. It's possible he found another rich patron, but with all the effort he'd been putting into Bruno, it's a little unlikely he could have come up with one this fast.

"First, though, I think I'll give that real estate agent up in Wisconsin a call to see if the resort Blanton was trying to get Bruno to invest in is still on the market. Speaking of which, have you given any further thought to the painting class idea?"

"Yeah, though I haven't come to any decision yet. So many things to consider. How many people would want to sign up? How would I advertise it? How much would I charge?

"And that set me off on a bunch of other things, like maybe I could buy a couple movable wall panels and put them up front when you take the paper off the windows, and display some of my paintings on them. But then I started looking at what's available in movable panels, and they ain't cheap."

"Well, on that score, let me talk to Arnie and see if maybe we can figure out how to make them ourselves–at least temporary ones. I think it's a great idea for you to put up some of your own work, maybe with a note on the window or door about how someone can reach you if they're interested. And maybe you might want to give Ralph a call and kick some thoughts around with him."

"Yeah, I could do that. Maybe we could have him over for dinner one night."

"Sounds good."

Shortly after Steve left the next morning, again insisting on taking the el, to spend the afternoon painting, Elliott went online to the Wisconsin real estate agency's website. The photo of the resort Blanton wanted was still up but with a "Sold" banner across it. He wasn't surprised.

Although he doubted the agent would be open on a Saturday, he called. The phone was picked up on the second ring.

"Superior Realty."

A female voice this time, and Elliott was rather relieved he wouldn't be talking with the same person, who might remember his earlier call.

"Yes, I was calling about the resort I saw on your website a few weeks ago, and was wondering if it were still available?"

"I'm sorry, sir, it was sold just last week."

"Ah, too bad. Someone from Chicago got it, I'll bet."

"No, the buyers are from New York. They plan to turn it into a retreat of some sort."

It took a moment for that to sink in.

"I see," he said finally. "The buyer wouldn't be a Mr. Blanton, by any chance?"

"No, it was a company called the Ferrell Group."

"I see. Well, I thank you for your time."

"But if you'd like to give me your name and phone number, I'd be happy to contact you if a similar property becomes available."

"Thank you, but I can always just check your site. I appreciate your help."

New York? A retreat?

His immediate impulse was to call Cabrera and Guerdon–or, since it was the weekend, to at least leave a message for them. Yet he realized that would be premature in the extreme. He had absolutely no way of knowing if Blanton were involved. If the woman had just said the buyer was from New York, he probably would have let it drop. But that it was going to be used as a retreat just seemed too much of a coincidence.

Whether Blanton had any connections in New York, he didn't know.

His reverie was interrupted by the ringing of his cell. An automatic check of the caller ID showed it was Steve.

"Steve Gutierrez! How the hell have you been? It's been too long."

Steve laughed. "I know, I know, and I hope I'm not interrupting you, but I was wondering. Did you just get a really strong whiff of Old Spice? I was working on a painting, and it's like someone held an open bottle under my nose."

"No. No Old Spice, but..." and Elliott related the results of his call.

Steve said nothing for a moment, but when he spoke his tone reflected his puzzlement.

"This is getting curiouser and curiouser. Why would I smell it and you not? You think it has something to do with your call?"

"Well, that the phone call and the Old Spice pretty much coincided is a good indication it does. And as for the 'curiouser and curiouser' part, I wonder what the link is between Blanton and New York, and exactly who it was who bought the resort?"

"You're going to tell the police about it, aren't you? Have them check into it?"

"Yeah, but we're walking on some pretty thin eggshells. I don't want Cabrera and Guerdon–or Brad, for that matter–to think I'm trying to use the police as a private detective agency. They already think I'm strange–including Brad."

"*You* could hire a private investigator."

"Yeah, I could, but do I really want to? I'm way too far into this John/Bruno paranormal thing as it is. I don't want it to intrude any more into my private life–*our* private lives–than it already has."

"Like we have a choice?"

"Let's not even go near that one."

"Okay. Well, I'd better get back to my painting. How about brunch tomorrow? Or dinner, and that way you could just stay over. Better a walk down one flight of stairs than driving six miles."

"Around six?"

"See you then."

⁂

Elliott went to bed early, hoping to hear from John. He segued seamlessly from closing his eyes to being at a cocktail party. One of Bruno's, he knew-without-knowing, as is the nature of dreams.

–Well, this is a first.

He turned around to find John standing behind him. Though John had never appeared to him before, other than as a voice in his head while he slept, he recognized him immediately from the postmortem photo Brad had shown him shortly after John entered his life. The shock almost woke him up, and his mind swam toward the surface of consciousness only to be pulled back down, back to the party.

–What the hell is going on?

The dream-John smiled.

–I'm not sure. But it's interesting.

Cage was snorting lines of coke from a silver tray, using a rolled-up thousand-dollar bill, while Ricky leaned against one wall crying. Rudy and Blanton were at the buffet table grabbing fistfuls of money from an array of dishes filled with currency. Walter Means stood at the far end of the table wearing a Nazi SS uniform, sipping from a glass of champagne while viewing the scene with a combined look of boredom and disdain. Around the room, groups of guys sat on the floor, spoons in hand, scooping coins from what looked to Elliott like pig troughs.

He spotted Steve across the room, looking at him with bemusement and shaking his head.

Then everyone was gone except Bruno, who stood at the glass door to the balcony, looking out over the city. Elliott could see his face reflected in the glass. He was not smiling.

Bobbing to the surface of consciousness, Elliott opened his eyes to look around the darkened bedroom then drifted back to sleep.

–As I said, that was a first.

No images, no dream, just John's voice.

–And I hope to hell it's a last. What was *that?*

–A dream. But not yours.

–Bruno's? I'm having Bruno's dreams now? This is going way, way too far.

–Don't panic. If you'll remember, when we first got together you had a couple of mine. Mountains. Remember?

–Right. But nothing like this! Dr. Freud would have a field day.

–I'm sure he would, though the symbolism could have been a little subtler. But like I said, don't worry about it. I think it could be a sign of real progress.

–I'd say it was about time.

He'd just gotten out of the shower when his land-line phone rang. Padding into the den while vigorously toweling his hair, he picked up the receiver.

"Elliott Smith."

"Ell! Hope I didn't wake you."

"No, I just got out of the shower. What's up?"

"This is gonna sound weird, but I had the oddest dream last night..."

❧

Stopping on the way to Steve's to pick up a bucket of chicken, Elliott drove into the garage under the deck at five-forty-five, walked to the front of the building and went upstairs.

"Drink first?" Steve asked as Elliott handed him the bags containing their dinner.

"Definitely!" He followed him into the kitchen.

As he set the oven on warm and opened the door to put the bucket of chicken in, Steve pointed to the refrigerator.

"Beer okay?"

"Sure."

They returned to the living room and sat down.

"So, that was John standing behind you? Nice-looking guy, from what I could tell."

"Yeah, he is...was. It was really good to actually..." He paused and made a dismissive wave with his beer."Well, figuratively...see him, even for a few seconds."

They had briefly compared their recollections of the dream during their earlier phone conversation, and the details each recalled were basically identical. They had cut their conversation off after about ten minutes to get on with their day, agreeing to talk more about it when they got together. Getting on with the day had proved to be easier said than done, and the dream stayed in the forefront of Elliott's mind.

"What do you think it all means?" Steve asked, returning from the kitchen after getting them another beer and checking the oven.

"Remember that dream we both had when we first got together and I was trying to find out who John was and who killed him?"

"The one about the mansion on the lake?"

"Yeah, that one. John was just testing his wings, so to speak, and I think last night Bruno was doing the same thing. But even if he does start communicating more directly with John, that still doesn't mean he knows who killed him. I just hope he might somehow be able to point us in the right direction."

"Maybe you'll be able to communicate directly with Bruno yourself."

Elliott looked at him, long and hard.

"Lord, I hope not! And I hope to hell he doesn't try to go through you, either. That's a big door I don't think either one of us wants to open."

Steve considered that for a long moment.

"You're right. But what do I do if he tries?"

"Good question. I'll ask John to make it clear to Bruno that if he wants our help, everything is to go through John."

Steve didn't look convinced.

"I just hope it works." He took a long swig of his beer and suppressed a belch before saying, "Have you decided for sure about telling the police about the resort and the infomercials?"

"I think so. I'd really like to know where the money's coming from, and they're in a better position to find out than I am...than we are."

Steve grinned. "Hey, that's okay, Ell. I appreciate your including me in all this, but it's your ball game. I'll be happy to do anything I can to help, but I'm just basically an interested spectator with a really good seat. That's another reason I'm with you in hoping Bruno doesn't try to get me more involved–it would just muddy the waters."

Elliott hoped his relief did not show too clearly.

"Thanks, Steve, I don't want you to ever think I'm holding things back from you. And two heads are always better than one when it comes to sorting some of this stuff out. I'm glad you're here...for a lot of reasons."

"Well, if dinner weren't ready, I'd suggest a side trip to the bedroom right now."

Reflecting Steve's grin, Elliott said, "Yeah, you'd better stoke up on the calories. I think you'll need them."

❧

Just before heading out the door Monday morning, he called the 23rd to leave a message asking detectives Cabrera and Guerdon to give him a call and was surprised when, just he and his crew were breaking for lunch, the two detectives showed up at the worksite.

"We were just down the street when we called in and got your message. Figured we'd stop by."

"Glad you did," Elliott said. "Let's go in the back where we can talk."

With a nod to Arnie, Ted and Sam, he led the detectives to his all-but-finished office, where he'd brought in a couple of folding chairs from home a week before.

"So, what's up?" Cabrera asked as Elliott closed the door behind them.

Neither of the officers sat down.

He told them of seeing the infomercial, of calling the real estate agency, and of learning that the resort's purchaser was from New York. When he finished, both detectives remained silent for a moment.

"We understand your interest in this case, and appreciate the time you've put into it," Cabrera said. "We'll talk to Blanton to see what he has to say about this latest information, but to be frank, Mr. Smith, this isn't the only case we're working on, and our time and resources are limited. While it might be significant that the New York buyers plan to use the lodge for the same purpose Blanton had in mind, it's also entirely possible it's just a coincidence.

"And the fact of the matter is that, while several people had a reason to kill Caesar, we still haven't been able to find any solid evidence that anyone did."

Anticipating Elliott's protest, Guerdon stepped in.

"That Caesar had drugs in his system is a fairly good indication it might have been foul play, but there was a party going on, and chloral hydrate is considered a recreational drug. We can't be sure whether the other men in the apartment had also taken it, so..."

Elliott caught just a hint of Old Spice.

"We'll look into any possible connection between Blanton and whoever bought the resort, but we just want you to understand there's only so much we can do."

"I understand. And I really don't mean to make a pest of myself or add to your workload, but there are just a lot of small details that might really mean something."

"True in every case, and we find not being able to follow up on all of them as frustrating as you do. But we do the best we can."

"I know, and I think I said before, I don't envy you your job."

"And we don't mean to discourage you," Guerdon said. "If you come across anything solid, don't hesitate to call."

He extended his hand, which told Elliott the meeting was over, and after exchanging a handshake with Cabrera as well, he led them to the front door.

❧

Elliott called Steve when he got home to tell him he'd picked up the paint for the gallery space, then told him of the visit from Cabrera and Guerdon and their not-so-subtle hint they thought he was more a nuisance than a help.

"Sorry to hear that,"

"I'm not surprised, really. They're right."

"So, what now?"

"I'm not sure. I'll have to think about it."

"You want to come by for a drink tomorrow night after work?"

"Sure. I'll see you then."

❧

It was nearly eleven-thirty by the time he got to bed, but it seemed as though his head had just hit the pillow when John was with him.

–Busy time.

–Yeah, I was wondering why I hadn't heard from you since our little group-dream thing. What's going on with Bruno?

–We're talking, sort of...it's a little hard to explain. Anyway, he knows about your talking with Cabrera and Guerdon today, and he's really concerned they're giving up on finding out what happened to him.

–I don't think that's true at all. But they did have a point about their not having the ability to track down every single possibility. I have to admit, the New York thing is *a bit of a stretch.*

–I'm not so sure. I get the feeling there may be some connection between Blanton and New York, but I haven't a clue what it might be. We're not conversing that fluently yet, but I'll keep trying.

–Please, do.

–Oh, and I did mention to him that everything will go a lot smoother if he just concentrates on trying to communicate more clearly with me rather than spreading himself thin trying to involve you and Steve.

–Thanks, but how did you know I wanted to ask you that? Oh, that's right. I keep forgetting you know what I'm thinking.

–Sometimes. Only sometimes. Not always. We've talked about this before. Don't start getting paranoid on me.

–You're right. So, I'll just wait to hear if you can find out anything more about Blanton and New York.

–Well, one of the things about being dead is that time doesn't have the same urgency it does for the living, and until the, uh...let's call them the new arrivals...get a handle on it, things can either drag out or fast forward so quickly it would give the living whiplash. That's pretty much what's going on with Bruno now.

❧

Though he wasn't dead, Elliott could understand the concept of time's ability to cause mental whiplash. He thought of those periods as "blurdays"—one day blending into the next with no clear dividing lines.

Painting the entire gallery area, the two offices and the bathroom blurred Tuesday and Wednesday, and the arrival and laying of the new flooring Thursday and Friday took care of the rest of the workweek. Plus, he'd talked to Cessy two or three times and Brad once, and heard briefly from John on Wednesday, only to learn Bruno was circling Blanton's New York connection without actually making it clear yet.

Larry called to say he'd lined up a couple of potential properties for Elliott to consider for his next project. Work on the basement storage areas and getting things organized there would take up a couple of days the following week, but after that, the Armitage project would be finished and it would be time to move on.

He'd also, in addition to talking with Steve every day, had dinner and a sleepover at Steve's on Thursday. That Steve was busily making plans for the opening of the gallery, even though he didn't talk very much about it, was evidenced by his suggestion they have Ralph over for dinner Sunday.

"Maybe he can bring over a portfolio of his work so you can see how talented he is."

Elliott grinned. "I'd like to see it, but I hope you don't think you have to get my approval for anything. If you decide you want to work with him when the gallery opens, that's fine with me. This is your baby."

"Yeah, but we're partners, don't forget."

"Believe me, I won't."

⁂

He spent Saturday catching up on paperwork, getting things ready to transfer to his new office and researching on the internet for office desks and chairs. He looked forward to the extra room in his den removing the two file cabinets currently there would create. He also drove by the properties Larry had mentioned and made a note on two he wanted to take a closer look at.

Because Steve wanted to finish his current painting, they decided to skip their usual Saturday night get-together. Ralph had accepted Steve's invitation to dinner Sunday at six-thirty, and Elliott planned to go over around three to transport a few office things and do a final clean-up of the ground floor–sweep, pick up leftover material from the floor laying, throw out the trash.

Steve brought him down a cup of coffee as he was finishing the sweeping.

"This is really beautiful, Ell," he said, looking around. "When are you going to take down the paper from the windows? I'm anxious to see it in full light."

"I wanted to talk to you about that. I was thinking of having Ted build a stand-alone modular panel for you first. We can hang one of your paintings with a display light and put it in front of the first support post. All the focus would be on the painting, and it might give people an idea of what's to come."

"That's a terrific idea, Ell!"

"So, if you can do a sketch of what you want the panel to look like, and what kind of covering you want for it, I can give it to Ted tomorrow."

"As it happens, I already did a couple, and have a good idea of the fabric. I'll give them to you later, and you can tell me if Ted thinks they're practical."

While Elliott drank his coffee, Steve wandered around the empty space and the two offices, taking everything in.

"This is great, Ell. Really great. I never dreamed I might really have my own gallery someday. And I never could have if I hadn't met you."

"That's nice of you to say, but don't sell yourself short."

Steve grinned. "Think we've got time for me to show you a little appreciation before I have to start dinner."

"Here?" Elliott asked, both a little surprised and instantly turned on.

"Who's to see? The windows are covered in paper. And we could step into your office so you could have a seat and make yourself more comfortable."

"'Ya talked me into it."

❧

Ralph arrived a few minutes after six, a quilted black messenger bag over one shoulder and a bottle of wine in his hand. Elliott had only seen him twice before, at Bruno's parties, but his recollected favorable impressions were verified. A little taller than he remembered, but with the remembered striking up-tilted eyes, flawless skin and silky black hair.

Steve fixed them all a drink.

"Why don't we take a run downstairs to show Ralph the ground floor before it gets dark? We can take our drinks."

Elliott noticed he hadn't referred to it as a "gallery."

Ralph, after a "grand tour," was duly impressed.

"This will make a beautiful gallery. The whole building is fantastic. I remember it from when I was a kid and my grandmother lived right down the street. What a change!"

It was pretty clear he and Steve had talked about the plans for the gallery, and that Ralph shared Steve's enthusiasm.

When they returned to the apartment, Steve excused himself to see about dinner and suggested Ralph show Elliott his portfolio while he was gone.

"You don't mind?" Ralph asked.

"Not at all."

Retrieving his messenger bag from the chair where he'd set it when he came in, he followed Elliott to the couch.

Though Elliott didn't consider himself a connoisseur, he recognized Ralph's talent and liked most of what he saw of his work; what he didn't care for he chalked up to personal preference. As Steve had told him, Ralph was both a painter and a sculptor, working in several different media.

❧

Dinner went well, and Elliott decided he definitely liked Ralph. The conversation centered on art, and Steve brought up the subject of holding art classes in the gallery space, which Ralph thought was a great idea. They agreed there was a lot involved–and a lot of details to work out–before they could start, but they'd get together again to talk about it.

Eventually, the conversation got around to Bruno.

"I didn't know him all that well," Ralph said in response to Elliott's question, "but I liked him, and I resented the fact Rudy was always trying to take advantage of him."

"You work for Rudy?" Elliott asked.

Shaking his head, Ralph said, "No, but I did for awhile. I really needed the money for school, and Rudy paid well. I'm sure not proud of having to hustle to make a living, and although he likes to sugar-coat it by calling his boys 'escorts,' they're just glorified hustlers, and he's just a pimp."

"I noticed that whenever I saw him he was always with at least two really good-looking guys."

"Part of his operating procedure. I met Bruno when Rudy took me and two of his other 'escorts' to one of Bruno's parties. We were sort of an hors d'oeuvres tray. Rudy does that a lot at gatherings. If the host doesn't find something he likes, maybe one of the other guests will."

"So, when did you leave Rudy?" Steve asked.

"I got fired when I just couldn't perform for some of the guys he set me up with. Now I schedule temp work around my class load, which just barely keeps my head above water. But I manage."

"Can you tell me what you know about Rudy and Bruno's relationship?"

"To be honest, I was getting a little concerned for Bruno. Rudy likes people to believe he's their best buddy, but if he thinks you're crossing him some way, he'll tear you to shreds. Everything was fine with Bruno as long as he let Rudy lead him down the garden path, but I heard him making some really mean comments when Bruno wasn't around. He called him 'the fatted calf,' and I'm pretty sure Rudy saw himself as the butcher.

"I know he was really upset when Bruno started balking at the plan for him to finance some bar deal–and I hope you don't mind my saying so, but I think Rudy blames you for that. I don't know how involved you might be with him, but I know I wouldn't want to cross him–he doesn't show it, but he's got a real temper."

"I never had anything directly to do with him, so I'm not worried. Do you know anything at all about the bar deal?"

"Not much, but I do know he really was serious about buying it–he never mentioned which bar it was, but I heard it might be Sidekick or Roscoe's or Spin. And I know he was really counting on Bruno to back it."

Elliott couldn't help but wonder just how unhappy Rudy really was when Bruno made his announcement at the party the night he died.

❧

Ralph left around ten, and Elliott accepted Steve's invitation to spend the night. By the time he had finished reciprocating Steve's earlier-in-the-day thoughtful gesture, it was nearly midnight before they got to sleep. Elliott was hoping to hear from John, and...

–I think Blanton lived in New York. And I think the guy he bought the Jennys from is also from New York.

–I remember Bruno telling me the original owner wanted them back, and that he'd been dunning Blanton. So maybe Blanton killed Bruno to steal the stamps and resell them to the original owner?

–That's pretty much the impression I'm getting from Bruno. We've gotten to the point where we can actually talk–that is, use actual words and sentences–though there are still a lot of areas where he reacts rather than responds. Generally, Blanton is one of them. He's still conflicted over the idea Blanton might have stolen from him–let alone killed him.

–Great. But now the question is, what do I do about it? Cabrera and Guerdon made it pretty clear they didn't want me coming to them with every hunch.

–You could ask Brad, see if he has any suggestions.

–I could, but I hate to impose on him, and I'm not sure what he could do in any event.

–Hey, like chicken soup, it can't hurt.

–I suppose.

–Oh, and Bruno says thanks.

Chapter 11

Cessy called Monday shortly after dinner to tell Elliott she'd heard from Steve.

"He says he's seriously considering conducting a basic painting class, and that he has a friend who might also do one on sculpting. I told him I'd spread the word, and that I thought it was a wonderful idea. Of course, I'd told him that before."

They talked for their usual five to ten minutes before Elliott, who had decided to follow John's advice, asked to speak to Brad.

When Brad came on, Elliott outlined his latest conversation with Cabrera and Guerdon, his contacts with the real estate agent handling the Wisconsin resort and the information that it had been sold to an organization called the Ferrell Group in New York, who planned to make it into a retreat. Then he told him about the missing stamps and the possibility that Blanton had lived in New York–he didn't elaborate on how he knew–and his theory that it was Blanton who had stolen the stamps.

"Since Cabrera and Guerdon say there hasn't been any blip on the stamp market about a recent sale of Inverted Jennys–and Blanton is smart enough not to make any huge deposits in his bank account, even if there were–I'm wondering if he might not have made a deal with the original owner to exchange them for bankrolling his projects without having his name directly on any of them. That way, there wouldn't be any direct bank-to-bank money transactions. I've never heard of the Ferrell

Group, but I'd like to know who's involved in it and if Blanton has any connection to them."

"Hmmm...possible. But Cabrera and Guerdon are right–they really can't look into anything that isn't a little more solid than possibilities and maybes. Contacting an individual is hard enough, but trying to track down a specific unknown individual in a company based strictly on conjecture is a real stretch."

"I understand. But where does that leave me?"

"Well, depending on how deeply you really want to get into this, I do have an idea."

"I'm listening."

"Bennie Lassiter, my first partner when I joined the force–I think you met him at my birthday party–retired and moved to New York. The retirement lasted about six weeks before he got bored and decided to take out a private investigator's license. If you want to contact him, he might be able to check some things for you, and I'm sure he'd appreciate the business."

Elliott remembered that Brad had offered a toast to Lassiter and his retirement at the party, and while he couldn't get a mental picture of the man, he'd undoubtedly met him in the course of the evening.

"Yeah! Definitely. Can you get me his number?"

"Sure. Hold on a second. He sent me a business card. Be right back."

Elliott quickly went for a pen and piece of paper. Picking up the phone again, he could hear voices in the background but couldn't identify them. Probably the kids.

"Okay. Got a pencil?"

"Yep." He wrote down the information. "I'll give him a call."

"If you talk to him, give him my regards."

"Will do. And thanks."

❧

During coffee break the next morning, Elliott called the number Brad had given him. The phone was answered on the second ring.

"Lassiter Investigations, Ben Lassiter speaking."

Elliott introduced himself and quickly outlined the situation.

"I don't have any idea who or what this Ferrell Group is, but I suspect it or someone in it is acting as a cover for Clifford Blanton. I know it's like looking for a needle in a haystack, but would you be willing to see what you can find out?"

"Sure. No guarantees, but I can try."

"Great. Do you want to fax me a contract, and will you need a retainer?"

"Let me do a little preliminary checking first and get back to you. No great rush on the contract. If you're Brad's brother-in-law, I can always go after him if something goes wrong."

Elliott laughed. "Yeah, he'd love that."

They hung up after Elliott had given Lassiter his phone numbers and his home address.

❧

The week passed quickly in the usual flurry of details–moving the file cabinets from the condo to the new office, ordering office furniture, dividing the basement into storage areas, talking with Larry to set up appointments that coming Saturday to check out the two potential next projects he'd driven by.

Ted built a free-standing panel to display one of Steve's paintings once the paper was removed from the front windows, and Steve suggested they have a small party Sunday to show off the completed gallery space. After some debate as who to have over, they settled on just Brad, Cessy and the kids, and Button and Paul–both of whom had asked to see it as soon as they could. They agreed on a much larger gathering when the gallery actually opened.

John was notable by his absence, and Elliott was curious as to what was going on with Bruno, but knew John would tell him when he had anything he thought Elliott should know.

He'd just gotten home Thursday night when his land-line rang.

"Mr. Smith, this is Ben Lassiter. I've got some information for you."

"Elliott, please. What did you find out?"

"The Ferrell Group is run by an Edmund Ferrell, who went through a messy and expensive divorce. Recently, the bulk of the divorce settlement was overturned when it was learned his ex-wife, who her lawyers had painted as a latter-day Mother Theresa, had been sleeping around on him for years. And it turns out Ferrell is a noted stamp collector. He's on the board of the American Philatelic Society and has written articles for the *Philatelic Literature Review*.

"And I was able to find out through their personnel department that one Clifford Blanton worked for the Ferrell Group from two-thousand-one to two-thousand-six."

Elliott noted a strong scent of Old Spice, which dissipated quickly.

"Brad was right–you're good. Look, Detectives Cabrera and Guerdon are a little tired of hearing from me. Would you be willing to talk to them directly to tell them what you found out?"

"Sure. George and I go way back. Would it be easier if I gave him a call? It might speed things up."

"That would be great, I'd really appreciate it. As soon as you've talked to them, send me a bill for everything up to now–and a contract, if you need one for your files. We can go on from there if there's anything you might do Cabrera and Guerdon can't."

"I'll do that. Give Brad my best."

❦

–Progress!

–Finally. I gather Bruno's aware of what's going on. I caught a strong whiff of Old Spice while I was talking to Lassiter.

–Yeah, it's pushed him back a step or two, I think, but hopefully he'll recover fairly quickly.

–There are still a lot of questions I hope the police will be able to resolve.

–Specifically?

–If Blanton did throw Bruno off the balcony, how did he manage it? I mean, he was one of the last to leave the party, but neither Ricky nor Cage mention him coming back. I asked you some time ago if you could find out the last things Bruno remembers about the party, and you never told me.

–Sorry, that was while he was still in "swirling cloud" mode. I'll try again.

❦

His latest conversation with John set Elliott off on a chain of questions.

While entering the building without passing the front desk wasn't easy, it was possible. The rear service entrance was always locked, requiring anyone wanting to get in to either have a resident's passkey or to buzz the front desk for admission.

It was general knowledge the security cameras covering the service entrance were frequently out of order.

As a further safeguard, there was a door between the lobby and the hallway to the service entrance, which also required either a passkey or a buzz-in, but this could be bypassed by entering at the same time as a resident or preventing the door from closing properly. The elevators couldn't be seen from the front desk, and although the desk had a bank of security monitors, the attendant was often either busy or distracted and couldn't watch them all at the same time.

As for how Blanton might have gotten back into Bruno's apartment without being seen, Bruno always left the kitchen and front doors unlocked during his parties, and probably never got around to locking them that last night.

He'd not had any word from Cabrera or Guerdon by the time the detectives' shift was over, so he resigned himself to waiting until Monday.

❧

With only a few more days of work ahead for his crew, Elliott began shifting gears to prepare for his next project. Since there was always a lapse between projects, he began working on a list of needed maintenance and repairs for his other properties to keep the crew occupied.

Again mildly concerned he was spending too much time at Steve's, he suggested they spend Friday night at the condo. Since he was meeting Larry Saturday at eleven o'clock to look at the prospective new properties, he could get Steve home in time to spend the afternoon painting then go over later in the afternoon to start setting up his office.

He waited for Steve to get home, then they stopped at the store to pick up some steaks for dinner. On the way, he filled Steve in on his talk with Lassiter and his hopes Lassiter's call to Cabrera and Guerdon might spark some activity.

Marco buzzed them into the main lobby, and Elliott took the opportunity to ask a question that had been niggling at him.

"Marco, I'm curious. Have the police returned the security tapes for the night Bruno Caesar died?"

"The lobby tapes, yes. Yesterday afternoon, as a matter of fact. Brian wasn't in, so they left them with me."

"They kept the service entrance tapes?"

"No, they didn't take them. The back cameras were out of order that night."

Elliott wondered if it was a coincidence or something more sinister.

"Those things really need to be replaced," he said.

"It's been on the condo board's agenda for the past two months, but nothing's been done about it yet."

"Well, thanks for the information."

"My pleasure. Have a nice evening, gentlemen."

As they were about to turn toward the elevators, Marco buzzed the front door open.

"Gentlemen!" a familiar voice proclaimed. "What a pleasant surprise. It's been a while."

"How are you, Rudy?" Elliott asked as they walked to the elevators.

"Things couldn't be better."

One of the elevator doors opened just as they arrived, and an elderly man got off.

"Cage and I are going to dinner with some backers for the senior condos project. There's still time for you to get in on it, you know."

"Thanks, Rudy, I appreciate it, but my plate's pretty full right now."

"Well, keep it in mind. I'll give you a call."

The elevator stopped on 35, and Steve and Elliott got off, exchanging a brief wave with Rudy as the doors closed.

"Ya gotta give him credit," Elliott said, retrieving his keys from his pocket. "He never gives up."

Setting the grocery bag on the counter while Elliott opened the refrigerator door, Steve passed him the steaks, butter and tub of sour cream, putting the baking potatoes aside.

"So, he's already got his hooks into Cage," Steve observed.

"Looks that way." Elliott shut the refrigerator door and opened the freezer compartment for ice cubes as Steve fetched glasses.

"Of course, there's the little matter of Cage's not having Bruno's money yet," Steve observed. "But he seems pretty confident Cage'll get it."

"If Cage's folks are in as poor health as he says, it's only a matter of time. And even if they aren't dead by the time the estate closes, I'm sure Cage can find a way to get it from them. I have no doubt at all Rudy will use the availability of Cage's impending fortune as a web to catch other prospective investors in his schemes."

"Do you think Rudy might have killed Bruno so he could get money from Cage?"

"I wouldn't put it past him. Rudy knew Bruno was getting wise to him even before their talk the night of the party, so whatever Bruno said to him couldn't have come as any great surprise. Rudy's nothing if not shrewd, and from what I gather, he'd already started laying the groundwork with Cage long before then."

"And what do you make of the Clifford Blanton...uh...Ferrell Group?...link."

"Hard to say, although it definitely points a finger in his direction. But I see one problem in his being the one who killed Bruno."

"What's that?"

"Bruno's murder was premeditated. The killer had to get the knockout drug in advance of the party and put it into whatever it was put into. Clifford would have had to know in advance Bruno was cutting him off, and from everything I can tell, he didn't. The only way to know for certain is if John can find out from Bruno exactly what happened during their talk at the party."

"Yeah, but if it was the stamps he was after, that wouldn't rule him out. Killing Bruno would be the only way he could get them."

"True, but it could also have been just a matter of opportunity after Bruno died. Ricky said Clifford came to see him the morning after and sat with him until he fell asleep. A perfect chance. He knew it was unlikely Ricky would be in any condition to notice right away that the stamps were missing. He knew their value, knew the original owner–almost definitely Ferrell–wanted them back, and knew he couldn't risk trying to sell them himself. I'd guess he made a deal for Ferrell to back him financially on the retreat and the infomercials in exchange for the stamps. What they'll do about Ricky's having the certificate of authenticity is another matter."

"You think he might go after Ricky to get it?"

"It's possible, but he has no way of knowing Bruno gave it to Ricky, and I hope Ricky's put it in a safe deposit box by now. Of course, after everything is said and done, there's no guarantee Ricky will end up with the stamps, anyway. That'll be up to the court to decide. Bruno's note didn't specify it was the stamps he was referring to, just that he wanted Ricky to have something to remember him by."

"Yes, but we were with him when he opened the envelope, and we can verify what was in it. That should count for something."

"It might. We'll just have to wait and see."

"I was thinking of that note that came with the certificate. Do you think Bruno knew something might happen to him?"

"I've wondered about that, too, and I hope John can find out for us. But I haven't seen anything that's happened since his death to indicate he thought he was in danger. I honestly think he was just being cautious. I think he gave me the envelope rather than Ricky so that, if he'd lived and he and Ricky had broken up somewhere down the line, he could just ask for the envelope back and no one would be the wiser."

⁂

It was a warm night, there was a pleasant breeze from the lake, and they opened the balcony doors to take advantage of it. After dinner and some TV, Steve said, "You've got an air mattress, right?"

"Yeah, why?"

"Well, it's a nice, warm night. What say we blow it up and go spend some quality time on the balcony? We've never done it out there before."

Elliott grinned. "Sounds like a plan. But watch the bucking–I don't want either one of us to follow Bruno over the rail."

It was just before midnight when they went to bed.

⁂

–No, Bruno wasn't concerned for his life. He was concerned for the stamps, though, and after your talk, he didn't want both the stamps and the certificate to be in the same place.

–Then why didn't he put the certificate in a safe deposit box?

–I think he was just being cautious. He knew a safe deposit box would go to his heirs in the event of his death. He wanted to be sure Ricky got the stamps. And he trusted–trusts–you.

–Well, obviously you knew I was going to ask about Clifford, too.

–Let's just say I anticipated it. Bruno told him he hadn't been aware of exactly how much he lost in the market until he insisted on Means's laying it out for him. He said Means had full confidence he would regain most or all of his losses when the market turned around but felt Bruno's knowing the full extent of his losses would needlessly upset him.

Means said Bruno had to curtail his spending, period—especially on costly and highly speculative projects like bars and retreats and infomercials. Bruno assured Blanton that, when stability returned, he'd be more than happy to help him in any way he could. That's why he was so disturbed when you found out about Ferrell and New York. Despite his misgivings, Bruno really believed in the guy.

—So, now that he's more...uh...together...does he have any idea who killed him?

—Not a clue. As I've pointed out, omniscience is not a perk that comes with death. The only things he knows now that he didn't know before he died are the things he learns from you. Oh-oh, I think you woke Steve again. We'll talk later.

Steve was once again propped up on one elbow watching him.

"John, I gather?"

"John. Nothing new, just going over some things."

"Ah, okay." Steve lay back down and draped his arm across Elliott's chest, pulling him into a spoon position. A few minutes later, both were asleep.

⁂

In order to meet Larry at eleven o'clock at the first property, they had a quick breakfast out, and Steve was home by ten-fifteen. On the way, they talked about setting up the portable wall panel.

"Decided which picture you're going to hang?" Elliott asked.

"I haven't made up my mind yet. The Devereux Gallery has the one I was thinking of, but I can't ask for it back at this point."

"How about your portrait of Manny?"

"Possible, but because I do mostly architectural stuff, maybe I should put up one of those. We'll see. I plan to rotate them every week, anyway."

⁂

Larry was, as usual, right on time. The building was a three-story Gothic limestone six-unit with arches over the leaded-glass windows above the entry and at the tops of the flanking first-floor windows. The small front yard was an unkempt jungle, and the roots of an almost-dead tree in the small space between the sidewalk and curb had uplifted a section of the sidewalk near the curb. From the looks of it, the building was empty and had been so for some time.

"Don't judge a book by its cover," Larry said with a grin, noting Elliott's reaction.

"You know I don't."

Larry had worked with him so often he instinctively knew what would appeal to him and what wouldn't, and never wasted Elliott's time. He always came prepared with a packet of information–taxes, assessment, utility costs, and any history he could find–for each building.

The property, which Larry explained had been empty for more than a year because of an only recently resolved squabble between the heirs of the deceased owner, largely fit Elliott's requirements. Built just prior to the start of WWI, it had large rooms, high ceilings, fireplaces and several of the small design details that, to his mind, indicated quality.

There didn't appear to be any major structural problems, but it was rundown. The asking price was at the high end of the general range of other properties in the area, although it didn't reflect the condition of the building and the expense that would be required to get it back in shape.

Elliott followed Larry to the second property, an eight-unit that looked fine from the outside but proved, inside, to be in considerably worse shape than the one they'd just seen. It would, in Elliott's opinion, require a complete gutting.

"I'll keep looking," Larry said as they parted ways on the sidewalk.

"Thanks. And I'll go over your packet and give the first one some more thought."

"Do that. I'll call you soon."

❧

He made a quick stop back at his condo to pick up a box of office supplies. As he got off the elevator on his way out, he noted two men wearing caterers' uniforms getting on the service elevator with a cart of what appeared to be party materials.

"What's the occasion?" he asked Marco as he passed the front desk.

"The Means's anniversary party. They've reserved the assembly room and have been hauling stuff in all day. A big deal, apparently."

Elliott wondered if Mrs. Means would insist on cranking up the air conditioning so she could wear one of her mink coats, and if she had handwritten all the invitations.

❧

Not wanting to interrupt Steve, when Elliott reached the Armitage building he went directly to the gallery area and began setting up his office, making a note to call the phone company to install a phone with an automated answering system. Steve had suggested he might want to decorate the office walls with photos of all the properties he had renovated and kept. When Elliott admitted he didn't have any, Steve volunteered to take them. Elliott also planned to frame and hang the colored drawing Steve had made of the Armitage building.

It was nearly five-thirty by the time he finished placing the furniture where he wanted it and unloading boxes. Steve was still working when he went upstairs.

"Why don't you fix a drink?" he said as Elliott opened the door. "I'll just be about ten more minutes."

Elliott was watching the news when Steve joined him in the living room.

"Finished?" Elliott asked. "I made your drink and put it in the fridge. You just have to add the ice cubes."

"Thanks. And yes, it's finished. Let's give the paint a chance to start to dry, and you can have a look at it in the morning, if you want."

"*If* I want. Like I wouldn't?"

"My dad always told me never to take anything for granted."

"Right."

⁂

Sunday morning, after breakfast, Steve showed Elliott the painting—one of Elliott's favorite buildings, a beautiful old Victorian former home on Belmont near Halsted sandwiched between two hulking, characterless commercial buildings. It, too, had been converted into commercial space, and though the signage was limited, the contrast between past and present was almost palpable.

"Beautiful," Elliott observed.

"I'm glad you like it. I think we'll hang this one downstairs today."

"A good decision. How about now?"

"We've got to get to the store to pick up stuff for this afternoon."

"This is more important. We'll go to the store afterwards."

Once downstairs, they set the panel in front of the forward-most central support beam. They decided to leave the paper on the windows and do an "unveiling" just before everyone came downstairs to see the finished space. Arnie had installed floor plugs at the base of each pillar to facilitate using display lights when needed, and the ceiling track lights could also be rotated to act as spots. It took several minutes to install the display light, and when it was exactly where Steve wanted it, they stepped back to admire the effect.

"We're good," Steve announced.

"Yep."

Button and Paul were the first to arrive, followed shortly by the Priebes. After half an hour of general conversation and the usual information exchange that goes on among people who have just met, Elliott said, "BJ, you want to lend me a hand downstairs for a minute?"

Jenny, of course, wanted to go along, but Elliott said, "We'll be right back. Why don't you help Steve get everybody some more to drink?"

Going first to the garage to retrieve a ladder, they entered the ground floor through the alley-side door. It only required a minute to take down the paper covering the front windows, but several more to fold it up, take it to the trash cans in the alley and return the ladder to the garage.

"You want to go upstairs and see if everybody's ready to come down?" Elliott asked, unlocking the front door.

"Okay."

As he stood by the front windows looking at the results of so many weeks of work, even he was impressed. Turning toward the street, he noticed a car he recognized from the neighborhood drive slowly past, its occupants gawking. He smiled and waved.

"I'm so glad everybody liked the space," Steve said as they finished cleaning up.

"What's not to like? It's your painting that really sets the whole thing off. I think even BJ liked it, and he's about as stoic as they come."

Steve grinned. "Yeah, he could be the poster boy for 'teenage cool.' But anybody could pick him out of a lineup as being Brad's son."

"How about I buy you dinner? You pick where."

"A good idea. I was just thinking I could really go for a bowl of hot-and-sour soup at that place on Broadway up near you."

"We can do that. Then, since we're so close, we could spend the night at my place, and I can get you home in time for work in the morning."

"That's doable."

⁂

Checking his answering machine as soon as they got back to the condo, Elliott noted he had a message.

"Elliott, Adam. We were wondering if you and...Steve...might like to come over for dinner Tuesday evening. We've been meaning to do it for a long time now, and if you don't mind a middle-of-the-week evening... We're anxious to tell you about our trip. Anyway, just give us a call."

Steve, who had followed him into the den, raised an eyebrow in a silent question.

"Adam and Jesse–the guys whose house I just redid. The ones who hired Ricky as a houseboy. They just got back from Europe."

"Ah, right."

"You up for it? It'd give you a chance to see their place."

"Sure. I never pass up a free meal."

Elliott returned Adam's call immediately to confirm. When he got off the phone, Steve pointed at two large, full black garbage bags in the corner where the file cabinets had been.

"Nice accent pieces."

Elliott grinned. "Yeah. I meant to haul them down to the garbage room but haven't gotten around to it."

"We can take them down now, if you want."

"Nah, I can get them later."

"Be easier if we each took one."

"Well, if you don't mind."

"Not at all," Steve said, walking over to pick one up. "Jeez, what do you have in here, barbells? These things are heavy!"

"Several years of old phone books and a boatload of outdated business catalogs from when I cleaned out the file cabinets before I moved them. Now that I have an official office, I can have all my business stuff sent there."

They took the elevator to the ground floor, then went down the back hallway to the garbage room. Raising the metal accordion door to get into the room, Elliott noticed that one of the large wheeled garbage bins was overflowing, and the floor around it was stacked with several boxes he recognized as the same ones that had been delivered to the Means's. The top of one of the boxes was torn off, revealing about a dozen empty champagne bottles.

"Fillion Fils?" Steve said. "Never heard of it. Either really fancy or really cheap."

"Go with 'really fancy,'" Elliott said. "These are from Walter Means's anniversary party, and the Means's don't do cheap."

"Ah, how the other half lives." Steve sighed. "But I forget, you're one of the other half."

"Watch it, Buster, or you'll be riding the Fat Lip Express."

"Yeah, like that'll happen. But there's another express I wouldn't mind riding..."

"Good God, man, do you always think of sex?"

"You'd prefer I didn't?"

"Not at all. I just asked."

⁂

Monday was a wrap-up day, and Elliott completed the work schedule of maintenance projects on his other properties, which should keep his crew busy. He realized he was behind schedule in his customary Tarzan-through-the-vines swing from one project to the next. He usually had the next project pretty well lined up before work on the current one was finished.

Normally, he looked at several potential properties before making a decision and had only seen two this time. However, the more he thought about the limestone six-unit Larry had shown him on Saturday, the more favorably he viewed it.

He went over Larry's packet of information carefully, relied on his memories and impressions of the place and jotted down some rough estimates of cost. He decided to call Larry to go through the building again and perhaps take his crew. Although he usually waited until he was pretty sure he was going to make an offer on a new property before taking the crew off a job for an inspection, he figured since they were nearly done with the Armitage building, he might want to expedite his decision.

"We can do it this afternoon, if you'd like," Larry said when Elliott called to see about a revisit, and they arranged to meet at the property at two o'clock.

⁂

Having the building completely empty facilitated the inspection and allowed a more accurate estimate of its condition. The rear porches needed considerable work, and it was agreed the rear stairs should be completely replaced. Several of the side and rear windows were also in very poor shape and would have to be replaced.

The kitchen and bathroom fixtures and appliances were at least a half-century old, and the basement utility room equipment equally reflected the building's age. The electrical boxes still used fuses, and the efficiency of the furnace and water heaters was questionable. The roof appeared to be in good condition, with no indication of leaking, and no significant structural problems were evident.

Elliott, as always, kept a running mental tab on what each repair would cost, and Ted, Arnie and Sam took notes within their specific areas of expertise. On their return to Armitage, they gathered in Elliott's office to go over them with him, including their rough estimate of the cost of their part of the job. The consensus was that the ratio of potential work involved to the profitability of the results was favorable. Elliott took note of the team's individual and usually fairly accurate cost estimates to compare with his own, and spent the rest of the afternoon going over them.

He was also aware, throughout the day, that nothing was being done to resolve the question of who had killed Bruno.

⁂

Cessy called shortly after he got home and, after their usual chat, said Brad wanted to talk with him. Curious, since it was usually he who initiated talks with Brad, he said, "Sure," and held the phone while she went to get her husband.

"Did you hear from Frank or George today, by any chance?"

"No. I was hoping to at some point but haven't yet. I've been fighting the temptation to call them, but...What's up?"

"Well, I assume they will be calling, but knowing your curiosity I thought I'd fill you in. I talked to them this morning, and it seems they're zeroing in on the guru for Caesar's murder. They talked to Bennie and subsequently contacted the NYPD to ask them to look into the stamp collector...Ferrell? It turns out he does have a set of four Inverted Jennys, but he insisted he's had them for years. However, the certificate of ownership was a recent re-issue. He claims the original was lost or destroyed, though he couldn't be specific.

"The NYPD also checked into his finances and found that, while there's no direct financial link between him and Blanton, Ferrell has a foundation that issues grants and which did, in fact, fund a 'metaphysical retreat' in Wisconsin and something called 'Inner Peace Media.'

"Frank and George had checked your building's surveillance tapes, and they show Blanton leaving shortly before one a.m. They figure he managed to get back in through the rear entrance, though at this point there's no way to verify it because the cameras for that door weren't working. They don't have enough for an arrest yet, but they're hoping to find a final link."

"Thanks, Brad, I really appreciate it. And if I do hear from either Guerdon or Cabrera, I'll let it all be a surprise."

"Do that."

❧

Continuously pushing away thoughts of Bruno's death and the investigation into it, he spent Monday night going over his notes on the six-unit and refining his calculations of projected costs against potential profit. He then came up with a purchase price he could live with. While he liked the building, it wasn't one of his favorites. If the owners were willing to go along with his offer, fine. If not, he would keep looking.

He notified Larry Tuesday morning to approach the owners with an offer then spent the rest of the day giving his crew their assignments, ordering supplies for the various jobs, waiting for the installation of his business phone, and general busywork.

When Steve got home, they had a quick drink before Elliott showered and put on the change of clothes he'd brought with him. They left for Jesse's and Adam's early enough so Steve could take a look at the new prospective property.

"Interesting. I like the leaded glass. Not much you can do with the outside, but with some creative landscaping and lighting..."

Elliott grinned. "Two great minds with but a single thought."

❧

Though Steve had never met Adam or Jesse, he seemed perfectly at ease, a trait that always impressed Elliott. While Adam saw to fixing drinks and Jesse asked Elliott's advice on building a gazebo for the back yard, Ricky invited Steve to see his room.

When they returned, Elliott noticed Steve kept glancing at him as though he wanted to tell him something, but since there was no easy opportunity to do so, they just went on with the evening.

After Adam brought their drinks, Ricky excused himself to go to the kitchen to see about dinner.

As if anticipating the question, Jesse said, "When we hired Ricky we certainly didn't intend for him to be a cook, too, but he volunteered, and we were delighted he did. It sure makes it easier on us. And he's a hell of a lot better cook than Adam."

"I'm really glad it's working out for you," Elliott said.

"We owe you for sending him to us," Jesse said. "He's been a huge asset."

⁂

They left around ten o'clock, and as they headed for the car, Elliott said, "You looked like you wanted to tell me something when you came back from Ricky's room. What was it?"

"Did you notice the drip candle on Ricky's dresser?"

"The one in the champagne bottle? Yeah, why?"

"Did you get a look at the bottle?"

"Not really."

"The label is almost covered, but I could still read the brand."

"And?"

"Fillion Fils. Sound familiar?"

It did.

Chapter 12

Wednesday morning, Elliott called Ricky as soon as Steve left for work.

"Hi, Elliott. You just missed Jesse and Adam."

"That's okay. It's you I wanted to talk to."

"Me? What's up?"

"Can I come over? Now?"

There was an understandable hesitation before: "Uh, sure. Is something wrong?"

"No, I think something's right. I'll explain when I see you."

Within less than fifteen minutes, he was ringing the doorbell. Ricky opened the door almost immediately, his expression a mixture of confusion and concern.

"Come on in," he said. "Would you like a cup of coffee?"

"No, thanks. I didn't mean to alarm you, but I wanted to talk to you as soon as I could. Can I see the candle in your bedroom?"

Ricky's obvious confusion deepened. "Sure."

He led Elliott to his room and unnecessarily pointed to the bottle and candle.

"Can I ask where you got it?"

"From Bruno's party, the night...the night he died."

"Did he serve champagne at the party?"

"No. He deliberately didn't order any champagne. I guess he wanted to make a point or something."

"So, where did this one come from?"

Ricky paused, brows furrowed. "I don't know. I went into the kitchen to get a couple of ice cubes, and it was sitting on the counter."

"Right inside the door, by the sink?"

"Yeah. How did you know? I took it in to Bruno, and he asked me where it came from, and I said I didn't know, and he said we should open it, and we did."

Picking up the bottle, careful not to knock the candle off or break off any of the dripped wax, he saw Steve had been right–the label said "Fillion Fils." And he saw, as he tilted the bottle slightly, that it was not empty.

"There's still a something in here!"

"Yes, I know. We each had two glasses, and there was a little left over, and then that's about all I remember. The next day, when I started cleaning up from the party just to take my mind off what had happened, I found it and realized it was the last bottle of champagne Bruno had ever had or ever would have so I couldn't just dump it out.

"I took it into our room and put a candle in it and lit it in memory of Bruno. I let a little wax run down so it wouldn't just be a candle stuck in a bottle, and then I blew it out and I don't think I'll ever light it again. Now, every time I look at it, it's almost like Bruno is still here." He studied Elliott's face as if he were looking for...something. "What is this all about?"

"Let me make a phone call, and I'll tell you."

❧

Detectives Guerdon and Cabrera arrived about two hours later, looking more than a little put-upon and far less than happy to see Elliott.

"So?" Cabrera said as they entered, "what's so important you couldn't tell us over the phone? What do you have?"

Elliott told them.

❧

Two weeks passed. No visits from John. No scent of Old Spice. Not a word from Cabrera or Guerdon. Elliott had no idea what was going on with their investigation, or with Rudy or Cage or Blanton, and while he tried to convince himself it didn't matter, his frustration continued to build.

He'd made an offer on the limestone six-unit, and it had been accepted after the usual dickering. Returning to his condo on a Saturday afternoon while Steve worked on his latest painting, he found a message from Brad on his machine and immediately return the call. He'd talked with Brad a couple of times since his meeting with Cabrera and Guerdon, and was told they were waiting for the test results on the remaining contents of the bottle.

BJ answered the phone, and Elliott asked to speak to his dad.

"Just a second."

The silence lasted far longer than a second, and Elliott realized how impatient he'd been lately.

Finally: "Hi, Elliott. I've got some news for you–a couple of things, actually. Walter Means has been arrested for Bruno Caesar's murder, and his wife's being charged as an accomplice. The lab results show definite traces of chloral hydrate in the champagne bottle.

"Means is denying everything, but it turns out he's been living way over his head for years, and had been steadily losing clients. When the market tanked, he was on the brink of losing everything. He'd apparently been dipping into Caesar's funds for quite a while. He believed Bruno was on to him and was going to report him. Caesar's signatures on paperwork authorizing stock sales were forged...by Means's wife.

"As for the murder, we figure that Means had easy access to the stairwells, and his chances of encountering anyone there at one-thirty in the morning were next to nil. Bruno's kitchen door was unlocked, so all Means had to do was open it just far enough to reach in, put the bottle on the edge of the sink and return to his unit. When he came back a while later and saw the bottle was gone, he took a chance on going in.

"Exactly how he got Caesar out onto the balcony and over the railing isn't clear, and Means, of course, swears he's innocent. But they've got enough against him to make a pretty airtight case."

Elliott felt some of the emotional weight lifting off him.

"I still have a hard time imagining how Means could have been so stupid as to drug a bottle of champagne so obviously linked to him."

"Well, I think you told me once you thought Means was an arrogant SOB. He probably assumed, correctly, that by the time the drugs were discovered in Bruno's body, all the evidence would have been removed. And maybe he thinks everybody drinks Fillion Fils champagne."

"Yeah, but he didn't count on Ricky's keeping the bottle, and not emptying it out."

"I just thought you'd like to know. I'm sorry George and Frank didn't keep in touch with you, but..."

"I understand, and I really appreciate your keeping me posted like this." He paused a moment. "You said there were a couple of things?"

"Oh, yeah. While the NYPD couldn't find any direct money link to... damn, I can't think of his name!"

"Clifford Blanton."

"Right! Anyway, those stamps he claims are his are being held until the rightful owner can be determined."

"That's great! Again, Brad, I can't thank you enough."

After hanging up, Elliott resisted the temptation to call Steve and, instead, stood in front of the sliding doors to the balcony, looking out over the city and going over the conversation.

As to the ownership of the stamps, he had little doubt Cage, either on his own or with Rudy's encouragement, would claim them. Elliott had heard nothing of or from either man in weeks, and was happy to keep it that way; but he decided that if anyone contested Ricky's right to the stamps, he would turn the matter over to his own lawyers to handle on Ricky's behalf.

His reverie was interrupted by the phone.

"Ell, hi. I know we were supposed to get together for dinner tonight, but I'm really getting close to finishing my painting, and I want to keep working on it until it's done. Do you mind?"

Deciding not to bring up his conversation with Brad until they were face-to-face, he said, "No, that's fine. You go ahead. I think I can survive a Saturday night alone. Let's just not make it a habit."

Steve laughed. "We won't, believe me. Brunch tomorrow, for sure. Around eleven?"

"You got it."

❧

He planned on just spending the evening relaxing but found himself going over the past few months and feeling a familiar, indescribable sense of discomfort. Sitting in front of the TV but not really paying attention to what was going on, he let his mind wandering further and further afield, until he just closed his eyes and allowed himself to drift off.

—You're doing it again.

—What?

—Exactly the same thing you did with me and with Aaron—going through your own version of postpartum depression.

—Yeah, I suppose you're right. It's just...well, damn it, there should be more. It shouldn't just fizzle out, like air out of a punctured tire.

—And so I ask you once again—what did you expect? A knock-down-drag-out fight? Swat teams? A car chase, with helicopters? An earthquake? That's fine for movies and books, where "The End" is the end. But life just ain't like that. It goes on after the crime has been solved and the bad guys get their just desserts. One of the reasons we read books and go to movies and watch TV shows is because at the end everything is tied up with neat little bows. Real life is one long loose end. Get used to it.

Elliott felt himself sigh.

—So, tie up a couple loose ends for me now.

—If I can.

—Why absolutely nothing from either you or Bruno in two weeks? Does he even know what's going on? I mean, we've spent months trying to find out who killed him and why, and when we do find out...nothing. Nada. Zip.

—Again, I'm sorry. Really. I've tried to tell you how differently time works for us, but I can't expect you to understand. Sometimes, it's pretty much parallel, other times...it's not. When you're distracted or upset or there's some big trauma, time still keeps moving for you at exactly the same pace. For us, it doesn't.

Look, I wish I could explain things better, but...I'd say the best way to describe why you haven't been aware of Bruno lately is that when he realized what had happened to him, time stopped. He's...adjusting.

—And when he adjusts?

—Well, then what happens is pretty much up to him. Since he's found out what he's been staying around to find out, I assume he'll just go though the gate. I can't imagine he'd feel any need to stick around.

—So, that's it?

—Pretty much, I'm afraid.

—Thanks. I feel a whole lot better. Anticlimaxes are always a lot of fun.

⁂

He awoke about two-thirty, still in his chair. Feeling groggy and drugged, he turned off the TV and went to bed.

He was still in a foul mood when he woke up around eight, but several cups of coffee and a long shower helped. Plus, thinking back over his conversation with John, he realized John was right. Books are books, movies are movies, TV is TV, and life is life.

He called Steve before he left the condo to be sure brunch plans were still on. Being told they were, he headed on over.

"So, the painting finished?" he asked as Steve let him in.

"Yep. I think you'll like it. Wanna see it?"

"Of course!"

With a courtly sweep of his arm, Steve said, "Right this way."

Elliott followed him to the studio, where the painting stood on an easel facing the window. Walking around it, he saw it was a full-color oil version of the pastel Steve had made of his vision for the Armitage building before any work had been done on it. As with all of Steve's work, he was in awe of the detail and the sense of non-photographic reality it conveyed.

"This is beautiful! I don't know how you do–" he began, and stopped short when he realized Steve had painted the suggestion of a male figure in the third-floor turret window. Steve almost never put people in his architectural paintings, and had done so only once before that Elliott knew of.

"Very deliberate this time," Steve said, seeing Elliott's reaction. "It's Bruno in his old apartment. I figure I owed it to him. I know he was happy there, and if he hadn't told you about this place, none of this..." He gestured around the room. "...would have happened."

A slight scent of Old Spice came and went.

"You're welcome," Steve said.

End

Special Thanks

Zumaya Enigma and the author wish to thank the Smithsonian National Postal Museum and its staff, especially Collections Manager Elizabeth Schorr and James O'Donnell for their assistance in acquiring the image of the Inverted Jenny for the cover of Caesar's Fall.

Located in the old Post Office building next to Union Station in Washington, D.C., the Museum was created by an agreement between the Smithsonian Institution and the United States Postal Service in 1990 and opened to the public in 1993. If you can't visit the museum itself, we encourage you to visit their website at www.postalmuseum.si.edu because it's almost as much fun.

If you are visiting DC, though, consider stopping by 2 Massachusetts Ave., N.E. and learn how the US Postal Service has been a vital part of the nation since almost before it was born.

ABOUT THE AUTHOR

With the release of *Caesar's Fall*, book 3 of the Elliott Smith paranormal mysteries, DORIEN GREY places a 17th book on his shelf of published work, joining the 13-book Dick Hardesty mystery series and the stand-alone Western/adventure/romance novel *Calico*.

ABOUT THE ARTIST

CHARLES BERNARD is an illustrator and graphic designer who has worked for Columbia House and the Famous Artists Schools in Westport, Connecticut. He has created cover art for various publishers, including story illustrations for *Analog Science Fiction and Fact* magazine.